NOW SAY YOU'RE SORRY

NOW SAY YOU'RE SORRY

A REESE CLAYTON AND EMERSON LAKE NOVEL

BARBARA FOURNIER

Stevie
May God Bless You

Barbara Fournier

The characters and events in this book are a work of fiction.
Names, places and incidents are the product of the authors
imagination. Any similarity to real persons living or dead
is coincidental and not intended by the author.

Cover and interior design by Caroline Teagle Johnson

ISBN: 978-1-7366109-0-9 E-Pub
ISBN: 978-1-7366109-1-6 Paperback
ISBN: 978-1-7366109-2-3 Hardcover

DEDICATION

This book is dedicated to those family members we lost during the COVID-19 pandemic beginning in March of 2020.

My brother Richard Biittig. Just nine days later, his wife Barbara Biittig

My nephew Robert Biittig. His sister, (my niece) Lori Biittig Warner shortly after.

My sister-in-law Millie Biittig

My sister-in-law Carolyn Biittig

My brother-in-law's mom Jean Mieczkowski

May you Rest in Peace

CHAPTER 1

I'm told to be very still, to close my eyes tightly.

"Do not cry." the voice echoes through my ears. "I will hold you; I will love you."

My wrists scream as he holds them above my head. My thighs throb from his weight, the cloth covered buttons on the sheetless mattress press into my back.

"I will enter your body, for now you are mine and I am yours. I am all that you asked for in your letters to Santa. When I am finished, I will bathe you in warm water to ease your pain. But now you must say what I want to hear. NOW! SAY IT NOW!" he screams with urgency in his body and fury in his soul. "SAY IT!"

I give in. "I'm sorry. I'm sorry." My fear and my hope, I will not survive. I cry inside, I hate throughout. Someone help me, please!" No one hears me. No one ever hears me.

"911 what's your emergency? 911 what's your emergency? Are you there?" Covering the mouth piece with her hand, the dispatcher signaled her supervisor. "Don't know what this is, if anything. No one has said a word." She removed her hand from the speaker. "Help is on the way I have your address. Try to stay on the phone with me even if you are unable to speak out loud. I'm still here with you. Please don't hang up."

CHAPTER 2

"I'm glad to be headed out early. It's hot and I could swear I heard someone say you were buying drinks at Riley's," Emerson Lake chuckled, elbowing his partner in the side.

Reese Clayton raised an eyebrow, "Seriously, are you ever going to open that wallet, Detective? Let those moths breathe a little."

"Excuse me, Detective," the captain's voice snapped from behind him.

Emerson spun around, "Yes, Captain?"

"You and Detective Clayton head over to this address. 911 call came in. The officers on scene just found a body."

"Got it, Captain."

Detectives Reese Clayton and her partner Emerson Lake of the Cromwell, South Dakota Police Department headed for the parking garage, suit jackets slung over their shoulders, keeping the same pace. Emerson got in the driver seat, Reese the passenger.

As they sped along Braxton Avenue, Reese pondered, "You know something, Lake? I was just thinking how it never ceases to amaze me how I always have to buy breakfast after we have a wild romping night of hot sex. Shouldn't the guy pay for at least a cup of coffee? I mean really?"

"Ah, real meaning of life question there, Reese, but the answer will have to wait. We're here." He gave her broad smile and a wink.

"Okay," she smiled back at him, "but you are buying me dinner tomorrow night."

"What have we got?" Reese asked the uniformed officer waiting for them at the end of the driveway.

"You are not going to believe this, detectives. One for the books, for sure."

"Where's the body?"

"This way, next to the fireplace in the living room."

Both squatting down for a closer look. "Shit! What the fuck is this?" Lake declared.

"I told you, Detectives."

"Who called it in?" Lake asked the officer.

"We don't know. The call was placed from this address, but no one was here when we arrived. Either the caller didn't want any part of this discovery or had something to do with it. Paramedics arrived when we did. When we knocked on the door it swung open. We identified ourselves, but no one answered. That's when we saw the body."

Both detectives could easily see this was going to be a long night. A man in his mid to late forties, lay in front of the fireplace. Most of his body wrapped in Christmas paper.

"What else did you find so far?" Lake questioned the uniformed cop.

"We're checking for prints now. Looks like the victim may

have had company. Both bedrooms have unmade beds. One has the sheets pulled half off the mattress. That room may have belonged to a child. There is a children's book on the night stand and the room is painted pink with some stuffed animals strewn around. Looks more girlish. So far, all we know for sure is the home is owned by a man named Adam Chandler. I'm guessing that's him; we'll know shortly."

"There's no sign of a struggle, no pool of blood or spatter anywhere, and I can smell chlorine," Lake stated. "Someone thought they did a fine job covering up their tracks. Hopefully Forensics will find something."

"Why the hell is he wrapped in Christmas paper?" asked Clayton. "Where do you even get it this time of year? It's early June for Christ's sake."

"This guy must have really pissed someone off. I mean they didn't just kill him and take off…they set a scene…I guess it wasn't good enough to just plunge a butcher knife directly into his chest. It looks like they glued his eyes shut and tied a bow on his penis like a star on top of a damn Christmas tree!"

The body was released to the Medical Examiner around 9 pm, but by then the media had gotten wind of what had happened. While Reese was trying to re-enter the crime scene, reporters were already hovering over her like vultures to red meat, shoving microphones in her face. No matter how much crime scene tape there is, the press always manages to avoid it.

"Boy, that ticks me off," she whispered under her breath.

"Detective," a woman interrupted, pausing to look for the name on Reese's ID, "Rose Baker here from News Channel 11. Can you tell us what happened? Was this murder or a suicide?"

"The investigation is still ongoing. When we have more details there will be a press conference. Now please let us do our job."

"Brittney Chase with News 24. Who found him? Do you have a suspect? Any witnesses?"

"There are no statements at this time. Officer, move the press behind the tape please." She then turned around and went back to the crime scene. This was part of the job, but no one said she had to like it.

"There has to be someone that saw something or heard something." Emerson declared as Reese re-entered the house. "It was a nice night. Must have been someone walking their dog or having a beer under the stars or maybe even a teen looking to feel-up his girlfriend on the benches."

"Really, Detective?"

He just laughed at her. The other officers pretended they didn't hear a thing.

"Something tells me it's time for a door-to-door with the neighbors. Reese, you and I will start here. The rest of you head to the park on the east side of the block. Everyone, heads up. We have a killer on the loose with a sick sense of humor."

CHAPTER 3

"I'm Detective Lake and this is Detective Clayton," Lake said displaying his credentials on the lanyard around his neck. "May we ask you a few questions? Mr.?"

"Minh Nyung," answered the very proper sounding man in his late fifties or early sixties.

"Mr. Nyung. May we ask you a few questions?"

"Maybe." He stepped out onto the front porch. Please, have a seat," he offered, gesturing toward the wooden rockers.

"We're fine. Thank you," Reese replied.

"What's this about?"

"Do you know the gentleman who lives two houses down? An Adam Chandler?"

"I don't know much about him except for one thing."

"What's that sir?'

"He's no gentleman."

Reese shot a quick look at her partner, raising an eyebrow.

"How's that?" Emerson continued.

"He was okay when they first moved in."

"They, Mr. Nyung?" asked Detective Clayton. "Who else lives

there?"

"He had a wife; I don't recall her name; and an adopted daughter. Her name is Kei Lien. The wife died during childbirth, so did the baby. They adopted Kei Lien several years before the wife died.

"Continue, please," said Lake.

"Like I said, he was okay in the beginning, but turned into a raving lunatic after he lost his wife and baby. Claire, that's it. Her name was Claire," he said slapping his forehead then running his hand through his straight black hair. "Anyway, he would yell and scream at everyone, even Kei Lien. Like it was her fault. I heard him one morning yelling at her because the laundry was hung on the clothesline wrong. So, what happened at the Chandler house, detectives? One of the neighbors heard on their scanner that someone died. Did he finally kill himself? No loss to the world if he did."

"We don't know yet. We're looking into it. Thank you for your time Mr. Nyung. If you think of anything else, please don't hesitate to call," Emerson handed him his card and then he and Reese walked back to the car.

"This case is going to be a nightmare I can feel it in my bones, Emerson," Reese said pulling the seatbelt over her shoulder.

"You might be right. For now, though, we need to take this one step at a time."

CHAPTER 4

Detectives Lake and Clayton, along with several other officers, finished speaking with all the neighbors. No one saw a thing. All anyone said was the Chandlers kept to themselves and that they would hear crying sounds from inside the house from time to time. They figured it was Kei Lien missing her mother.

"There was no sign of the daughter in the house where the victim was found. I'm guessing we won't find any adoption records either, at least not in Cromwell, but that's not unusual." Reese began to think about different options to learn of Kei Lien's past. Churches, adoption agencies. "The name Kei Lien sounds like, maybe Vietnamese. What do you think?"

"The possibilities are endless and the probability of finding where she came from is, at best, one in a million," Lake answered. "With privacy laws alone, this could go on forever. We need to find this missing girl, Reese. She could be a victim, or a suspect, and who knows how long she's been missing."

His phone rang.

"Lake. Yes, Captain. Got it. Let's go, Reese. You're with me. Another murder."

CHAPTER 5

"Cromwell Police, Officer Manning."

The woman on the other end was hysterically screaming and crying into the phone.

"Ma'am, I can't understand you."

"Allen, it's Teresa. I need help now!"

"Teresa? Calm down I can't understand what you just said."

"I need help. Please help me. Hurry, Allen. Send someone to the house. Martin is dead!"

Allen immediately got on the radio to alert officers and paramedics.

Nearly losing his balance getting out of his chair he barged into the Captain's office.

"Captain, I just got a call from Teresa Kelsey. She says Martin is dead. I'm on my way over there."

"Where? What the hell happened. Did she say?"

"At the house, she didn't say what happened just that he is dead. She's hysterical. I'll put someone else on the desk."

"Just go. I'll take care of it. I'll contact Clayton and Lake and tell them to meet you there."

Moments later police and emergency teams arrived with lights and sirens blaring. In the house, Teresa sat in total shock staring at the body of her husband, police Sergeant Martin Kelsey, in front of the fireplace. A butcher knife through his heart, a bow tied to his penis, eyes glued shut and the rest of his body wrapped in Christmas paper.

When Manning arrived on scene, the first words out of his mouth were "Oh, fuck." He managed to maneuver Teresa off the sofa away from the fireplace. "What happened Teresa? Can you tell me anything? Did you see anything or anyone in the house?"

She just stared into nowhere, not saying a word, her hand to her throat breathing heavily. He put his arm around her back and her other arm over his shoulder and took her out of the house into the fresh air where she collapsed in a heap.

"I think she's in shock," Allen yelled to the paramedics.

They rushed over, got her on the gurney, placed an oxygen mask on her face and quickly loaded her in the ambulance and sped away.

CHAPTER 6

News spread fast about the Sergeant. Every media hound in the area showed up. Microphones and cameras hovered over police as soon as an opening allowed. They all got the same answer, *no comment*.

The whole city knew the Sergeant and no one could understand who would want to hurt him, except maybe a drunk with too many DWI arrests. Or, possibly one of the local socialites who couldn't get their kid out of trouble for hosting parties involving underage alcohol or a little too much weed. Other than that, Cromwell was pretty quiet.

Detectives Lake and Clayton arrived on the scene shortly after the Captain notified them.

"Is there anyone left at the precinct?" Clayton asked. "Looks like the 4th of July with all the lights."

"Lucky us," Lake replied. "The press is adding to this nightmare."

"What a way to start your week. Right, detective?" Manning asked sarcastically.

Manning wasn't a huge fan of Lake and everyone knew it. He

didn't care for his attitude.

"I'm headed back to the office," he continued. "I'll fill the captain in on what we have so far."

Emerson just tossed a look at the police officer as he walked away. Another officer was walking with them toward the house to keep the media at bay.

"Where's the body?" Clayton asked. "Did anyone disturb it in any way?"

"No. His wife was in shock and could barely breathe when we arrived. Paramedics took her to the hospital. Body is in the den next to the fireplace. His whole body, well most of it, is wrapped in Christmas paper. Butcher knife through his heart. If that wasn't weird enough, his eyes appear to be glued shut and there is a bow tied around his junk."

"Junk? Is that a new age description for a penis, officer? If so, ditch it. Be professional."

"Sorry, detective."

Lake turned to Clayton.

"Looks like we have a serial killer on the loose."

CHAPTER 7

Everyone available from the Cromwell Police force was told to meet in the squad room. Detectives Lake and Clayton were already tossing their ideas around while adding information to the board. The room itself was more like an afterthought when it came to how it was designed, but at least the paint color was a little more calming than the rest of the precinct. A lighter shade of blue. Someone once joked that they must have run out of paint and sent the next best thing to dull drab. The room was filled with mostly folding chairs in rows with a few rolling desk chairs mixed in. There was a board in the front. Part push pin, part dry erase board. A podium stood in front of the room.

"What have we got so far?" The whole room stood at attention out of great respect for their new Captain. Kimimela Brown was the first female Lakota to hold the position of Captain. First impressions to her were bullshit. Show me what you got was more her style.

"Take it easy. Sit," she directed. "This is one of us. We need to find who did this and why. No mistakes. Everything by the book. Got it?"

In unison, "Yes Captain."

"Detectives Clayton and Lake will take the lead here. Anything you need...warrants, more boots on the ground...whatever is needed, I'm available 24/7 on this one. I will notify the judge in case we need him spur of the moment. Detective Clayton, take it from here."

"Thank you, Captain. Listen up people. We want to make sure there are no mistakes here. Cross your t's and dot your i's. We do not want a mistrial when we catch this guy. Now let's go over what we have. Maybe something will click."

"Who says it's a guy, detective?" a female voice from the back of the room pierced the silence.

You could almost see the daggers in the Captain's eyes, but she let the detectives handle it.

"Who the hell are you and who let you in here? This is police business." Lake barked.

"Rose Baker News 11. So, if it wasn't suicide or accidental, it must be murder. Everyone wants to know what is happening and the Cromwell P.D. is not cooperating to keep the public informed. Again sir, are you sure it was a man?"

Detective Lake was furious that a stranger could enter the squad room undetected. "Someone please see to it that Ms. Baker is escorted out of the building right now!"

Officer Manning stood to escort the reporter out of the room.

"And furthermore, Ms. Baker News 11, this is official business, not a goddamn circus." Reese shouted at the story monger.

The Captain gave Reese a slight nod. Lake continued.

"Okay, we know of two murders in Cromwell so far. Names of the two victims. Adam Chandler and Sergeant Martin Kelsey.

Presumed cause of death in both cases is a stab wound to the chest. We have both butcher knives in evidence, they appear to have come from the same set, although they are the same size which is unusual for a knife set. No fingerprints on either knife, unfortunately. The only person willing to say anything substantial about victim #1, Adam Chandler, was a neighbor a few houses down on Braxton Ave. His name is Minh Nyung. He claims Chandler was a real nasty son of a bitch. Always yelling. Says Chandler has an adopted daughter named Kei Lien who no one has seen recently. It might be helpful if we can locate where the wrapping paper was sold. It had to be somewhere it could be sold in bulk and all year round. It takes a lot to wrap a human being, yet alone two."

"Detective?"

"Yes, Officer Sorenson." Reese answered the recruit.

"What if it was more than one person that did this? You would have to be damn strong and agile to wrap a dead body alone."

"Good point. We already figured as much." Lake noted.

Detective Clayton agreed. "Certainly true. Anything is possible. Lots of questions here. Who? Why? How? And will there be more? Not a lot of answers. That needs to change fast."

Captain Brown moved toward the doorway and once again everyone stood.

"I appreciate the respect, officers, but it's not necessary. What I do want is answers. Get to work and watch your backs. Detectives, keep me in the loop."

CHAPTER 8

Detectives Lake and Clayton gathered what little evidence they had so far from their desks and headed in to meet with the Captain. They were halted by an officer escorting a woman in uniform, a postal uniform.

"Detectives, this young lady says she needs to speak with you both. She says she may have something for you concerning the death of Mr. Chandler."

"Officer, will you tell the Captain we will be delayed a few minutes?" Reese politely asked.

"Of course."

"I'm Detective Clayton. This is my partner Detective Lake. How can we help you?"

Emerson pulled an extra chair up to the desk. "Please have a seat."

"Thank you. My name is Linda Abrams. I'm the letter carrier for the Chandler household. I heard, like everyone else in this city, about the death of Mr. Chandler. I also read in the paper something about wrapping paper. Christmas wrapping paper to be exact."

"Well, Ms. Abrams, don't believe everything you read."

"I know. I just thought you might like to have these letters. I have been delivering mail to the Chandler household for a lot of years and didn't think twice about mail addressed to Santa, at least when it was Christmas time and their child was a little girl. But the last 10 years, maybe more, I have found these stuck in the mailbox once in a while or sometimes on the ground. I didn't think much of it at the time and just stored them in my locker. That is, until I heard about Mr. Chandler's death. They are all addressed to Santa, the North Pole," her voice began to crack. "After this happened, I had to open one, Detectives. I just had to."

"So, you believe they may have something to do with his death?" Lake was very close to her face.

Clayton interjected. "Detective Lake, would you mind getting Ms. Abrams a bottle of water, and would you mind grabbing one for me as well? Thanks, I appreciate it."

As Lake left the room, he gave Clayton a quick nod.

"So, Linda...may I call you Linda?"

"Yes, of course."

"How often would you say this happened?"

"Hard to say. I don't really remember how often, but the last one was probably late April, early May of this year. It's in the box, I just don't know which one it is."

"And you never opened one before today to see what it said?"

"No. They may mean nothing. I don't know, but I just have that eerie feeling, do you know what I mean? Sort of like a mother's instinct. I probably should have inquired about them long ago."

"Here's your beverages of choice, ladies."

Lake, now wearing a smile on his face and very polite, handed the mail carrier her water.

"Thank you. I think I should take mine to go. I have to get back to my route. If that's okay with you both?"

"Of course," Clayton said. "I'll have the desk sergeant take your information and if we need anything else, we will contact you. Thank you for your help."

Clayton escorted Linda back to the front of the station and then hurried back to Lake.

"Let's take everything into the Captain's office. She is waiting for us anyway."

They showed the Captain the letters, repeating the letter carrier's story.

"Did you arrest him?" The captain asked. "That's a federal offense."

"No not that kind of letter," Detective Clayton replied. "They are letters to Santa. Oh, and the carrier is a woman."

"Well let's see what we have."

Each one opened a letter. Each one had the same look on their face.

Dear Santa,

Could you bring me someone to love me? I want to be hugged and kissed and made to feel special. I know I am too old to believe in Santa, but I have nothing else to hold onto. If you can, send someone whose touch is warm and gentle with arms that

*will hold me every day. A special someone that
will love me no matter what I have done in the
past. I have been a good girl Santa, for most of this
year at least. Better than most other years. Please
remember Santa, I always say I'm sorry.*

"What the hell?" Emerson was first to speak. "This is written by a child, but the requests are not for toys, or books or pets. This kid just wants someone to love her."

"This one, too," Captain Brown said tossing it onto the desk. "It's written in a child's handwriting with crayons, but she says she is too old to write to Santa. Is she an adult? What was happening in that house that she would have to say she was sorry for? Another thing, how do we know this was written by a female? Do we know that Kei Lien was the only child living there?"

"The neighbors only mentioned a daughter and the letter carrier mentioned picking up the letters years before when Kei Lien was just a little girl. I think that letter carrier might be right about her motherly instincts after all."

CHAPTER 9

Kei Lien went to the kitchen to start dinner for her father, a task that was turned over to her almost immediately after her mother died. She had thought long and hard, day after day, about using the butcher knife that she now held in her hand to end the pain that had taken over her every waking moment. The time would come soon. She remembered she left the laundry basket next to the clothesline in the back yard, so she set the knife down and went outside to retrieve it. She turned around to head back in and was startled by a man peering over the chain-link fence. The only time anyone arrived at their home was when Santa would send another gift. He was a much younger man than usual maybe only a few years older than her. Maybe twenty-four or twenty-five.

"Hi, I'm Daniel Nyung. I live just up the street. I've seen you a few times out here and I just thought while I was out for a walk, I'd stop by to say hi. What's your name?" he asked.

She glared at him. "Are you a gift from Santa?"

"What?"

"I just thought..." her voice trailed off. "Never mind. Where did you say you live?"

"Just a few doors down the street. Do you live here with your parents?"

Kei Lien stared at him wondering what this guy was up to. "I can't talk right now. I have to make dinner."

"Oh, I'm sorry," he said feeling uneasy. "I didn't mean to bother you. It's just that we've been neighbors for a long time and yet we've never been introduced. I just wanted to see if maybe we could get some friends together sometime and go over to the Dipper for an ice cream? Or maybe we could go for a cup of coffee someday?"

Daniel, being more of a loner, found it difficult to make friends. The few people he knew were more acquaintances than friends.

"But I can tell you're busy. I'm sorry. I'll let you get back to making dinner." He turned and started to walk away.

"Maybe," she replied, surprised at herself. "Daniel?"

"Yeah?"

"Don't say you're sorry, I'm not. It's Kei Lien, by the way."

"What?"

"Kei Lien Chandler. That's my name," she smiled.

Daniel smiled back at Kei Lien. He was confused by her remark about not saying sorry, but glad he now knew her name and got a maybe on the get together. As he walked down the sidewalk headed toward home, he glanced back and saw an older man going up to the front door of the Chandler's house. The only thing he heard when Kei Lien opened the door was *gift from Santa.*

That's fucking odd, he thought to himself. That's Sergeant

Kelsey.

What had Kei Lien done to cause the police to come to her door and why would the Sergeant tell her he was a gift from Santa?

In a split-second, Daniel leapt from the sidewalk and ran across the grass in between the houses. He managed to squeeze himself through the tall shrubbery that surrounded the back and sides of the house. He heard voices coming from a slightly open window around back. He moved closer and crouched down below the sill. What he heard was unbelievable. The Sergeant was having sex with Kei Lien and not just any sex, she was sobbing. It didn't take long for Daniel to realize that she was being raped.

He didn't know what to do. Should he try to help her? Would he be arrested for interfering? How would he explain why he was eavesdropping?

When the Sergeant finished with her, he said, "Now stop crying. You asked for this. Don't tell anyone. Now say you're sorry."

Kei Lien did as she was told.

After hearing the front door open and close again, Daniel immediately knocked on Kei Lien's bedroom window. It startled her. She cautiously went to the window and peered out. Daniel stood facing her. His forehead wrinkled with worry. Red scratch lines all over his arms from the shrubs.

"What are you doing here?" she asked, still trying to wipe away her tears.

"Are you okay?" he asked, knowing full well she was not.

Kei Lien once again began sobbing.

"Let me take you away from this awful place," Daniel said.

"Let me help you. Is this the way your father is treating you as well, Kei Lien?"

Kei Lien just hung her head and nodded yes.

"I can't come with you now, but I will meet you after dark somewhere. After I cook dinner for my father. After he goes to sleep."

Why am I telling this guy all this? she wondered. I don't even know him.

They agreed on an old barn near the Dayton County line. Kei Lien hoped she could find it. It had been a very long time since she ventured out of the yard, yet alone out of the area.

CHAPTER 10

Minh Nyung was just sitting down to eat when he was startled by someone banging on the front door and ringing the bell frantically.

"Who's there?"

"I don't know what to do or where to go" the shaky voice replied.

Minh cautiously pulled the curtain back to look out the window near his front door only to see a young woman. Her face covered in tears and what appeared to be blood on her legs. He immediately opened the door.

"What happened? Have you been in an accident?"

"I need a place to stay. I don't want to go home anymore. It's all my fault. I asked for this and I'm sorry. I'm sorry." Through the gasping, sobbing sounds and the runny nose, her voice lowered. "Does Daniel live here?"

She was weak and trembling.

"I know who you are. I think the police are looking for you. They thought you were dead. How do you know my son?"

Her eyes rolled back in her head. She passed out.

CHAPTER 11

"911. What's your emergency?"

"My name is Minh Nyung. I need an ambulance at 211 Braxton Ave. A young woman came to my door asking for help. There is blood on her legs. She just passed out."

"Help is on the way, sir. Please stay on the phone with me. Is she breathing?"

"Yes, barely. Could you contact the Cromwell Police Department and ask for a Detective Lake or a Detective Clayton? I believe this is the girl they are looking for."

When the paramedics arrived, they jumped into action. One placed an oxygen mask over her face to help her breathe. Kei Lien started to move a little. The other, a young man, attempted to find out where the blood was coming from, but was stopped by her screams.

"You're not Santa! Stay away from me!"

"Miss, we are just trying to help you," he said, while trying to restrain her.

She kicked him so hard she laid open a gash on the young man's face with the heel of her shoe. He fell backwards, but regained his balance quickly.

"Miss please, you need to let us help you. You're bleeding. Calm down and breathe normally."

"The oxygen will make you feel better," said the female attendant. "Can you give us your name and where you live? Is there someone we can contact for you? We're going to take you to a hospital."

Minh who was watching this all unfold pleaded with her, "Kei Lien, please let them help you."

With that she rolled over, got her legs under her, threw the oxygen mask, and ran like she had wings on her feet. Before the paramedics knew what happened, she was gone.

The call from the 911 dispatcher jolted Emerson Lake straight up in bed. Shaking the cobwebs out of his head, he picked up the phone. "Lake" he said still groggy.

The 911 dispatcher gave him the information. He hung up, tossed the sheets back and contacted his partner.

"Reese?"

"Who the hell else would answer my phone?"

"Get dressed."

The paramedics and Minh were waiting inside when the detectives arrived. They were baffled by what happened. Not wanting to admit how they allowed the patient to escape.

"She ran toward the back of the house, through the bushes," Minh explained. "I tried to follow, but she was too quick. Everything happened so fast. I can't believe it. Detective, the last thing she said to me was, 'Does Daniel live here?' Daniel is my son. He's not here now and I have no idea how she even knows him. He has never mentioned her."

"When your son comes home, please contact us. We will need to ask him a few questions," Clayton replied.

With that, she gave him her card with her contact information.

"Thank you, sir. You did the right thing calling 911 and having them contact us as well."

On the way out the door, one of the paramedics stopped Detective Lake. "While I was trying to assess the injuries, she became violent and kicked my face."

"I see that."

"That's not it. She screamed at me and said 'You're not Santa'. I don't know what the hell that means, but it took me by surprise for sure."

"Are you sure she said Santa?"

"Yes, very sure. As sure as the hole she left in my face."

Emerson smirked. "Thank you. Anything else we need; we know where to find you. Here's my card as well."

"Mr. Nyung, Detective Lake or I will be in touch tomorrow. Unless your son comes home sooner."

CHAPTER 12

Two bodies were on slabs in the morgue. No doubt they were murdered and by the same person or persons. Chief Medical Examiner for Dayton County Sara Hunter and her colleague Bill Oosterhout had received these disturbing bodies within hours of each other. Now it was up to them to determine cause of death. Seemed obvious, but still had to be done by the book.

Blood from each of the bodies was sent to the lab to check for abnormalities, narcotics, DNA. The gift-wrap was sent up as well. And then it began. Checking the bodies for bruises, broken bones, other knife wounds, bullet holes, even checking for needle marks.

"Sara, look at this? I don't think the knife killed Mr. Chandler."

Sara changed rubber gloves and stood next to Bill. "What did you find?"

"There are stitches at the base of his skull and it's not from brain surgery, either. Unless the surgeon was drunk. What do you make of it?"

Sara Hunter had seen what she thought was most everything in her twenty-year career. This was a new one for sure.

"Let's check the Sergeant. Help me roll him on his side so we can look."

There it was. A poorly stitched incision at the base of his skull.

"Shit," was all Sara could say. "We need to find out why they have matching incisions."

Sara began removing stitches from Sergeant Kelsey. Sara was always professional, but she was finding increasing pleasure in cutting him up little by little. The town's beloved Sergeant may have had everyone else fooled, but Sara knew better. He was a little bit too friendly you might say. Being the M.E., she would have to be in the same room with him at times. More often than not he would stand way too close to her. She could feel his breath around her hair and ear. The touch on her shoulder now and again was just too much. She asked him nicely one day to please remove his hand and step back a bit. He was not happy at her suggestion or her subtle accusation of him being in her space, but he did as he was told.

When the autopsy was done, neither Sara nor Bill could believe their findings, it appeared someone had hit him in the back of the head.

"There are definite fragments of something still visible," Sara said.

"Why do you suppose whoever did this stitched him up?" asked Bill.

"Probably because they didn't want to take away the startling effect of the butcher knife plunged in his heart. Which would mean he was already dead, or near dead, when he was stabbed. Or, maybe he was stabbed first. Either way, more questions than I can or want to answer right now anyway. We need more to make a solid cause of death."

Bill proceeded to open Adam Chandler. He found mostly the same kind of fragments, possibly pieces from the stone fireplace, but then noticed a very small piece of metal.

"Sara, what the bloody hell is this? I've seen some strange objects in the dead, in all cavities of the body, but this is bizarre."

CHAPTER 13

Once again at Cromwell Police headquarters, Detective Clayton was at the board trying to figure out this whole scenario. She needed time to absorb all that happened.

Captain Brown, appeared at her side, "What have we got so far, detective?"

"I'm just adding to the list. Chandler's daughter was found alive at a neighbor's home and now escaped into nowhere. How did her father get away with not sending her back to school after the mother died? Why did the teachers not report that she wasn't in school? Neighbors heard her crying in the house and assumed it was because she missed her mother. How many years could she or would she do that and why did no one investigate? Was she really crying because she missed her mother? Where did the blood come from on her legs? Was she assaulted? Or, did she murder her father and the Sergeant? The list is growing."

Walking in late to the conversation, Lake commented, "The list just got longer. Bill Oosterhout just called. It seems during the autopsies; he and Sara discovered a dog tag placed in the back of Chandler's head. It has one word etched on it. Santa."

"Did they find anything in Kelsey?" asked the Captain.

"That's all he said. I told him I would check in later with Sara."

"Reese, we need to pay Teresa a visit in the hospital. Maybe she remembers something by now. Quite a mess. Don't you think, Captain?"

"Indeed, Detective Lake."

On the way to Cromwell Medical Center there was little conversation between Reese and Emerson. Both knew the other's breaking points and respected quiet when needed. Their relationship had grown over the years. Grown from friends to good friends and occasionally friends with benefits. Nothing more than that. Of course, the rest of the precinct thought differently. How could it not happen? Reese was very bright, had a great sense of humor, and was stunning. Long brown hair always neatly pinned at the back of her head when on the job. Rock hard abs, a gold shield and packing heat. What's not to like? Emerson, with his aqua blue eyes could turn heads on a dime. His face was chiseled with a strong jaw line. Six foot two, short black hair with a hint of gray around the temples. Handsome. A little more intense than Reese. Being in law enforcement hardened his views on the world's problems with no room for gray areas. Reese and Emerson were in their mid-forties and yet the two of them looked like they had just walked off a magazine cover.

Reese smiled at her partner as they entered the parking lot. "Ready for the scent of alcohol swabs and disinfectant?"

"Are you ready for me, hot lips?"

She smiled and just shook her head back and forth as they walked into the hospital, preparing to talk to their murdered

Sheriff's wife, Teresa Kelsey.

"I'm Detective Emerson Lake, this is my partner Detective Reese Clayton. We're here to speak to Teresa Kelsey. She was brought in earlier this evening?"

After scanning the computer screen, the woman at the front desk replied. "Hmmm, I'm sorry, but I have no record of a Teresa Kelsey in our computer system. Maybe she was brought to a different hospital."

"And just what hospital might that be Nurse…uh…Carter?" Lake asked, scrutinizing her security ID. "The only other place is an hour away at least. Makes no sense. Could you look again?"

Nurse Carter glared at him. She deserved more respect than this arrogant ass was giving her.

"Call St. John's to see if she might have been taken there. I have patients to tend."

She wrote down the number, and passed it to him across the top of the counter.

"Have a nice day, Detectives."

"Guess she told you," Clayton teased. "Maybe you could have been nicer?"

"Bite me, I'm in no mood." Immediately regretting that remark, he gave her a wink.

Cromwell Medical Center was much the same as any hospital these days. Understaffed and overcrowded. Patience is a virtue, just not with Emerson Lake. He did make the call, but was much nicer to the person who answered. He even said thank you. Both he and his partner looked at each other, bewildered.

Teresa Kelsey was officially missing.

CHAPTER 14

The sunlight was nearly gone in the almost forgotten cabin hidden among the trees. Almost three miles separated the cabin from the nearest road. A dirt road. It had been a very long time since laughter, or any type of happiness, rang through here. Now it stood cold and damp. Most of the weathered shingles from the roof lay on the ground. Water, the color of rust from the pump, lay in the kitchen sink. Would take a while to clean that. No modern-day facilities either. An old outhouse sat tilted in the back yard of the cabin. Whatever was left in the single hole must have been long ago absorbed into the earth.

When he first found the run-down cabin, he imagined a family living there, a happy family. Lots of children even though it must have been crowded. He imagined a large dining table, one that looked like a picnic table, but meant for indoors. Nice kitchen, not modern by any means, but workable. A place to have family dinners. A place called home. Could this old falling down structure of someone's memories once again be filled with warmth? Maybe I should try. Should I try?

If I focus and do one thing at a time, his thoughts racing, I just might be able to restore this run-down cabin. It was in the thick and lush woods of the mountains. I don't believe I ever saw a park ranger anywhere near here. Probably because it isn't considered as park property. But it is mine now. I'm taking it over, like it or not. I think I can get a few guys together to help me. The ones that stand on street corners in that nearby town. They're always holding up signs that say looking for work. I'm sure they can use the money even if it is just for booze and drugs. First, I will need some help with cleaning it all out and fixing the well pump. I hope its deep. It will need to be pumped many times though to prime it. Boring task, but worth the effort. Nothing tastes as clean and pure as water from an old fashioned well. Plus, this type of supply should last forever; if it can catch the run off from the mountain, I would think. Just have to wait and see, I guess. I'll need to find some shingles. Somewhere there are no questions asked. There will be no permits needed because no one that matters will know about my cabin. I will have to use logs from the woods to replace some of the walls being eaten away. The outhouse will do for now. But one important thing I will need to finish the cabin is a lot of bricks, bright red bricks. To hang the stockings with care.

CHAPTER 15

"Daniel, where were you last night?"

Daniel, still half asleep, was not prepared for the question. His father repeated himself, this time in a much harsher tone.

"Just out. What's going on, dad? I'm 24 years old. You've never questioned where I've been before. What's the matter?"

Minh went through the whole story about the incident with Kei Lien the night before. How she had run off when paramedics were trying to help her.

"Daniel, when I told her I knew who she was she surprised me by asking if you lived here? How do you know her? The police want to talk to you. They need to ask you a few questions. I told them I would call when you got home, but I never heard you come in. I'm going to make that call. I'd like for you to be here when they arrive. Got it?"

"Dad, I have seen her in her back yard, but yesterday was the first time I ever spoke to her. I was just looking to make a new friend. You know how hard that is for me."

"Well, we will wait for the police to arrive so you can explain okay?"

"Got it. I'm going to take a shower and have a bite to eat before they get here."

"There are scrambled eggs and a few sausages left. No orange juice though. I could have sworn I bought some."

"I drank it. I was thirsty last night when I got home. I'll be ready by the time they get here dad, go ahead, and notify them. Daniel finished his breakfast and headed for a shower.

"Thank you for contacting us. Your son is here?" Detective Lake inquired.

"Yes, he is. Daniel," he summoned. "Detective Lake and Detective Clayton are here." Daniel appeared in the living room; hair still wet and a second cup of coffee in hand. Introductions were made.

"Daniel we would like to know how well you know Kei Lien Chandler?"

"Like I told my father, I just met her yesterday. I've seen her before, but never had spoken to her. This time I said hello, told her my name. I could see she was close to my age…a pretty girl under all that anger."

"Anger?" questioned Detective Clayton. "What do you mean by that?"

"Well I was just trying to make a new friend; she just about took my head off. Told me she couldn't talk right now, she had to make dinner for her father. I told her I was sorry to have bothered her and started to walk away. She yelled to me as I was leaving and said don't say you're sorry, I'm not."

"Was there anything else?" asked Detective Lake.

"That's all I can think of."

"Well thank you for the information."

"Daniel," Reese said. "Where were you last night?"

The question took him by surprise. "Just out walking around town seeing what was happening in the local hang outs."

"Can anyone verify your whereabouts last night? Another friend perhaps?"

Minh chimed in quickly. "Wait just a damn minute detective. Are you accusing my son of something? Now furious with the detectives' statement, he opened the front door. I think we are done here! Have a nice day Detectives."

The detectives headed out and got back into their car.

"Well that went well, don't you think? For Christ sake, what the hell were you thinking throwing that out there so fast Lake? They are the only family on the block willing to talk to us."

"I know. I trust the father, but wanted a reaction from the son and didn't get it."

When they were gone, Minh asked his son, to not say anything further to the police, any police, not without a lawyer at least.

Daniel agreed and left the house for a while. Said he needed fresh air. He decided to take a bus to the next town Willow Falls. Once there he sized up the men standing on the corner holding signs with the words *Looking for Work* printed on them. He wanted to rebuild the cabin in the woods. Make it a happy place once again. A safe place. Now with all that has happened within the past few days, he wondered if this was possible. He made mental notes of the men he would choose and took the next bus back to Cromwell.

CHAPTER 16

Daniel's birth father was a soldier, killed, driving his deuce and a half truck over a land mine. He never knew about the pregnancy. Daniel's extremely curly blonde hair and height no doubt came from his birth father. His mom later married Minh Nyung and they moved to the states.

They lived in California for a few years before moving to South Dakota. They sent him to college hoping Daniel would be a doctor one day. A parent's dream. He was an extremely intelligent young man. He made it through the basics and started medical school. He came back home when the news arrived that his mom was diagnosed with stage 4 breast cancer. He spent what seemed like forever watching his mom suffer the torture of going through chemo and radiation. The vomiting, day after day, dry heaves because food of any kind was not an option for her. Countless doses of medication that didn't help. Losing her hair by the handful until she was bald. Watching his stepdad hold her hand to comfort her and hold her head while she vomited nothing. Rubbing lotion on her to prevent sores on her scalp. It was difficult because she did not want Daniel to see her this way and certainly did not want him to help with her care. According to her, mom's care for their children, not the other way around. He did what his dad allowed him to do while watching her wither away praying for recovery and wishing it to end at the same time. Nightmare for her and a definite nightmare for him and his dad. He couldn't return to medical school. If he couldn't save his own mother, then why do it at all was his response to his stepdad. Minh could not argue with that. He knew all too well the heartache of losing the love of his life. He also knew that life with a stepson without a mother would be one of his greatest challenges.

Daniel began a job in a park preserve in Cromwell. The pay was decent. He could be alone. Another benefit of being in the preserve was he could hide away from all the people that made fun of him. The squirrels and deer didn't care what he looked like.

CHAPTER 17

Daniel waited, for what seemed like forever, for Kei Lien to meet him at the barn. While walking around the property he began to envision the torture that his new friend had endured. How long had this been going on? She had said her father was one of the men and I know the Sergeant was another. Was it possible there were others? Many others? Would make sense. Why else would her father keep her away from the public all these years?

Daniel checked his watch. 2am. He couldn't stay any longer without his dad worrying. He grabbed the insulated bag and hung it on a nail protruding from the railing. If Kei Lien did show up, at least she would have something to eat and drink. Saltines, cheese and OJ wasn't exactly a gourmet meal, but it was all he could steal from the house without being noticed. He started walking back out to the road.

Kei Lien never did show up at the barn that evening. Instead she decided to run for her life. Run somewhere no one would find her. She stopped at the edge of the woods and remembered that there was a camp a few miles in. Maybe it's still there and I could hide for a while, but how would I get food? Maybe that's not a good idea after all. Wait, I think I remember a lake. Yes, there is definitely a lake. She remembered being there with her mom and dad once. She had dropped a toy in the water. The water was so clear she watched it slowly sink and could still see it when it gently landed at the bottom. I'll go there she thought. I can go in the water and clean off. Maybe then I will feel better. My stomach really hurts.

When she came upon the lake, it was a beautiful sight. The moon was shining a beam of light across the water making it glisten. The lake was partially surrounded by ponderosa pine, some elm that casted shadows on the lake's surface. It was clean and cold. She felt very sick and her body was extremely sore, partially from the hike to the woods, the rest from her final encounter with her father. Nausea overcame her and she vomited on the shoreline. The skin on her bloodied legs felt raw when she entered the water, but soon the pain subsided, the cold water numbed her body.

Although the name of this crystal-clear lake eluded her, it became hers and hers alone for tonight. The water may have been cold, but it felt like a clean, calming bath for her. And she did not have to listen to her father telling her it was her fault while he washed her sore body and broken spirit. And for sure she did not have to say I'm sorry to anyone. She would have to find food soon, but not just yet. For the first time since her mother died, she felt clean.

CHAPTER 18

Teresa Kelsey lay wide-awake in her bed at the Strasburg Hotel, wondering what to do next. How was she going to make it through the next few days? She had told the paramedics to bring her here after they were far enough away from her home. The home she always imagined. The home she was supposed to live in and have a family and devoted husband. The home that was now crawling with reporters and police. The home where her prince charming lay murdered in front of their fireplace. How was she supposed to plan a funeral for Cromwell's beloved Sergeant Kelsey? The thought of trying to be the grieving widow nauseated her. How come he was not happy being with me? I should have…her thoughts trailed off. I planned our future. I had him ready to run for Mayor and climb that ladder to success. Why did he need to have another woman to make love to? Did he think I didn't know? All women know, eventually anyway. The words were a jumble in her mind. Teresa Kelsey decided it was time to face the public about her husband's death. She contacted Cromwell Police and asked to speak to one of the detectives on the case.

"This is Detective Clayton."

"Reese? This is Teresa Kelsey. I know you've been trying to locate me. I'm sorry I disappeared like that. I just wasn't ready to face the police, or the community for that matter."

"Why didn't you go to the Medical Center? And where are you now?"

Teresa was hesitant about giving the detective answers over the phone and nearly hung up, but decided it would be better to get it over with.

"Why did you run, Teresa? I need to ask you a few questions about your husband's death. Are you okay? I'll come to get you. Have you spoken to anyone else? Where are you?" Reese was stalling while Lake had someone else doing a trace. Emerson gave her the thumbs up. They had a location. Strasburg Hotel.

"Teresa, what happened? Can you tell me now?"

While Reese kept Teresa on the line, a squad car in the area of the Strasburg was dispatched to the hotel. The patrol men arrived and asked the desk clerk for Teresa's room number. "I'm sorry sir, but there is no Teresa Kelsey registered here."

"She has to be here. We just had the phone traced to this hotel."

With that, the grieving Mrs. Kelsey appeared in the elevator doorway. There was nowhere for her to go.

"Mrs. Kelsey, I'm so sorry. There was no way I could warn you about the visitors."

"It's fine, Randall," raising her hand to stop him from saying anything else.

"Mrs. Kelsey, we are so sorry for your loss," said one of the patrolmen. "We have been trying to find you. The Medical Center said you never arrived. What happened?"

"Never mind, officer." she said abruptly. "Please take me to the Cromwell Police Department. I need to talk to Detective Clayton."

One of the officers turned as they were leaving the hotel and said to the clerk, "We'll deal with you later."

Once back at the precinct, Teresa was greeted with condolences on her husband's death by most of the department. All except for the two people heading up the case.

"Right this way," Lake said, as he led her to an interrogation room. "My partner and I would like to ask you a few questions."

"Do I need a lawyer?" she snarled.

"I don't know, Mrs. Kelsey. Do you?"

"You are not under arrest and may leave at any time," Reese interjected respectfully. "We just want to ask you a few questions about your husband's death. Is that all right with you?"

"I'm afraid I don't know much. I panicked when I saw him on the floor like that. I was scared there might have been someone still in the house. I called the police. I was hysterical. Allen came just after the rest of the emergency response team arrived. He took me out of the house. That's really all I remember. I didn't see anyone or hear anyone. When can I see Martin?"

Ignoring her well-rehearsed statement, Lake asked, 'Why didn't you go to the hospital with the paramedics? Better yet, why didn't they take you to the hospital in the first place?"

"Because I asked them to take me to my hotel where I could rest without people hanging over the top of me asking me all kinds of stupid questions. I needed to think how I was going to handle an onslaught of reporters and still plan my Martin's funeral."

"Your hotel?" Detectives Lake and Clayton asked in unison.

"Yes, the Strasburg Hotel is mine. Is that so damn hard to believe?!"

"No. We just never knew you were the owner Mrs. Kelsey," Reese gently patted her hand to comfort her.

"Did your husband know Adam Chandler?" Reese continued.

"I know my husband was fooling around on me. We were hoping to work through it all. I also know his wandering eye led him to the Chandler house quite frequently. Adam Chandler seemed to know who would pay for the women he provided. I think he was running a brothel. I think he was paying women off the streets to service men at his home. Not that he had to pay. Adam was a very attractive man. Suppose he could get anyone. He might have had something to do with all of this. Do you think you should talk to him? I know my husband would frequent his home, or whorehouse, as I call it. I want to see Martin now."

"We are so sorry," Lake said. "But the medical examiner is not finished with the autopsy and we need to find the cause of death."

"Cause of death?" Teresa said exasperated. "Detective Lake, are you sure you know what you are doing? Could it possibly be the 10-inch butcher knife that was stuck in his heart? Idiot!"

"Mrs. Kelsey, please be civil," Clayton admonished. "We are all trying to be patient with you. Detective Lake does know what he is doing and that, Mrs. Kelsey, is trying to find the person or persons that murdered your husband. Now let's try to get through this mess."

"Bullshit!" Emerson bellowed. "Teresa you are a pain in the

ass…my ass to be exact! This can go either way. You can help us or we can throw your snooty butt in a cell until you can learn a little respect. Got it?!"

She put her head down for a brief second and apologized. All while thinking to herself, he is going to be a problem.

"We have more questions to ask you," Clayton said. "Would you like a cup of coffee or a drink of water before we begin?"

"Thank you," she smiled at Reese. "That would be nice." She glared at detective Lake. Not that he cared.

Clayton had an officer bring in a cup of coffee for Teresa. She took a long sip and winced at its bitter taste.

"Now, are you comfy?" Lake was tired of her nonsense.

"I'm just fine detective. Ask away."

"Where were you before you found your husband on the floor?"

"You know? I believe I will wait to answer any of your questions. That is until I have my attorney sitting by my side. I would like to go back to my hotel. You know. The one that I own."

Lake sneered at her. "You are free to go. We will be in touch again soon. You and your lawyer."

On the way out of the precinct, Teresa looked back and said to them both, "I expect to see my husband by morning."

She walked out the door, thinking to herself. Did they really believe I would fall for that good cop bad cop thing?

CHAPTER 19

Kei Lien, very weak now from hunger and plain old exhaustion, went to the old barn where she was supposed to meet Daniel. It was getting closer to daylight and she knew she had to find shelter.

She found the bag of food that Daniel had left. At least she hoped it was Daniel. Cheese and crackers tasted fresh enough. Although she wasn't sure about the juice, she figured what could it hurt. The sugar made her feel more alive and yet ready for sleep. She climbed into the loft and covered part of her body with the old hay that remained there after the barn was abandoned. Sleep came quickly.

Dreams and nightmares rolled into one. Fears of someone lurking over her…touching her…entering her…causing her pain. Pain inside her tortured body and pain in her heart. She jumped out of her sleep screaming, "I'm sorry!"

"I'm right here. No one will ever hurt you again. I promise." Standing over her was a man in a Santa Claus suit. Could this be real she thought or was this part of her nightmare? She scrambled to her feet and began to run to the end of the loft. She stopped at the edge, turned around, and he was gone.

CHAPTER 20

Daniel went back to the barn to see if Kei Lien had been there the night before. He found the empty container of orange juice and the insulated bag had only wrappings from the cheese. She had been there. Now angry with himself for not staying longer, he hit the barn door with his fist. He heard rustling of the hay above in the loft. He climbed the ladder slowly to see who, or what, made the noise. He yelled, "Who the hell is in here?"

An old drunk rolled out of the hay scaring Daniel causing him to nearly fall off the ladder.

"I'm looking for a friend of mine. I was supposed to meet her here."

"No one here but me." the drunk muttered, falling back into the hay with a thud.

Daniel left not knowing if it was the drunk or Kei Lien that ate the food.

CHAPTER 21

After Kei Lien got her bearings, she decided it wasn't safe to return to the barn alone and headed out to find Daniel. She found the walk back was a bit more calming to her soul. She remained hidden as best she could, but enjoyed the sounds of the squirrels rustling around, watching the birds soaring from tree to tree and the fresh smell of the earth.

She finally made it back to the neighborhood, but the problem was she couldn't remember which house she had gone to the night before. She had been so frightened she had not even paid attention. It was sheer luck she even ended up at Daniel's house. She began sneaking through the backyards of the houses on her street. Trying to avoid being seen, she crawled through shrubs, bushes and trees leaving scratches on her arms. Eventually, she ended up in her own backyard and saw all the police cars. She was sick to her stomach and feared they would see her. Yellow tape surrounded the home. The home she was brought up in and often prayed she would find a way out of. Staying out of sight, she slipped back into the prickly bushes and continued her search for the house where Daniel lived. Not easy from the backyards. She came upon a back porch a few houses from her own. She let out a sigh of relief when she saw Daniel sitting in a rocking chair, drinking something out of a mug.

Daniel saw her immediately through the rustling of the bushes. "Kei Lien," he lowered his voice to a whisper. "Stop. I'll come to you." He checked to see if his father was near and then jumped off the porch without touching a step. He climbed into the shrubs not really knowing what to expect.

Kei Lien was shaking with fear not understanding what was happening all around her. The fear of not knowing what would become of her now. Who would take care of her? She was scared of what her father would do to her this time if he found her. The last time she ran away, she came back only because of what she had seen and her father punished her for making up such stories. He took a belt to her bottom and that aroused him. Once again, he had his way with her. She was now afraid that Daniel might want to hurt her too.

"What happened to you yesterday? Why didn't you come to the barn?"

"I did go to the barn, but it was late and you weren't there." Hanging her head low she told Daniel, "I was late because after you left, I made my father dinner and expected him to go right to sleep. But he came to my room instead and made me do the bad things to him. I can't remember. I don't want to remember anymore Daniel, I don't. I heard a lot of voices and knew I couldn't take one more Santa gift. So, I ran to my bedroom and crawled out through my window. I started running. I was trying to be really quiet, but I was crying. My legs hurt all over. I didn't know where I was, so I just ran up to a house and started knocking on the door and ringing the bell. I don't remember too much after that until a man in white tried to pull up my dress. I kicked him hard and was able to run away. I kept running. When I went to the barn, you weren't there."

"Did you find the bag of food I left for you?"

"I found a bag with some orange juice and some other stuff. I had hoped you left it for me. Thank you. I ate and then was so tired I fell asleep in the hay. I've been hiding ever since." She was crying again.

Daniel took a step forward to comfort her, but thought she might run again. "I know a place you can go until we figure this out together. It's not real nice yet, but I'm sure we can fix it enough for you to be safe for now. It's an old run-down cabin about three miles into the woods. I'm going to try to make it a nice home again someday. If I bring some stuff from here, I'm sure you will be safe." He knew the cabin wasn't ready to live in. He just wanted her out of the mess where her father had been found dead.

"I think I know that place. I don't know how I remember it. I almost went there last night to hide, but I was so hungry and tired I didn't think I could make it that far."

Daniel found it odd that she would know about the cabin, but decided not to question her. "You must be hungry again by now. Stay behind the shrubs while I get some food for you. Okay?"

She nodded her head yes, all the while wondering if Daniel was safe to tell things to. Would he call the police? Would he really bring her food? Would he help her? Would he tell anyone what he saw and heard through her open window? She took the chance and waited for him to return.

CHAPTER 22

"Daniel, what the hell are you doing? What's all that for? I probably shouldn't even ask, but I will anyway. Who and what are you hiding?"

"Please, just trust that I know what I am doing, Dad. Probably for the first time in my life. I promise I will replace everything I take from here when I go to the store. I just can't go right now. Okay?"

"Just tell me. Is she all right?"

"She will be."

"You do know that the detectives aren't accusing her of anything, that I'm aware of, and just want to make sure she is Mr. Chandler's daughter? They, like myself, are worried about her physical and mental state. Does she even know that he's dead?"

Daniel didn't know how to respond to that question. He wasn't so sure if she wasn't the one that killed him. And if she did, did he want to know?

"I have to go. Love you."

"Be careful son. I love you, too."

Daniel left through the back door with all that he could

carry for now. He was pleasantly surprised to find Kei Lien still hiding in the bushes.

"Ready? We need to get some food and water into you before we take that hike into the woods."

CHAPTER 23

Chief Medical Examiner Sara Hunter and Bill Oosterhout finished the autopsies on Adam Chandler and Sergeant Kelsey. The findings were so different from anything that they had ever seen. The results were more of a guess than a conclusion. It was either the result of the knife wound to the heart or the hole in the brain. It was hard to say which one was the fatal blow. Either could be lethal, both combined definitely were. It appeared that both murders occurred within a very short period between the two locations. The only thing different between the two bodies was what they found in Chandler's brain. A dog tag with one word Santa.

"Do you think the lab has anything that would change our findings?" Bill asked.

"I'm hoping for a miracle, but I highly doubt there will be any other evidence to verify which came first, the chicken or the egg. Or, in this case, the brain or the knife. Put them away for the night. I'm ready for a hot bath and a cold glass of wine. Then, maybe sleep. I wish there was a better answer to all of this. It will be dreadful to tell the relatives."

"The police and the press won't be happy either. One for the books. I'm going to start with a cold beer and then a shower. If I take a bath I may drown. See you in the morning."

"Good night."

CHAPTER 24

"We need some sort of diversion, Boss."

"I know. Who do we know that would be able to make up a story about an unsolved third murder?"

"I can do that," offered the third person in the room. "I can even get a body for you."

"Really? And just which cemetery do we dig up to get one?" the Boss asked sarcastically.

"We don't need a cemetery. I know a place where there are a few buried bodies. Shallow graves. Easy to get to."

"Okay," pausing for a moment, "if you say so. Now, where do we stage these bodies and how many are there?"

"Six," he grinned, allowing drool to run down his bottom lip.

"Stage? Stage! That's it, Boss!" exclaimed his cohort. "What about the Bradford Theatre? Talk about an encore performance."

"Yes! We could display them as a family wrapped in Christmas paper on stage in front of a fireplace prop. How do you know you can get six bodies?"

"I know because I put them there."

"So, you're sure you can find them?"

"Yeah."

"Okay, let's get those lame brained detectives in such a tither that they will be running around like chickens with their heads cut off."

CHAPTER 25

"I need a drink."

Clayton knew that meant Lake was looking for company for the evening. It was their secret code.

When Emerson reached Reese's apartment in the park district of Cromwell, he did the traditional, *you know who* knock at the door. Reese still looked through the peephole anyway. Force of habit. She opened the door. He grabbed her around her waist while kicking the door shut with his foot. His mouth was planted on hers in a split second. He walked her to the bedroom never once removing his arm from around her waist. Once there he said to her, "Is this all right with you?"

"Absolutely detective. And by the way, hello, come on in."

Emerson gave her a quick grin and proceeded to remove her T-shirt. And with one flick of his fingers, her lace bra was now on the floor. He grabbed her breast and rubbed her nipples until they were hard, the feeling made her rise on her toes and lean in for more. He kissed her neck and bit a little on her ears at the same time. She began to unbutton his starched white shirt and loosened his tie enough to pull it over his head. He then unzipped his suit pants and let them fall to the floor. His boxers were next.

Reese was kicking off her sandals when Emerson reached inside her jeans to feel the warm and moist spot, he called his happy place. He then inserted his finger as she moaned for more. He removed her pants with one hand. Her lace panties with the other, while she searched between his legs for what she wanted. He then picked her up and positioned her on the bed. He got on top of her and entered his happy place, moving in and out of her carefully while she almost demanded for him to go deeper and harder. But he wasn't ready for her to finish yet. He removed his penis and grabbed on to her nipples. Nibbling on them, then kissing her from her beautiful neck down to her even more beautiful thighs, lingering between them for quite some time. Reese was about ready to explode when he finally re-entered her with absolute need and desire. This time he took long and hard strokes to make them both moan and finish together.

No words were spoken during this passionate meeting of bodies. Reese wanted to say I love you, but knew there wouldn't be a return word of affection. Because of their careers. At least she hoped that was the reason. They stayed attached to each other until he softened and then rolled off her. Exhausted. Reese got into the shower while he slept. She was just about to get out when the shower door opened.

"I need to shower, too," he said with a mischievous wink.

"I thought you were asleep."

He then rubbed the bar of soap on her wet body and then on himself. He then picked her up, wrapped her legs around his waist and positioned her near his once again aroused manhood.

"Round two. Are you ready?"

"Not in a slippery shower. Let me down before we kill each other in here. Can you see those headlines? Later, okay?"

CHAPTER 26

Officer Allen Manning went to the Strasburg Hotel to visit the newly widowed Teresa Kelsey. He knew she would be there from the conversations he overheard at the station. He also knew the trouble that was about to be brought to his career. Lake and Clayton were pissed that he sent her to the hospital without an officer.

Once at the Strasburg, Allen went to the front desk.

"My name is Officer Manning from the Cromwell Police Department. Would you please tell Teresa Kelsey I would like to see her?"

"Yes sir, I will let her know you're here."

Allen happened to notice the nametag on the desk clerk's pocket. Randall Cummings.

"Randall, do I know you?" he asked, staring at the name tag closer. "Are you from around here? You look vaguely familiar, but I don't remember from where. How did I not get a chance to meet you?"

Allen stuck out his hand and waited for Randall to offer his up for the handshake. He did hesitantly.

"Nice to meet you Mr. Manning…oh I mean…Officer Manning," Randall stuttered.

"It's fine, Randall. This isn't an official visit, but thank you."

Randall spoke in hushed tones on the phone before hanging up.

"Mrs. Kelsey said she'd meet you in the café."

"Thank you, Randall. Have a nice day."

As he went into the café, he felt very uneasy. He knew that guy from somewhere. He made a mental note of the meeting as he found Teresa already waiting for him. Drink in hand and one for him as well.

"Good thing I'm off duty. Thank you."

He took the drink and offered a toast, clinking his glass against hers.

"It's so nice to see you feeling better," he continued. "You two were together for a long time. Is there anything at all that I can help you with? Do you need help making Martin's arrangements?"

"How very kind of you. If I find difficulty with anything or anyone, I will certainly contact you. I appreciate the gesture, though."

"Is there someone bothering you? Just tell me. I would be glad to help."

"It's just the thought of those pesky reporters trying to dig up information that is no one's business."

"I'll see if we can put a guard out here to make sure no one that's not supposed to be here stays away."

He shuffled in his seat trying to think of how to switch topics. He finally decided just to go for it.

"Had anyone threatened your husband or you, that you know of? Maybe a business partner of yours? Or a person Martin might have had a run in with on the job? You know how it is out there. People will shoot you for a routine traffic stop."

"I can't think of anyone at the moment, but I will let you know when my mind clears out from the shock of seeing him like that."

"Yeah, you're right. I should let you get some rest. But just know I'm here for you." He stood to leave, patting her shoulder. "Everything will be all right."

On his way out of the hotel, Allen paused at the desk where Randall was busy with the computer. Randall looked up from what he was doing and said, "May I help you, Officer?"

"Can I ask a favor of you?"

"Of course, sir. How can I help?"

"If any reporters try to bother Mrs. Kelsey, call me. Right away. Here's my personal number."

"I will do that. Glad to help."

"Thank you, Randall. Have a good one."

"You as well."

Until I can remember this guy, Allen thought to himself, it's good to keep him on my side. Keep him thinking I'm trying to protect Teresa.

CHAPTER 27

It was easy to dig up the bodies. They were not too far from the cabin and not too deep in the ground. The only extra work was to clear away all the leaves and forest debris that accumulated over the years. There wasn't much left of them. Not heavy at all, but enough bones on each one for that shock value.

I will carefully put them in the van and take them to the Bradford Theater. I don't want the boss to yell at me for mixing up the bodies. Everyone knows they will be brought to the morgue to be identified. I can't believe how excited I am to see them all again. It was such fun to watch them die. Not mom though. I love her. I'm sorry, but you shouldn't have slapped me. You shouldn't have said you were going to put me away again.

When they met at the theater, it was agreed that each one of the bodies had a purpose in how and where they would be displayed on the stage. An afternoon class for the town's seniors would be starting in two days. Just something for the old folks to keep their minds busy. These types of classes were offered several times a year. In two days, they would probably never be offered again.

"You want me to get the furniture from the props room?"

"Yes. A few cushioned chairs, a sofa and a table as well. Grab a few big sofa pillows to put on the floor."

"Got it."

"Mom and two children on the sofa. Knitting needles on Mom's lap. Two more children on the pillows on the floor facing a cardboard television. And dear old Dad, well of course, we will wrap him in Christmas paper and place him in front of the fake fireplace."

"Won't that be a nice family reunion scene? Let's move quickly. We don't want anyone realizing we are in here. By the way, how did you get the doors open, Boss?"

"It's called a key, idiot. You didn't see any broken windows or a busted lock, did you?"

"That wasn't a very nice thing to say to me," he mumbled to himself. "I don't like that word." He walked away.

Within an hour the stage was set. Everyone was in their places just as planned. Except there was no butcher knife or evidence of brain surgery.

"Now let's get out of here and watch the Cromwell Police think they are doing a great job solving two murders. Surprise!"

CHAPTER 28

Cromwell Senior Citizens Arts Club met on a weekly basis to draw, paint, and put on a little show for the area now and then. They were a creative group of people. They approached the theater on Tuesday afternoon ready to rehearse a song and dance show that everyone agreed (for a change) would be a tremendous amount of fun.

Sometimes there were 12 seniors. Other times maybe 20. Nice size group for a senior citizen club. This time all of them wanted to partake in the fun. They entered through a side door that led to a meeting room, where they all took a seat. They were discussing the particulars of the show. Roles, what music to play, the dance moves, etc. Once that was done, they headed to the stage to evaluate where everyone should be positioned during the production. It was a tremendous amount of preparation. When Alice, the group's leader, along with a few others started up the steps to the stage, she was puzzled.

"What is going on here? No one told me there was another show taking place at the Bradford."

Suddenly, there was a blood-curdling scream from one of the

other women.

"Dear God! These are real bodies!" shouted John, a senior in his mid-eighties. He began gasping for breath and clutching his chest.

Leaning in for a closer look, Alice shrieked, "Lord almighty! He's right!"

"Call 911," John whispered before falling into the arms of two men standing nearby.

Screams of sheer terror were coming from the ladies. Men were ushering them off the stage as fast as possible. Alice, knowing she was the leader, kept yelling orders to everyone, not really knowing what the hell just happened herself. The two men got John outside to the fresh air before he collapsed.

"Help is on the way! Hold on, John."

They each took turns doing CPR on him.

"Did anyone call 911?" Alice yelled.

Within minutes, police cars came from all directions. Reese and Emerson came to a screeching halt. Reese jumped out and ran to the man lying on the ground and took over CPR until the paramedics arrived. They stabilized him and put him in the ambulance.

"Hopefully, they can save him," Alice said.

"And you are?" Clayton asked.

"I'm Alice Warner," she said through tears. "I'm in charge of the show that is scheduled to be playing here soon."

"One of the officers will take a statement from you, Ms. Warner."

Both Reese and Emerson walked into the building where all hell was breaking loose. The seniors were all talking at once. They were visibly shaken. Their nerves shattered. Camera flashes were going off everywhere to capture the evidence and crime scene.

"Officer Manning," ordered Lake, "please take these people into the meeting room and get their personal info along with statements about this afternoon's events. No one leaves until we clear them. Got it?"

Manning knew this order was strictly meant for him after the incident with Teresa Kelsey. Allen wanted to slam Lake's face into the wall for making him feel like more of an ass than he already did. Teresa had acted like she really passed out. What was I going to do, stop her from getting medical attention? Moron.

One by one, the seniors were released and told they would be contacted if further information was needed. Alice was the last to make a statement. Allen had known her for a long time, so taking her preliminary info was fast.

"Tell me what happened when all of you arrived here today. Did you see anyone else in the building?"

"No, I didn't, and I don't believe anyone else did either. But you would have to ask them. Who do you suppose those poor people are or I should say…were? What a disturbing scene, to walk onto that stage thinking it was set up for a different show and then suddenly realize they weren't props. The bodies, they were laid out to look like…well I don't even know how to describe what they looked like."

Avoiding her question, Allen continued. "Can you tell me how you knew they were real bodies? I mean did you touch them at all?"

"No, I did not touch anything, damn it! I may be old, but I'm not stupid," she stiffened, "John yelled they were real, grabbed his chest in pain and all hell broke loose. When I looked closer for myself, I knew he was right. I've been to enough theater productions in my lifetime to know what a fake set of bones look like. More plastic than real. These weren't plastic. By the way, being a senior citizen just means I have a whole lot more life experience than you. I'm not stupid. Are we done here?"

"I'm very sorry, but all of us are just trying to piece together what happened and making sure no stone is unturned. We will be contacting you if we need any more information. You can go now, and Alice, thank you. You are indeed a smart woman. Are we okay?" he asked with a little wink.

With that she turned to walk out and, as she did, gave him a shy grin.

The M.E. arrived quickly, as well as her associate, Bill.

"Sara, I hope you will be able to give us cause of death and how long they have been dead. More importantly I also need to know who they are. Our relatively small city is turning into a big city crime spree."

"They don't look fresh, that's for sure. May take some time to get you those answers Detective Lake, but we will get on it as soon as we get these victims back to the morgue. Please make sure all these bodies, at least what's left of them, are bagged separately. That way we will be able to piece them together. Without causing a jigsaw puzzle effect, I hope."

Once again reporters were on scene in a flash. Trying their best to get answers and to get an award-winning story. And that it would be. Once again, the response, no comment, from police.

"Another body placed in front of a fireplace," Lake mused. "Wrapped in holiday paper. If we can just figure out what that one piece of the equation means, we might have a better chance of cracking this case."

CHAPTER 29

"It's okay, my precious little one, I'm here to love you like you asked in your letter to Santa. I will see right through you and touch you with my warm body and love you. Now close your eyes tight."

Kei Lien screamed in pain as this monster of a man climbed on top of her and brutally raped her for the first time and then, with tenderness, washed her with warm water and told her not to tell anyone because this is what she asked for in her letter to Santa. He then said to her, "Now say you're sorry." She did as she was told.

Kei Lien was forced into this life of torture, which she believed was her fault. Like he had said, she asked in her letter for someone to love her.

Kei Lien was born to Asian parents that loved her very much. So much so that they wanted her to have a better life in a free country, the United States of America. They had heard if she went to America, she could be anything she wanted to be without fear. They made a deal for adoption with a group unknown to them and probably unknown to most of the families looking for better lives for their children. A local store owner told them that adoption was quick and easy. Word came of a couple that would take Kei Lien to a new home and would pay the parents a good deal of money for letting her go with them to the States. The deal was done. She was only one year old.

When Kei Lien was brought to America, her new family showered her with love. They taught her the good in life, love, and laughter. She was happy. They gave her a nice home to live in with a beautiful bedroom of her own. Pink everywhere, lace pillows and a nightstand that held a little Golden book titled, *The Night Before Christmas*. They bought her new clothes and taught her to speak English. Claire and Adam Chandler were loving parents in every way. They even taught her how to write to Santa Claus every year, something most American parents look forward to. It was a new life, a good life, for Kei Lien. A life she would not have had living in a foreign country as a female.

Her new mom, whom she loved like no other, had taken ill. During an unexpected pregnancy, Claire started to have very painful cramping in her lower abdomen. Then a slow trickle of dark watery blood ran down her legs. Claire knew she had to get into bed and get her feet up. Within an hour, the pain in her abdomen had become unbearable and the bleeding was even heavier. There was no doubt that she was going to give birth prematurely. Kei Lien was a child, a frightened child, who tried desperately to help her mother. They both cried. Claire, because she knew what was happening to herself and her unborn child, and Kei Lien, because she couldn't stand to see her mother in pain. Claire told her daughter to run and get help. She tried to get her father's attention. Screaming at him waving her arms around frantically, but he could not hear her past the roar of the lawn mower. By the time Adam finally came into the house, it was over. She had lost the baby during the birth. Claire tried to protect her daughter from seeing the blood and the pain she was having during the miscarriage to no avail. It's something you can't un-see. Two hours later, Claire was gone as well. She had lost too much blood. Her beautiful daughter sobbed uncontrollably. She was barely ten years old.

Kei Lien was now left with a very angry father. His mind, now focused on the tragedy in his life, took his frustration out on this mere child. The child he once loved but now no longer wanted.

By the time Kei Lien was 13 years old, she had already written many letters to Santa, all asking for someone to love her. Each time, the answer would be delivered by her father. On occasion, it would be a total stranger that arrived. She would watch helplessly as each one paid to be her gift. They would tell her to close her eyes and be quiet and not to tell anyone. When they were done with her, the father would bathe her in warm water to stop her from crying and then he would say, "This is your fault. This is what you asked for. Now say you're sorry."

She was nearing the age of fourteen when she began to gain a bit of weight around her middle. She had no idea why she felt sick in the morning. She was not allowed to attend school after her mother died, so there was no education on pregnancy and babies. Adam Chandler realized what was happening to her and assumed the child wasn't his because of the other paid encounters. He found a wire coat hanger, unwound it, and inserted it into her to get rid of the baby and said to Kei Lien,

"It's the right thing to do." A memory of her mother trying to be brave, for the sake of her little girl, flashed before her eyes. Someone, help me, she thought to herself through rivers of tears. Please someone help me. But no one did. He then washed her with warm water while she screamed not only in pain, but at the horror she had just witnessed.

CHAPTER 30

Kei Lien and Daniel took their time on the three-mile hike through the woods. They stopped not too far in so they could refresh with some food. It was the first time Daniel was able to have a conversation with her and get to ask a few questions.

"What happened in that house that made your father attack you like that?" he asked gently. "Have others, besides the Sergeant, done this to you as well? You must be close to my age. Why did you stay so long?"

Kei Lien struggled to keep all that she knew inside for fear everyone would know this was her fault.

"Please help me to help you," Daniel continued. "I know it can't be easy. I want to be your friend and friends tell each other things that they would never tell anyone else."

She thought to herself...do I trust him? this young man that I know nothing about? Is he just another gift? Is this just a game my father wants me to go along with? He did try to help and get me to safety. He did leave food for me. And he hasn't tried to touch my body at all. All of this did make her feel good about him.

"It's all because of my letters to Santa. It's all my fault." She began to sob. "All I asked for my whole life was for someone to love me. That's why these men came to my house and that's why my father would also hurt me."

"What does that even mean, letters to Santa? Take a deep breath and start over. Please. I want to know. I want to help you as much as I can."

"I have been writing to Santa since I was a little girl. My mom and dad taught me how to write a letter to him when I was little. When mom died having the baby, the baby died too. But I still wrote letters to Santa, hoping I could find someone that loved me like my mom did and like my father used to."

"So, he blamed you?"

"Yes. He didn't want me anymore. He wanted his real child and his wife back. I didn't know what to do so I just kept writing to Santa."

"Then what happened?"

"He told me I was no longer welcome in school and that I would be the one to take care of him. Cook, clean, and do his laundry. And…" her voice trailed off.

"That's okay. You don't have to tell me anything else until you want to."

They continued the hike to the cabin. When they arrived, Daniel stopped abruptly before opening the door. He turned to Kei Lien, motioning for her to be quiet. He thought he heard someone inside. He thought he was the only one that knew about this place. But there it was again…rustling of leaves…twigs breaking. Daniel held his breath. His heart started to race a little faster. Suddenly, two squirrels leapt through the hole in the wall. Zigging this way and that…chasing each other up a tree. Daniel let out a little sigh of relief and it gave Kei Lien a smile.

"This is where I thought we could keep you safe, but it will need a lot of work to make it livable. I'm going to hire some locals to help. There are some things that I can't do by myself."

"I'll help you. Please, don't let anyone know I'm here. I can clean it up if you find me a broom, some rags and some soap and water."

"Kei Lien, these walls have big holes in them. That's how the squirrels got in and who knows what else."

"We can use the blankets you brought to hang over the holes in between the logs. Does that pump work?"

"Not yet, but I was going to see if I could make it work again. What if you need to use the bathroom, there is none except for that old outhouse?"

"There's also the woods if I need to. You could bring me stuff to use and some food and water to drink, maybe?"

"Well let's see how far we get today with cleaning it up, okay? No promises. I want to help you, but I want you to be safe first. Blankets won't help keep out the critters. I'll have to find some wood that will fit in the holes and maybe some dirt will help hold it in place."

Kei Lien started sweeping the floor, as best she could anyway. Not much hope for this place. There were nutshells and animal droppings all over. She needed water. She went to the pump and started the task of priming it. Over and over she would pull the handle up and down to get it to spit out some hope of water. Daniel stopped her and told her that they needed some water to pour down the spout to give it that prime. It had been sitting like this for years he guessed.

"When we come back, we will bring water with us in big jugs and something to clean the floors with, okay? You can't stay here until we know you will be safe. When we leave, I will ask my father to help us and maybe he will let you stay with us for a few days. I promise you, no one will hurt you there."

"No. My father will find me and take me away with him. I can't say I'm sorry to any more gifts from Santa. Please."

He knew then that Kei Lien did not know her father was dead. He wished this conversation were within earshot of those detectives. That way they would know she had no idea about the murder. He deserved to be dead after what he had done to this girl. Her childhood was taken away, along with her teen years. Not much formal education, although she had been schooled on the evil in life and knew more than anyone could imagine. Her father had taken her virginity and sold her into near slavery.

"What kind of animal does that?"

He realized he had said that out loud.

"Kei Lien, I can't leave you here. I promise to make sure you are safe. Please listen to me and trust me. I am your friend. I will never hurt you or let anyone else hurt you ever again. Do you believe me? Do you trust what I am saying to you is true?"

"You are my friend. You are my friend. You are my friend." She repeated these words over and over again. They were familiar, but she couldn't remember where she heard them before. She looked directly at Daniel and then hung her head in defeat. "What else is there for me to do?" Tears began to run down her face, which was caked with the sweat and dirt she had been sweeping. She thought for a moment. If Daniel doesn't help me, I will find another butcher knife. Just like the one in dad's kitchen sink and end it all just like I meant to do before. Before father gets another chance to hurt me. Yes. That's what I will do.

"Okay. I'll go with you. I'm so tired."

Daniel knew the fear in her voice was something to take seriously. Perhaps it was instinct from the little medical education he had in the past. "Let's take a different trail out so you can get to see the beauty in these woods. See the peaceful sights that I see every day. We can talk some more if you like. You can ask me anything you want to. Is that all right with you?"

She nodded her head, still not sure about anything. She was getting more confused by this person who seemed to really care about what happened to her.

CHAPTER 31

Some remains of the bodies were sent to two different medical examiners in the neighboring counties, to help get a little more control of the situation. More eyes...more answers. Maybe.

Over the next few days, Sara and Bill worked on the bodies that were already in the morgue as well as the new arrivals. Even though there was no knife found or other weapons, it appeared knife wounds were the cause of death in all the new victims. A large knife. At least as far as they could tell with what was left of the bodies.

"Bill, would you mind contacting the detectives to tell them our findings so far? Inform them about the knife blade. I'll check with the other M.E.'s to see what, if anything, they have to add. Oh. And one more thing. Would mind telling Detective Lake about the brain surgery and dog tag? He's going to flip when he hears that one. Hell, I still don't understand it myself."

"Of course," Bill replied. "Want coffee or something when I come back?"

"No, I don't think I could digest anything right now. You think you've seen it all in this crazy world."

Sara contacted one of the other Medical Examiners but there was no new information. The second phone call was to Mark Swanson, a good friend from the Wesley County Coroner's office.

"Mark, it's Sara Hunter. Have you found anything? I'm sorry. How are you? We haven't spoken in such a long time. How is your family?"

Sara was running questions at him so fast he couldn't even answer them.

"Sara, you need a drink! Give me a chance to at least say hello to you," he chuckled. "I was just about to call. Just as you thought, two of the bodies were children. But one of them had some dental work done. Not a lot to work with here. Decomposition is pretty bad. Appears they have been dead for quite a few years. I'm just guessing, but I believe they are related. We are sending the dental work to the lab."

"I thought the same about them all being related, but I need to stick with the facts. Now the police need to search databases for a missing family of six. Who knows where they came from, let alone who did this to them or why? Let's work on the type of soil left on the bones. Maybe it will help us find out where they were originally buried."

"Got it! Now go do something that is not related to death for about an hour."

Sara smiled to herself. "Thank you, Mark."

CHAPTER 32

Cromwell Police had immediately started running searches on missing families as soon as the bodies were discovered at the theater. Sara went upstairs to speak to the detectives but was disappointed when they weren't there. Instead, she spoke to Officer Manning.

"We are now looking for a missing family of six," she announced.

"Already on it," Manning replied. "This was done immediately after the bodies were found. Sara, you know the way this works like the back of your hand. What's going on? You don't look good."

"Oh, thanks," she replied with a smirk. "I've just been unnerved by this case. I feel like I should know more than I do by now. I wish I could explain it, but I can't."

"I get it, kiddo. We are all feeling overwhelmed. I'll let the detectives know what you found so far."

Downstairs, the new recruit, Officer Kenneth Sorenson, met the detectives as they walked through the door.

"You guys might want to take a look at this," he said, pointing toward a television set. "The news, national news, is talking about a possible serial killer on the loose in Cromwell, South Dakota. The phones are ringing non-stop with people asking for answers."

Emerson tossed his stuff on his desk without removing his gaze from the TV screen. There she was. Beautiful, long red hair and the greenest eyes he had ever seen. Her dream of becoming a national news reporter was right there in front of him. It wasn't her original plan of covering the White House, but it was close.

"Sir? Sir?"

Lake was speechless for a moment.

"What do you want to do?" the recruit persisted. "Should we set up a press conference, Detective Lake?"

"I'll take care of it, Ken," Lake finally said. "Find me a number for that reporter."

"Right away, detective. I'm on it."

I wonder how long before she will contact me? She certainly knows where I have been all these years. Brenda seemed to be staring right into his eyes through the television screen. Emerson Lake was deaf to the outside world in that moment. He could almost smell her hair and taste her lips. My God, she is beautiful. His thoughts turning into a jumbled mess.

"Hey, Lake. Isn't that the girl you used to date way back when?" Officer Manning interrupted. "Boy, she is a knock-out for sure."

Manning was treading on thin ice and he knew it, but after the remarks Lake had made earlier, it felt good to take him down a notch.

"Yes, she is. Anything else you'd like to comment on? Or

anyone else for that matter? Get back to work or the next job on your resume will be station janitor!"

Lake knew he could never go back to that time in his life, but seeing her again woke up that familiar tingle in his chest. He certainly didn't know how he would handle having her here reporting on this serial killer. And that is what this was for sure. A serial killer.

"Manning, tell Detective Clayton I need her in my office now."

"Really, Lake?" Clayton asked.

Lake turned around to see her standing with her hand on her hip. Close to her weapon.

"What the hell was that?" she asked. "Are you ordering me into this office? Because the last I knew we were equal partners here."

"Sorry, this case has got one hell of hold on all of us."

"Are you sure it's the case?" she whispered, hoping no one else heard her.

"Look, I don't need this crap right now, Clayton!"

"Neither do I," she said taking a step back. "And it's Detective Clayton to you, asshole! Your partner. Remember?"

CHAPTER 33

Emerson Lake was born and raised in Cromwell, South Dakota. He always wanted to be in law enforcement, worked hard to get there and now he was a highly-regarded detective. Not much ever happened in his city. Nothing major anyway. But he was still proud to have that title. Detective.

As far as his love life went, there had been several women, but none like the one that stole his heart. He met her around the time his career was about to take him in new directions. She was a real go-getter as well and wanted to become a top-notch writer for big city newspapers. Political press mostly. But she found her way to a D.C. television station WDC 23, and began reporting on air and in the field. She would take on any major story that came along, no matter where she had to travel. She had red hair and pale white skin, as most redheads often do, and a few freckles that kissed her nose. Six feet tall, Brenda Charles was nearly as tall as Emerson. She could easily have been a model. Lake had fallen in love with her almost immediately. Not always a good idea, but she felt the same way about him.

The opportunity for Lake's dream of becoming a detective was on track. It's what he always wanted to do. He also wanted Brenda to be by his side when he made it. He would have asked her to marry him in a heartbeat, but when he told her he had the good fortune to stay in South Dakota, everything changed. Washington D.C. or New York were more of what she had in mind. She asked him to give her the breathing room to try out her skills elsewhere. He agreed and hoped she would return to him quickly so they could marry and have a beautiful family.

After a few months of her being away, he realized she was in no hurry to return to their relationship and he reluctantly agreed to break it off.

Lake dated a few women after that, but nothing heavy until a certain very good-looking woman decided to join the force about a year after Lake and Brenda parted ways. Her name was Reese Clayton. Detective Reese Clayton. She was not what you would call a big city kind of girl, but certainly knew the ropes in this field. Lake was no longer top dog in the department. He now had an equal player at the table. Sometimes heated discussions flew back and forth between the two, which to the rest of the precinct was sort of comical, but they did not dare to laugh or even smirk in front of Lake.

After being partners for nearly six months, they both felt an urge that should never be allowed on the force. Too many things can and do go wrong. But you can't just stop on a dime when it comes to matters of heart, or in this case in matters of desire. The encounters didn't happen often, only when needed. Lake could certainly go back for more at any time, but knew it might cause a romantic issue. Something he was not ready for currently in his life. Reese would act the same, but that's all it was…an act. She really cared for her partner but knew it could cost them both their careers.

CHAPTER 34

Kei Lien and Daniel continued to walk through the woods, being very quiet for a while. It was a different path than Daniel had taken before. He knew the direction he was going. He had just never gone this way. Up ahead, after about a mile and a half walk in silence, Daniel noticed a narrow road. Not much wider than a path, but certainly a road. There were signs of tire tracks. Maybe it was tracks from an ATV, but they looked a little wider than that. This was good news for Daniel. It meant an easier way to haul stuff in to rebuild the cabin. Kei Lien stopped and looked around the woods in a way that Daniel had never seen before. He thought she had finally seen the good in life.

"Isn't it beautiful out here?" he asked. "So peaceful and alive with trees and animals. You know, mother nature at its best."

Kei Lien glared at him. "No. This is a bad place. A very bad place!"

She began to run away like a child afraid of a monster under her bed. Daniel grabbed at her wrist and she fell to the ground. She lay there screaming, "No! No! No!"

She kicked and punched at him until he finally said to her, "I'm not trying to hurt you, Kei Lien! I'm trying to help you!"

She was crying now, giving in to the exhaustion. She sat up; her eyes locked on his as he helped her get on her feet. Kei Lien brushed the dirt and leaves off her clothes, clenched her fists and suddenly pushed Daniel, knocking him to the ground. She ran farther into the woods. By the time Daniel could collect himself, she was nowhere to be found. He spun in circles trying to catch a glimpse of her. "Oh my God, what the hell just happened?"

He tried desperately to find her. Running in all directions. Calling her name repeatedly, but nothing. He was so distracted, he tripped and went headfirst into a hole, hitting his nose on a rock. First came the throbbing pain and then blood squirted out from his nostrils. He pulled his shirt up over his head and tilted his head back, using the T-shirt to apply pressure to the bridge of his nose. He prayed it wasn't broken.

When he was sure it had stopped gushing, he let go of his nose and looked to see what he tripped over. He nearly passed out. Not from the blood loss, but from the hole he was standing in. It was no random hole. This looked like a shallow grave! Terrified, Daniel scrambled up out of the hole. Once upright, his heart sank as he realized there were five more holes just like the one he crawled out of. He knew this wasn't random. The holes were neatly placed in two rows and he could tell they were freshly excavated. Daniel collected himself and started running as fast as he could. He knew he had to find Kei Lien. Was she aware of these graves? She said this was a very bad place. Is that why she ran? Did she see something she wasn't supposed to see?

He eventually came upon the ATV tracks again and decided to follow them. Sure enough, they led to the only road he knew about in the forest. It was farther down the trail, but much closer to the cabin than the path they had hiked.

"I don't know why I never saw this before," he thought out loud.

As soon as he got to the road, he caught something out of the corner of his eye. Kei Lien was huddled behind a tree. Shaking. Daniel slowed his run to a walk trying to catch his breath. He didn't want to startle her. He didn't know if he should try to talk to her.

"Daniel, I'm scared," she said and stood up next to him.

Daniel was a little more cautious this time. He didn't want to get sucker punched again. But his kind heart and common sense took over. "Follow me to Dad's house."

She nodded her head in agreement.

CHAPTER 35

There was still yellow tape around Kei Lien's house and a forensic team onsite as she and Daniel cautiously approached his home. Daniel let himself in and was met by a very upset father.

"Where the hell have you been and why are you bloody? I've been waiting for hours for you to return."

Kei Lien didn't know what to do. Was this man going to hurt Daniel? Will he hurt me? I can't run away again. She spoke up, which surprised both Daniel and his dad.

"It's because he was trying to help me and I wouldn't listen. I had seen where we were before, but I don't know when. It brought back such bad visions in my head. I thought he was going to hurt me, so I punched him in the mouth and ran."

"Kei Lien, what is it you remember? We are both trying to help you. The police have been trying to figure out if you are alive or if were you murdered like your father. No one wanted to scare you. Honest."

Daniel shot a look at his father, the kind of look that said shut up.

"Dad, stop. We need to call the police and get them here

before we say anything else about all of this."

Kei Lien was confused and afraid to ask. Was her father really dead? She watched as Mr. Nyung dialed a number into the phone.

"Cromwell Police. Officer Manning. How can we help you?" said the voice on the other end.

"Could you connect me with Detectives Lake and Clayton please?" asked Nyung.

"May I ask who is calling?"

"Nyung," is all he said.

"One of them will be right with you, Mr. Nyung."

Clayton and Lake were on two separate phones, both listening to what Mr. Nyung had to say.

"What can we do for you?" Lake asked.

"You can start by calling me Minh, Detective Lake. The name Nyung is too hard to pronounce. My son is here. With a visitor. I thought you might like to speak with her. Her name is Kei Lien Chandler."

"We are on our way," said Lake. "But please do not let any reporters near Daniel and certainly not the girl. Got it? This is already a circus; we do not need the hounds out and about, if you know what I'm saying."

"I hear you. Thank you."

They arrived at 211 Braxton fifteen minutes later.

"I think we should park away from the house," Clayton said. "So no one will catch on to where we are. There is enough commotion on this street. No need to draw more attention than necessary."

"You're right," Lake said.

"I'm right about a lot of things," Reese replied in a low condescending voice.

Emerson pretended he didn't hear her remark.

Once inside, Daniel told the detectives how frail Kei Lien was in her mind and body, but also how fear could change her in a flash.

Reese wanted to ask, which one was it when she knocked out your tooth? Mind or body? But she held it in along with her urge to laugh. She was still wavering on whether to believe this guy or not.

Daniel had been too frightened to even notice the missing tooth. Besides, his nose was still sore from hitting that rock when he fell into the hole.

"Kei Lien, I'm Detective Reese Clayton and this gentleman is Detective Emerson Lake. Do you feel well enough to speak to us about what happened before you ran away from home?"

"Is my father really dead?"

"Kei Lien, I'm very sorry, but yes he is. Did you see what happened to him? Or see anyone else before you ran?"

"I'm glad he's dead and I will never say I'm sorry again to him or any of his gifts. Never, never, never!"

"Dad, do you think Kei Lien needs an attorney present?" Daniel asked.

"No! No more presents! He's dead. He can't bring me gifts anymore!"

Daniel jumped in immediately. "She was raped repeatedly by her father and others he brought into the house. He told her they were gifts from Santa."

"How do you know this?" his father asked.

"Because I saw one of the so-called gifts go in the house and leave again. I was listening under her bedroom window when this man raped her and told her it was her fault because she asked for this in her letter to Santa."

"Daniel! Why didn't you stop him or call for help? What the hell were you thinking? You allowed a girl to be raped while you listened?"

"No, you don't understand, Dad. I was walking back to our house after speaking to Kei Lien for a minute. She said she couldn't talk. Said she had to make dinner for her father. When she first saw me, she asked if I was a gift from Santa. I didn't know what to say to that. It was such a weird question. When I was walking away, I turned around and saw a man at her door. I heard him say gift from Santa. I was curious, so I snuck through the bushes to find out why this man was there and why he made that statement to her. I heard them under an open window in the back of the house. Her bedroom. He was really hurting her, but I didn't know what was happening or why."

"So, you allowed this young lady to be raped without even calling the police?" Lake sneered.

"No! Wait a minute. I *couldn't* call the police. I was afraid of what would happen to her and afraid of being arrested myself," Daniel pleaded.

"Why didn't you come to me at least? I'm your father."

"I know, but this was different. I'm smart enough to know right from wrong for heaven's sake. I'm not stupid."

Reese jumped in. "Then why?"

"The one raping her was Sergeant Martin Kelsey. How do you call the police on the police? I knocked on her window when the Sergeant left. She was hysterical. I asked if her father was doing the same thing to her and she said yes. I wanted to take her away then, but she said she would meet me later after her father went to sleep. We agreed on an abandoned barn on the edge of town. She never showed up."

"We're going to need you to come down to the station…both of you. We'll need your statements."

Reese was angry. Daniel had allowed this girl (in a woman's body) to be abused. She knew when they were interviewing Minh the first time that something didn't add up.

"Wait! There's more. A lot more," Daniel interjected.

Reese glared at Emerson and back at the young man. "I'll bet there is."

"Let him talk." Lake jumped in.

He was already pissed that Reese was lashing out at this kid, when he knew it was really him that she was angry with since seeing this morning's news broadcast.

Daniel explained how they had gone back to the woods, to an abandoned cabin. But as they were walking back, Kei Lien got scared and ran away.

"I started chasing after her but fell into a hole and hit my nose on a rock. But it wasn't just a hole. It was a grave and there were six of them! I was so scared I ran to find Kei Lien and get the hell out of there. She was huddled under a tree near the road. That's when we came here. I really was trying to help her. Please, Dad. I really was. You have to believe me."

"How do you know those holes were graves?" asked Detective Lake.

"I don't, but it sure looked like a cemetery to me. Especially when I saw the remains of a human foot in front of me."

"Mr. Nyung," Clayton stepped in, "sorry Minh, I would like to get this young lady to the hospital to be checked out. Have a rape kit done. We will need a statement from you, Daniel."

"I want to go with Kei Lien to the hospital," Daniel replied. "She is too frightened to go alone and she has no idea what you are saying, Detective"

Reese reluctantly agreed with Daniel, she could see the fear on this young lady's face.

Emerson asked Minh to come with them. He knew this was going to get ugly. Daniel had already said enough to get him in deep water. Kei Lien was just thankful her father was dead. Emerson believed that Kei Lien went through hell in that house and would need a lot of help sorting through all of it. He believed Minh would be the best person to be at her side, along with Daniel, whom she was beginning to trust.

CHAPTER 36

"I heard that there were two victims that were the product of a little brain tampering so to speak. Is this true? Did you think that I wouldn't find out about the second one? I know everything going on in this town and this stab at being some sort of surgeon upsets me. You know I don't like being upset! You know if I give an order, I want that order followed correctly, right?"

"Yes, boss I know, but it was a mistake. Let me explain."

"Mistake? How in the hell do you make that kind of mistake?" Taking a deep breath, "Why don't you tell me what happened?"

"I did what you wanted me to do with Chandler. When I got to his house, the Sergeant was leaving. I thought, well, now would be the time to take care of business. I waited for a while to go in. The door was open a little bit. I figured the Sergeant left it open. I could hear Chandler yelling at his daughter. He was telling her it was her fault and to say she was sorry. Boss, I remember him saying that to her before. When I was in the house another time. No one saw me then either."

The Boss almost interrupted him to ask why the hell he was

in the house before but didn't. "Go on."

"I was going to ring the bell, but..."

"But what, you moron?"

He began to twitch. "I don't like that word."

"Okay, then what?"

"I just gave the door a little push. When I went in, Chandler was on the floor with a knife stuck in him. I swear I could hear the gurgling in his chest. I figured my partner had been waiting for him and now I could finish the job. I heard noise coming from the back part of the house and realized I wasn't alone. I was careful, Boss. I swear, but just as I got to one of the back bedrooms, I saw the girl trying to climb out the window. She was scared, for sure. I told her I would not hurt her, Boss. I kept telling her I was her friend. That's when she jumped out the window and ran. Boss, she was hurt. I could see blood, but I swear I didn't touch her. Boss, do you think...."

His partner interjected, "Did you know that fucked-up Chandler told all the men that had sex with his daughter that they were a gift to her from Santa? Sick bastard. Even the Sergeant didn't give a shit that she was just a young girl. Is that why you hired us? To protect the girl from being hurt again? Is that why you gave us the dog tag?"

The Boss ignored the question and turned back to the moron. "What happened next? I mean, after the girl ran?"

"I wrapped him up in the paper and glued his eyes shut like you said. I did add a little extra. I tied a ribbon around his thing. Then I high-tailed it out of there. I got to the Sergeant's house and saw he was already on the floor, too. His head was split open from the back. I started to put the dog tag in his brain.

I guess I was nervous, but then thought this is the wrong guy. So, I stitched him up, stuck the knife in him a little bit more and went back to the Chandler house and put the dog tag in his brain. No one saw me because I went in through the girl's bedroom window this time. Did I do it right? The way you wanted me to?"

He was cut off by his partner, "Where should we go from here? Do you think we did enough to make them look in other directions for the killer of Martin and that Adam guy?"

"I don't think we have to worry for now," the Boss assured. "They have their hands full trying to figure out who the dead family is, how they got there and who killed them."

"So, what's next?" the moron snorted back a loogie, but held back the urge to spit when the Boss glared at him in disgust. He swallowed hard and smiled wide showing his rotting, green teeth.

"Let's just stay away from each other for a while so we won't be connected to anything going on in this city. I'll set you up in a motel across the state line. You can go about your business. Maybe find a job somewhere. You know, look like you fit in the community. I will contact you when everything calms down here."

"What about this guy?" he said motioning. "Does he get to stay in town?"

"No. I found another spot for him," the Boss replied, trying to be as convincing as possible. "Now get your stuff together. Quickly. A cab will pick you up in an hour at Rosie's Bar."

The Boss turned to the moron's partner.

"You, on the other hand, will be picked up next to the Trixie Market. Don't be late or they will leave without you. I have already paid the cab drivers. We will talk soon, but I have a lot of work to do here."

Moron? The Boss really shouldn't call me that. I don't like that to be called names he thought clenching his jaw as he headed for the door. Am I going to be the one to take the blame for all of this, he wondered? Is my so-called helper being sent away so it looks like he had no part in all of this if things take a bad turn? I know one thing for sure, he thought, I won't let them get away with it. Even if I am blamed. He left to pack everything he owned in a brown shopping bag with frayed handles and waited at Rosie's Bar.

CHAPTER 37

"Detective Lake, there's a call for you. She says it's important."

Lake picked up the phone.

"This is Detective Lake. How may I help you?"

"Wow, Emerson, why so proper? How have you been?"

Emerson Lake's stomach dropped. It was her. The sound of her voice filled him with excitement, but also anger. Broken hearts cause a lot of different emotions. He had them all just from the sound of her voice.

"Brenda Charles, as I live and breathe, what could I possibly do for you after all this time? How are you?"

"I'm fine, Emerson. And you?"

"I heard you on the news talking about the murders in Cromwell. I'm guessing you're searching for a little inside info on what is happening in our beautiful city. The city you grew up in and left for bigger and better things."

"Emerson, I'm sorry for what happened between us. You also know we could not be happy as a couple in careers that were not meant for either one of us. You blame me, but I know you would not have been happy here in D.C. just as I was not happy in Cromwell."

Emerson couldn't think of a smart come back, because he knew for the first time since they parted, she was right.

"What can I do for you?" he asked. "If you are looking for the story of a possible serial killer among us, a little inside information perhaps, you can just...."

She stopped him. "Emerson I was simply hoping you could do an old friend a favor by giving me a shot at this story. As a courtesy."

"Could this be your award-winning story? Well, Miss Brenda Charles, I am also sorry about what happened between us, but I can't help you. This is an ongoing investigation."

"Don't be like that. It's just a story."

"The only thing I can say at this time Ms. Charles is, no comment!"

With that, he slammed down the phone. To his surprise the entire station started to applaud. He wasn't even aware they were listening. The only one not there at the time was Reese.

CHAPTER 38

Daniel told the detectives where he and Kei Lien had been when all of this happened. He didn't know exactly how far from the road the graves were, but at least knew the direction. Police, local and state with K9's would be out there looking for the shallow graves. And no doubt, they would find the place he wanted to call his own someday. It didn't take long to find the location. Daniel's directions were pretty accurate. He was also accurate about the six holes he saw. One contained the remnants of a foot, as well as a stone with blood spatter - later determined to be from Daniel's nose.

"They're shallow graves, all right." said a member of the search team. "Dug recently."

"This is a morbid burial site." another replied. "I wonder who was buried here?"

"I'd like to know what sicko dug them up."

The area was secured and forensic teams went to work collecting samples of the soil, bloody rock and the decaying foot. All would be delivered to the lab and to Medical Examiner Sara Hunter to review.

Officer Manning and the K9 officer still searching the wooded area with his dog came across the run-down, animal-infested cabin. Daniel's dream of a rustic home with a fireplace mantel to hang Christmas stockings were about to end. The cabin and surrounding area were cordoned off.

"We're going to need a much bigger search team." commented the K9 handler.

"How long do you suppose it has been empty?" Manning asked.

"No idea, but must be for a while. The walls are literally rotted out."

"I didn't think building permits were allowed in the Park Preserve. I'm going to head back to town and pay a visit to the County Assessor's office. See if I can find who owns this eyesore. I'll meet up with you back at the station." Manning gave the well-trained German Shepherd a pat on the head and a nod to his handler.

When Allen arrived at City Hall, he asked the clerk for a map of the Park Preserve so he could pinpoint the property lines. Once he identified the parcel and tax number, he searched for the deed. Turned out, that parcel was never purchased by the state of South Dakota. It had been grandfathered to remain as private buildable property and it was owned by John Francis Delamater. The same John Delamater that suffered the heart attack at the Bradford Theater. Allen quickly had the clerk print out copies of the records and headed back to the station. How is this possible? No one knew there was a cabin in the woods all these years? Sometimes talking to himself in the car helped him work through a case. He was hoping for answers. Not this time though.

Clayton and Lake were waiting for him when he strode into the station.

"Look, before you say anything, I know I took it upon myself to head to the Assessor's office, but you're not going to believe what I found."

Lake snatched the papers out of Allen's hands and Clayton peered at them over his shoulder.

"No shit! Well isn't that an interesting development?" said Lake. "Good job Manning. Good job."

Allen was surprised by the rare praise from Lake.

"Thanks. So, I think I'll head over to the hospital to have a little chat with Delamater."

"I'd like to hear what Delamater has to say myself," Clayton said as she grabbed her suit jacket from the back of the leather chair at her desk. "Let's jump in together, Allen."

"Let's hope he's still alive when we get there."

Clayton chuckled, "No kidding. We don't need one more dead guy on our hands."

Emerson watched as the two strolled out of the station like old buddies. Clayton twirling her keys on her finger, sly smile on her face and a strut in her step. *What the hell is with the sudden camaraderie between Allen and my girl? My girl? Wait. What the hell is the matter with me? Stay focused, Lake. There is enough going on without getting jealous.*

When they arrived at the medical center, Allen approached the front desk. "Hello, Miss. My name is Officer Manning, and this is Detective Clayton. How's your day going so far?"

"Pretty good. Thank you for asking, Officer."

Nice touch, Clayton thought to herself.

"What can I do for you?"

"We need to interview a patient that was brought in. John Delamater. Would it be possible to find out his condition and if he is healthy enough to speak with us?"

"No problem. Let me see what I can do." She started clicking away on her keyboard. "Ok, I see he is in serious, but stable condition. Let me call the nurses station on that floor to see if he is well enough to speak with you."

Clayton could not believe how helpful she was being. Big difference from the last time she was there with Lake. Obviously, Allen's approach was much better. Guess it's true. You do catch more flies with honey.

"Okay officers, you can go right up. It's room 8130. Take the elevators just down the hall to the 8th Floor."

"Thank you very much." Allen gave her a warm little smile. It made her day.

As they walked to the elevators, Clayton whispered, "Nice going, Officer," and gave him a fist-bump.

Mr. Delamater was awake, but groggy, when they entered the room. Clayton explained who they were and asked if he was able to answer a few questions. "We will make this as short as possible."

Allen started. "Sir, you own a piece of land in the park preserve along with a cabin, is that correct?"

"Yes, it was left to me by my grandmother."

"Did you or anyone else live in the cabin? It doesn't appear to have been occupied for some time. It's pretty run down."

"I used to rent the cabin to vacationers from time to time. It was a quiet retreat for people. I never advertised it though. It was all word of mouth. I figured it was a good way to make some extra cash under the table so I wouldn't have to pay taxes. I know I'm probably in trouble for that, but none of that matter's anymore."

"Why is that, Mr. Delamater?" Clayton asked puzzled.

"Because I'm dying and I know it."

Clayton and Allen gave each other a look then Allen continued the questioning.

"Do you remember anything about the vacationers that used to rent the cabin?"

"My memory isn't what it used to be, but I do remember one family in particular that stayed there. They were a bit peculiar."

"How so?" Clayton inquired.

"It wasn't for a vacation. The father specifically said he wanted to teach his children what it was like to have fewer things in life. How to manage with just a well and an outhouse. He said it would be a good learning experience for them and didn't care that the cabin was in rough shape. He thought it would make them appreciate the comforts of their own home more."

"Did he say how many of them would be staying in the cabin?"

"There were six of them all together, including him and his wife." Allen and Clayton exchanged glances both thinking the same thing. Six family members. Six graves.

"Oh wait, no, that's not right. There were seven. I remember he said that one of his children would be joining them after he was released from the hospital. That always stuck with me. Who would leave their child behind at a hospital if they were sick? It wasn't really any of my business, though. If I was getting paid,

I didn't ask too many questions."

"Do you remember his name? Do you have any records you may have kept on your renters?"

"No paperwork. It was all cash under the table. Why are you asking me all these questions?"

"It's part of a case we're working on. Anything you can remember would be very helpful."

John's eyes widened. "Oh my God, does this have something to do with those bodies at the Bradford?"

"We're not sure," Reese said. "Just trying to pursue all possibilities. But anything you can remember would be very helpful. The name of your renter would be a key piece of information in our investigation."

"Oh my, let me think. Oh no!"

BEEP! BEEP! BEEP! BEEP!

Alarms from machines behind John's bed began sounding. A nurse rushed in.

"I'm very sorry, you'll need to leave. Mr. Delamater is getting agitated and it's time for his evening medication. You can come back in the morning."

"We understand. Mr. Delamater, we just need the renter's name and then we'll leave you to rest." Neither Clayton nor Allen wanted to leave. They needed that name.

"I...I. I'm trying to..."

"Officers, please!" the nurse interjected. "You really need to go. You can speak to him in the morning."

"Of course. Thank you, Mr. Delamater. Get some rest and we'll see you tomorrow." Clayton patted John's ankle through the waffled hospital blanket and then ushered Allen out of the room.

Once back in the car, Allen sighed "We were so close to getting the name. It must be the family. The numbers seem to match up anyway."

"I know, but even if he does remember, it doesn't mean it will be accurate. It was a handshake deal. The father could've lied."

"That's true, but we can at least run it through the system. I mean a family that size just doesn't go missing with no report of it, do they? Fingers crossed Mr. Delamater survives the night."

"Fingers and toes!"

CHAPTER 39

M.E. Sara Hunter decided to do a little research of her own. She ran a computer search for missing families of six in the state of South Dakota. Nothing appeared on her screen.

Detectives Lake and Clayton were on their way to the lab when they saw Sara at her office desk.

"Any luck on the bodies? Who they might be?" asked Reese.

"Nothing so far, Detective. I was just trying to research missing families of six on my own, but nothing is coming up. How can a family that large fall off the map of South Dakota and no one reports it?"

"I know what you mean," Reese replied, "but we've expanded the search to missing persons across the entire country. And new information has us looking for a family of seven."

"Sara, we'll check back with you later. Reese, let's go. We have work to do."

Once out of earshot, he grabbed Reese by the elbow and dragged her face to face with him.

"What the hell is wrong with you? Why am I just hearing about this seventh family member now? You made me look like a fool in front of Sara."

His face was beet red and he was resisting an overwhelming urge to punch the wall.

"Oh, for God sake, Detective! Don't get your panties in a knot. I was going to tell you what happened as soon as I finished the report on John Delamater's statement. At least what we have so far. He is not doing so well. Our interview got cut short because his blood pressure or something was setting off the machines. The nurse made us leave, but we'll be headed back there in the morning."

"So, what you're saying, is he didn't have the names?"

"No, I'm saying he physically couldn't talk anymore. I'm not a fucking doctor. I don't know what happened to him."

"I'm sorry."

It was something he never said. He let go of her arm and just stared at her face for a second, not knowing what to do next. For some reason, he wanted to hold her close, but stopped himself almost immediately. She backed away, turned around and started toward her office. Emerson followed.

"Maybe we start re-interviewing some of the people we've already talked to," Lake suggested. "With this new information about the seventh family member, maybe we can pick up a new lead."

"That's a great idea. First up, the so-called grieving widow of Sergeant Martin Kelsey."

At that moment, Clayton received a text message.

"Aw fuck!" Clayton muttered.

"What's wrong?"

"Delamater's dead. He had a massive stroke."

CHAPTER 40

Being the daughter of a farmer in upstate New York, she made a promise to herself to never milk another cow. Farm life was not what she thought of as a profit-making endeavor. Having dated many of the locals, she knew that none of them would make enough money for her to be the princess she always thought herself to be. Every chance she got she would steal a few dollars out of the metal box her parents used to set aside money for needed household items. She certainly knew how to save for a rainy day, or in her case, a way to fund her departure from the farm. Plus, the money she had hoarded away all those years would give her a good start elsewhere.

She packed what she could carry in a small old suitcase she found in the attic, a brown paper bag and a lavender crocheted purse that her mother made for her to attend church with on Sundays. Walking for about three hours, she began to think this wasn't such a good idea without a vehicle. She sat down on a few boulders alongside the road. She grabbed a bottle from the brown paper bag, pulled out the homemade foil stopper she had fashioned and took a long drink of water. Daddy's old beer bottles came in handy to carry her water. She saw a car approaching and thought about standing in the road to stop it, but she didn't have to, he stopped anyway.

"Are you okay, Miss? Do you need some help?"

"I'm just trying to get to Albany. A friend was driving me, but she became ill and had to turn back. I told her I could walk the rest of the way. I guess it's a longer walk than I thought."

"When you are walking, yes. But I can get you there in no time at all. Here, let me take your bags for you. My name is Martin Kelsey."

"Teresa," is all she gave him.

He held her arm to help her up and then held the car door for her while she slid into the seat. Now this is what I am looking for, she thought to herself. A gentleman.

"Where are you from?"

She lied. "Syracuse." She didn't want him to call her parents.

They began a conversation that was polite without giving up too much information. As they drove, they laughed, talked about the scenery and small-town life and gradually became more comfortable with each other.

"We are getting close to Albany. Where would you like to be dropped off?"

She couldn't think of what to say because she hadn't planned on getting in a car with anyone.

"I have to trust that you will understand I have no place to go. I just needed to get away for a while to figure out what I want in life."

"You are a very beautiful woman, Teresa, I understand. Are you married?"

"No. Not yet. Maybe someday."

Martin placed his right hand on the seat close to her thigh. "Would you like to stay the night at my place?"

She didn't know what to do. As much as she wanted to stay with him, she didn't know what to expect. What he would do to her. Yet, she had nowhere else to go. Without a word, she nodded yes.

They arrived at his apartment soon after. Martin helped her with her things and led her into his apartment. She thought to herself, Teresa, you are an idiot for not making a better plan.

"I will stay the night only if we are in separate rooms, Mr. Kelsey. I am a lady, you know."

"Oh, of course. Separate rooms. But I hardly believe that as beautiful as you are, lady doesn't fit the bill. Am I right?"

With that, she clenched her fist, unclenched it again and slapped him across the face. "Who the hell do you think you are talking to? "she yelled.

She collected her things, turned, and started for the door. Martin grabbed at his face to make sure no teeth were missing.

"Wait! I'm sorry, but I had to make sure you are really the kind of person you say you are. You could be someone just trying to rob me in my sleep. Please, let's start over. Stay the night. Separate rooms. And I will take you anywhere you would like in the morning."

Since she had nowhere else to go, she reluctantly agreed. For the rest of the night, Kelsey was the perfect gentleman.

The next morning, they had a light breakfast. Toast with strawberry jam. Coffee for him and tea for her. They talked about the weather and other trivial things for a while.

"Look, I'm headed to South Dakota. There's a job waiting for me. The job I have always wanted. Sergeant in the Cromwell Police Department. I was born and raised there, but decided to spread my wings a little and came to New York for a while. Why don't you come with me? You can either stay at my house when we arrive, or I have a hotel where you can stay. My family left it to me. What do you say?"

Wow, Teresa thought, this guy is rich. If I snag him, my chance of climbing my way into the upper class of society is at my fingertips.

Teresa Kelsey was not born into money, even though she looked the part. She fell into it by accident, so she thought anyway.

CHAPTER 41

The young man at the desk called Teresa's suite to let her know she had guests.

"Mrs. Kelsey will meet you in the café."

Detective Lake thanked the young clerk before taking a very comfortable seat by the elevator doors. He was not going to trust her.

"Thank you for coming down, Mrs. Kelsey. How are you feeling?" Reese sounded genuinely concerned for her. "May we ask you a few questions about the night your husband was murdered? We promise to make this as short as possible."

"Please follow me. We can talk in here. The café is quiet this time of day. I'm sure no one will interrupt us. I'm in the process of getting things organized for Martin's funeral. That is if they ever release his remains to me. Seems like that autopsy is taking forever. Do you have any idea what's holding up the process? There is a lot of planning. He was so well liked in this community. People will expect a grand send off. Don't you agree? I thought a military type send-off would be appropriate. He did serve our Country and continued serving as Sergeant of Cromwell. I will expect law enforcement to be there in full dress uniform."

"Of course, Mrs. Kelsey." Detective Lake was doing his best to be polite.

"Mrs. Kelsey, the night of your husband's murder...I know this is difficult...can you tell us what time you found him and where you were before that? We are not accusing you of anything. We just need details of that evening. Do you understand?"

"Yes. I was here at the hotel taking care of some business that evening. Checking the books, upcoming reservations, things like that. I left the hotel around 7pm and drove to the pharmacy to pick up some prescriptions. You can check if you like. Mosley's around the corner. After that, I drove home and found Martin on the floor in front of the fireplace stabbed in the chest with a ten-inch butcher knife."

And there it was. That same statement from the other day. Emerson could barely hold his tongue. His first instinct was to arrest her right on the spot, but knew he needed more.

"I couldn't breathe when I called the station. Allen had a hard time understanding me. I guess I was in shock. It was only minutes before police and emergency crews arrived. Allen came in a short time later and took me out of the house and told the paramedics to take me to Cromwell Medical Center, but after I got some oxygen in me, I convinced them to take me to the hotel instead. They didn't want to, but I can be persistent."

No shit, thought Clayton. No shit.

Clayton took over.

"Did you hear anyone in the house at the time? See anything unusual besides your husband on the floor?"

"Not that I can remember. It's all kind of a blur and I was frightened and felt nauseated."

"Are you sure that's all you can remember?" asked Emerson.

"I don't know what else you want me to say."

"Thank you for your time, Mrs. Kelsey. We will be in touch and if you need help with the planning for the Sergeant's send-off, let us know."

Reese knew that Emerson was ready to pounce on Teresa because of the knife comment, yet she also knew they needed more proof. It was best to leave before either one of them let on about what they both already knew.

"Thank you, detectives."

Once outside, Clayton and Lake got back in the car and almost simultaneously said, "The knife!"

"How the hell did she know it was a ten-inch blade, Reese?" Lake mused. "It was still stuck in her husband's chest when the police arrived."

Reese and Emerson both knew she must have had help with this, just like the recruit Sorenson had suggested. It was much too hard to move a body alone.

CHAPTER 42

Daniel convinced Kei Lien that she really needed to be seen by a doctor. If not at the hospital then in a doctor's office. Daniel felt a quiet office would be best. All the activity at the hospital would agitate her even more than she was now. He convinced Detective Lake it was a much better idea. He also knew this was going to be very painful for her physically and emotionally. Detective Lake agreed and sent an officer with them. Daniel was so right. Kei Lien fought hard when asked to remove her clothing and even harder when they tried to examine her. The nurse and the doctor at the Glen Ridge Woman's Health Center were both female so that was a plus. If you could call any of this a plus.

"Kei Lien, have you taken a bath or shower since your last sexual encounter?" asked the doctor.

Kei Lien didn't know how to answer that question because she had no idea what sexual encounter meant. She just stared straight ahead.

"It would help us to know the person who assaulted you if you just give us a chance and answer our questions."

"Doctor," the nurse said quietly, "I'm guessing she does not even know what the word assaulted means."

Kei Lien spoke up. "My father. He always washed me in warm water after a gift from Santa."

"A gift from Santa? What does that mean?" the doctor asked. "I'm sorry Kei Lien, I don't understand."

The nurse looked at her and then at the doctor. It suddenly dawned on her that this girl was not just physically abused, but mentally as well.

"We need to tread lightly here," the nurse said. "This young woman has obviously been abused for quite some time now. Trying to find out who the person or persons is will not be determined from a rape kit. Not if she has been bathed after every episode. Kei Lien, may we ask you another question?"

"I guess."

"What does *gift from Santa* mean? Can you try to explain? We only want to help you. We are very sorry you had to…"

Kei Lien flew into a tantrum upon hearing that word…*sorry*.

"No! No! I'm never saying that word again! I can't have another gift or say that word ever again! I'm glad my father is dead! He can never bring me those gifts ever again!"

"He can never hurt you again. Kei Lien," the nurse said calmly. "Take a deep breath and take your time. Tell us what happened to you. We won't touch you, okay? Would you feel safer if we brought Daniel in here to sit by you?"

Knowing Daniel was right outside the door was comfort enough. Kei Lien started to calm down and her breathing became less labored. She was quiet for a few moments and then slowly began to tell her story.

"I write letters to Santa. Like my mom used to tell me to do. When she died, I kept writing them. A lot of them. Hoping Santa would bring her back to me. Then I asked for him to bring me somebody that would love me like she used to. My father said what he and the others did to me was my fault because I kept writing and asking for someone to love me. Then I'd have to say I'm…." her voice trailed off.

"Kei Lien, did you keep any of your clothes? Maybe some under clothes by any chance? Something that you did not wash?"

Kei Lien didn't know how to answer that question or why they would even ask it.

"I guess so. I don't like to touch some of those things, so I keep them together in a bag under my bed. If my father found out I'm sure he would be awful mad. He would do more bad things if he knew."

She sounded like a small child at times while being questioned. In reality, she was an adult. Just not a functioning adult.

The nurse and doctor stepped aside to talk privately.

"This poor girl has been tortured sexually for many years, I'm guessing," the nurse said.

"It sounds that way to me as well," replied the doctor.

It was nearly impossible to collect all the information they needed to conclude she had been raped. The doctor could see the bruising and scaring on the outside of her body but was unable to perform an internal exam without sending her over the edge. Once out of her room the doctor spoke to Daniel.

"Daniel, are you her guardian?"

"No. I'm just a friend trying to help. She is of age to make her own decisions, but I'm guessing she's not mentally able to do this, right?"

"Miss Chandler needs to be admitted to a hospital for observation and to see if she can be convinced to submit to an
internal exam. We need that exam to determine if she was raped
and assaulted. I think the only way we'll be able to do it is with
the proper medication to relax her."

Daniel didn't like the sound of that. His short-lived attempt
at a medical degree taught him a lot about medications and
their side effects. But he didn't have the power to make the
choice for her.

The nurse called Detective Clayton and shared the information about the clothing under Kei Lien's bed. The detectives had
already searched the house and nothing like that was logged
into evidence.

"Is she still at the doctor's office?" asked Emerson.

"I'm on the phone with them now," Reese replied. "They're
going to transport her to Cromwell Med."

"Let's go. We'll meet them there."

Detectives Lake and Clayton walked into Cromwell Med,
flashing their badges at the reception desk.

"Kei Lien Chandler, where is she?" barked Lake.

A very recognizable voice replied from the back-computer
station, "Oh, as I live and breathe. Are you going to be polite
to me this time or are we going to continue to have a problem?"

Reese chimed in, "We're sorry about the other day. My partner and I had a disagreement right before we arrived, and he
took it out on you. Isn't that right, detective?"

"Right. Sorry," he huffed. "Now could you direct us to Kei
Lien Chandler? Please."

"I'll look up that room number for you."

At least that's one fence mended, Reese thought to herself.

An officer was posted at the door to Kei Lien's room. Emerson questioned him a bit and then asked the nurse if it was okay to go in and speak with her.

"I think it would be better if I go in with you," Reese interjected. "She's pretty fragile right now and seems more comfortable with women."

Reese entered the room with the nurse as Emerson stood at the open door within earshot.

"Kei Lien," the nurse said, "this is Detective Reese Clayton. She'd like to ask you a few questions."

Reese quietly approached her bedside. "Kei Lien, it's very nice to meet you. I'm with the Cromwell Police Department and I'm here to help you. I'd like to talk to you a little bit if that's ok?"

Kei Lien nodded her head.

"Ok, great. Kei Lien, do you remember when the last time your father gave you a bath? Was it before you ran away?"

"I don't remember, but when I got into the lake I felt clean… really clean. The cold water felt good and I stopped hurting for a while."

"Oh shit," Emerson said under his breath.

"Reese," he whispered from the door.

Reese turned toward him. "Ask her what lake," he said.

Reese turned her attention back to Kei Lien.

"Kei Lien, do you remember which lake you were at?"

"I don't know. I want to go home. Do I have a home? Where should I go? What do I do now?"

It hit her all at once. Her mind was racing. Suddenly her arms began flailing uncontrollably and her eyes were rolling back in her head. The nurse ran to her bedside and held her steady as not to pull the tubes from her arms. She hit the call button.

"I need some help in here...the patient is seizing."

She looked back at Detective Lake at the door, "I think you and your partner need to leave now. It's too much stress for her."

Once back at the station, Captain Brown huddled up a team to start researching lakes in the area.

"Let's first go over where she began to run and then trace the path to the barn she slept in that night. How many lakes are in the vicinity? Which one would she go to?"

"It looks like three within close proximity, from what I can see on Google earth," one of the officers replied. "I hate these satellite maps. Give me a paper map any day."

"Luckily, two are not that big, Captain," replied Reese hanging over the officer's left shoulder. "More like good size ponds. The other is rather large. It would take a long time to search that one."

"Okay," the Captain said. "Then it looks like we have our work cut out for us."

Captain Brown assigned the search teams and gave them their orders.

"Remember, we are looking for a young woman's clothing. Stay sharp people."

"Detective Lake," Reese chimed in, "call for a K9 team to start on the biggest lake."

"Yes, ma'am," he jolted up to attention and saluted her.

The entire station erupted into laughter.

"That's enough!" shouted Captain Brown. "Get your asses out there and find that clothing!

"Lake," Reese sneered, "I'll deal with you later."

As the group began filing out of the conference room, Reese overheard snickering from two of the officers, "I'll bet you twenty bucks she does, too."

"Twenty-five?"

"Deal."

Reese stepped in front of the doorway blocking their exit staring them down.

"Is there a problem here officers? Anything you want to share?"

"No, Detective."

"Dismissed!" yelled the Captain giving Reese a look. "Is there something I need to know, Detective Clayton?"

"No, ma'am."

CHAPTER 43

Allen Manning, while sharing in the hunt for Kei Lien's cloth-ing, could not shake the feeling that he knew the hotel desk clerk from somewhere. He asked the officer with him, "John, do you know Randall Cummings? The desk clerk at the Strasburg Hotel? I know Dayton is a pretty big county, but I know I've seen him before, just not at the hotel."

"No, I don't know him personally, but I have seen him from time to time. Coffee shop, grocery store, I think. Why, what's up? Do you think he is involved with this case?"

"I don't know for sure. Let's just say it's a gut feeling."

"Where did you work before you came to Cromwell, Manning?"

"I was a transplant from the D.C. area. Always wanted a career in law enforcement. I considered being a bodyguard for hotshot politicians, but after I started training, I realized I could lose my life in a flash trying to protect someone who in reality, would give a shit less if his bodyguard died taking a bullet for him. So, I said my goodbyes and headed west. I tried a few security jobs along the way. Just wasn't my thing. Standing in a bank lobby for eight hours a day would drive anyone crazy. So,

I moved on. Still heading west. Never once did I ever consider South Dakota. It just happened that I loved the state."

"Yeah. Clean air, natural beauty, low population."

"I saw Mount Rushmore while traveling west and that was it. All of it seemed comfortable for some reason, like a hometown should. So, I decided to call it home."

"How did you get on the force?"

"I already had my college degree, so I was able to sign up right away for the local police academy and became an officer after graduation. What about you?"

"Born and raised in this area. Always wanted to be in law enforcement, too."

They continued their search around the perimeter of the lake. Hoping to find answers. It didn't matter to Allen if he went farther in his field or not. He liked what he did and where he chose to live. He had a secret though. One that could cost him his career.

CHAPTER 44

The search teams around the lakes were coming up empty handed. Detective Clayton was beginning to think they would have to bring in the big guns. FBI. Something she dreaded doing. It would be a black mark on her record and on her ego as well. So, she thought she would give it a little while longer before she caved. She decided to approach Sara Hunter again to see if there were any updates on any of the victims.

Sara Hunter had been the Medical Examiner for Dayton County for a little under twenty years. She was very good at her job, but this case frightened her for the simple reason that she might not be able to give Cromwell Police the information they expected. For the first time in her career, she was confounded by a case. Her inner voice kept saying 'What am I missing?' Shocking her out of her thoughts, her computer alerted her to new data in the case. She had set a notification alert ringtone that would knock most people out of their skin. At least she knew she had something. The dental records were back for one of the children. Database records confirmed the dental work was performed in the small hamlet of Jade, just south of Westin,

South Dakota. Patient name: Laurie Elizabeth Cole. She no sooner started to page the detectives when in walked Reese. The startled look on Sara's face surprised Detective Clayton.

"Hey Sara, what's going on? Did you find something?"

Sara took a moment to compose herself, "Yes, we have ID on one of the children. Her name is Laurie Elizabeth Cole. Dental records confirm it. The town is called Jade, near Westin. I was just going to contact one of you with the details when you walked in."

"Thank you, Sara, great job. I'll take it from here. Are you sure you are okay?"

"I'm fine. Just very disturbing cases and not sure if these six bodies have anything to do with the other two. Other than the stab wounds on all of them, where is the common thread?"

"We'll find it. At least we have something to go on now."

Reese looked directly into Sara's eyes. "Thank you for what you do, Sara. Send the information to me. I'll contact Detective Lake. I'm quite sure we'll be taking a road trip to Jade."

Sara decided to take a breath and get a cup of coffee in the break room. She thought it was time to relax a little before continuing her work on the autopsies. She selected a table that was semi-clean, wiped it with a napkin that she had dipped under the faucet. Better. That's better. Several police officers came in, got their coffee and candy from the machines, and rotated out again. Except one.

"Hi, I'm one of the new recruits here. My name is Ken Sorenson. I don't believe we have met."

"Sara Hunter," she said politely. She really wanted to tell him to go the hell away and leave her alone.

"You're the Medical Examiner. We've just never been introduced. Are you waiting for someone or may I sit down and rest my weary bones for a minute?"

The very last thing Sara wanted to hear right now was the word bones, but being the nice person she was, she nodded and motioned at the empty seat.

"This is some case isn't it?" Sorenson asked. "I mean, all these bodies at once. Must be a lot to handle in the morgue right now?"

"Yes, it is. Look, Mr. Sorenson…"

"Please, call me Ken."

"I just came in here to take a breather and collect my thoughts for a few moments. So, please forgive me, I don't mean to be rude, but I really would like to be alone for a while."

"Oh, sure, I understand," Sorenson said as he got up and headed to the doorway before turning back around. "Till we meet again, Sara Hunter."

Then he slipped out.

Sara smiled. He was good looking, but there was no way she was going down that road, not if she could help it. Sara knew she was not herself lately. She felt nauseated, had headaches and was weak after standing in the morgue so long. Everything pointed to the flu, but she was sure that wasn't it. Soon she would need to see her primary care doctor, but like all who have an ounce of medical knowledge, she felt she could deal with whatever it was that was making her feel like crap. She nearly fell asleep at the table, but the sound of voices jolted her back. She picked up her cup, did a fast swipe across the table with a napkin and headed back to work. Back to work on the body of that prick that probably raped his own daughter. Even though she knew it was unprofessional, when her colleague Bill wasn't around, she made a few extra cuts on him. Smiling after each one. Cuts that made her feel better. Like she was exacting a little revenge on behalf of this child.

CHAPTER 45

Detectives Lake and Clayton both packed enough clothes to last a few days, just in case. The trip to Jade was a little over a hundred miles away.

"Who knows how long we will be in Jade, Emerson, or what we will find on this family. I don't understand why there was never a bulletin sent out about their disappearance. Jeez, a family of six, possibly seven, appears to fall off the face of the earth and no one cares where they went or why they never returned. Again, I have to ask the question, why did no one from the school district look into their truancy?"

Before they had left for Jade, they had their Cromwell investigators go through the police records warehouse to check on missing persons files. They went back ten years, at least, and nothing. After that time period, everything was stored on computers and nothing was there either.

"First, Reese, we need the family's home address from the dentist and any other information his office may have regarding their employers or insurance coverage. Anything that will lead us to more details about this family."

Reese nodded in agreement.

For most of the rest of the trip, they sat in silence. Both were lost in their own thoughts about the case. Until they reached Jade. "This town seems really quiet, almost like an old-fashioned mom and pop type community," said Lake. "I can't imagine a business staying here and trying to survive. I don't see a whole lot of people out and about either. You think of a dentist and immediately think big money, but how the hell does that happen here?"

"Beats me, but it's clean," Clayton replied. "Homes look in good shape. Lawns are nicely manicured and no trash around either. I'm guessing we'll have to go to Westin to find a hotel room. Don't see anything here that even resembles a bed & breakfast, do you?"

"Not yet. I knew we should have checked into that before we left Cromwell. Such good detective work, don't you think? Aren't we supposed to be brilliant at what we do?"

"We are, or at least, I am," she smiled looking up from her phone. "According to this, we are really close to a motel. So, there you have it. Smart, aren't I?"

"Hey Reese, how do you feel about pulling onto a back road somewhere tonight and sleeping in the car, or if not sleeping then…"

"Screw you, Lake, if I'm not worth the price of a nice hotel room then you can sit yourself in the back seat and give yourself a *hand*, so to speak."

"Reese, I'm hurt," as he gave her a gentle tap on the thigh and a big smile.

"Is that what miss hotshot reporter Brenda used to do for you?"

Fun time was over. Reese immediately regretted the remark, but it was too late to take it back and she was not about to apologize. It wasn't her style. So, the conversation the rest of the way through town was kept to police business. The building where the dental office was located was very quaint. Not fancy by any means, but nice. Hometown nice.

"Doesn't this whole town remind you of Maine?" Clayton asked. "Well, minus the ocean and the crowds of people shopping in overpriced small shops?"

Lake, as angry as he was with his partner, got hysterical laughing at her. "How the hell is that description like Maine in any way shape or form? Is the Dakota air too thin? Are you getting lightheaded?"

"A little bit. Maybe I need a drink?" she chuckled.

"Hey! That's my tagline," he shot back. "Find your own."

He leaned over to her seat and gave her a short kiss. That was much more than she could have asked for.

"Later?" he whispered.

"Later," she replied. "Now let's get in that office so I can get sick to my stomach. I hate going to the dentist. Any dentist."

Once inside, the receptionist checked their IDs and showed them into the office. The gentleman was not young, but knew what he was doing for sure. The name engraved on his bronze desk plaque was Dr. Cavity.

"That's what I call myself for the children. They get a kick out of it."

"Clever," quipped Emerson. "We are here about the dental records for a child found in Cromwell."

"Your Medical Examiner notified me of the situation. Very

sad. She was a nice child. Only one cavity the last time she was in my chair. I guess the cavity is what might give you the information you need to find this bastard."

CHAPTER 46

Jade was such a small area that not much in the line of law enforcement was required. Even so, Lake thought it best to show up unannounced at the police barracks. This way stories couldn't be changed before they arrived. He had the same question as his partner: Why didn't anyone report the Cole family missing?

"Reese, do you want to go in as a team or split up?"

"I say a team. Two sets of eyes and ears are better than one," she answered. "Also, it's more intimidating when two detectives pull out shields. Don't you agree?"

Once they arrived at the Jade police station, the first thing they noticed was how helpful everyone seemed to be. They were very respectful of their shields. Some small-town law enforcement officers can be easily offended by other agencies coming into their world asking questions, making them feel inferior and incompetent. Not this station. While asking a few questions about the disappearance of the Cole family, one person, an older female probably nearing eighty, said that they left town on a vacation of some sort. Something they did now and then and this time they just never returned. None of them.

"Why did no one from the school report them truant?" asked Reese.

"The owner of the apartment they lived in just thought it was one of those cases where they skipped town, left no forwarding and no rent. Happens all the time. Not here so much, but it does happen."

She couldn't remember how long ago this was and seemed to be the only original employee of the station.

"The owner reported it, of course, but knew he was not about to file suit against these people, even if they were found. What's the point? Would cost more in attorney fees than the price of the rent owed. They were nice people. Kept to themselves mostly, but had a son that was not quite with it."

"Meaning?" asked Emerson.

"Mentally. He didn't live at the apartment for any length of time. When he would begin to act out, his father would place him back in the mental institution. You know, to protect the other kids."

"And no one report them missing?" asked Lake again.

"We didn't know they were considered missing. When the officers went into the apartment with the owner after he filed the complaint all that was left were the original furnishings that were part of the rental. All personal items were gone. That's why we considered it as a skipped town scenario."

"Thank you very much for your help, "Reese said. "One more thing. Do you happen to remember the name of the mental facility? Did Mr. Cole ever mention this facility to you?"

"I can't remember. I used to see him in the market occasionally.

We would chat a bit, but I don't recall him ever saying where he was placed. It couldn't have been too far away for him to keep bringing him back and forth. Let me see if I can get you a list of the ones nearby. Can't imagine there are many at all. This is a small town. Not just Jade, but Westin as well."

She printed out a list of hospitals and mental institutions within a hundred-mile radius.

"I'm sorry I could not be more help to you detectives. I'm not getting any younger. My mind isn't as good as it should be. I'm just grateful the Jade Police Department still allows me to work here a few days a week. If I didn't have this, I would be sitting home waiting to die."

Emerson gave her a wink and flashed his magazine cover model smile.

"Jade is lucky to have such a smart and beautiful woman on the job," he said. "Thank you very much for all of your help."

"Oh my," she blushed.

Once outside, he turned to Reese, "Well, how was that for giving an older woman a memory she can dream about?"

"Emerson Lake! It was a fine gesture coming from someone who's actually a big jerk."

They split the list of hospitals and institutions in half and began calling them from the motel they checked into not far from the police station, near the edge of the Jade town line. The fifth place on the list appeared to hit pay dirt. They arranged to meet with a physician the next morning around 10:30am. By now they were both hungry so agreed to stop at a chain restaurant near the motel. The food was good and plenty of it, as you would expect. While having their last sips of coffee, they came up with a plan for the next day. Questions that needed to be asked and who would ask them. Once back at the motel, Reese wondered if it was a good idea to share a room with the person who liked her enough to make love to her at will, but not enough to make any kind of commitment. Not enough to even say I love you once. Was she giving in to this man too easily? Giving him free reign to take her whenever he needed her and only when he needed her?

"Emerson," she yelled to him in the shower, "I'm going outside for a little fresh air. Maybe take a little walk around the lot to clear my head."

"Okay." he answered. "I'll be done in here in a minute."

The sky was very clear with stars. It seemed like diamonds scattered over the earth and reminded her how important these little, yet beautiful, moments were. Evenings like this made her feel how much she would just love to be a stay at home soccer mom. The kind of mom that cooked dinner for her family every evening before tucking the children into bed. Reading them a story and kissing them goodnight before snuggling up to a caring husband. Suddenly, she was snapped back to reality when she noticed a man lurking in the parking lot shadows staring at her. She placed her hand on her weapon, "Is there something I can help you with?"

She tried to make out the face with no luck.

"I'm going to ask you one more time. Is there something I can help you with?"

"No officer, but I might be able to help you. The guy that you and the other cop are looking for? I know the name of the hospital he was in. If you want to call that piece of garbage a hospital."

"Can I get your name? It would help to know whom I am speaking with. My name is Detective Reese Clayton."

"I know who you are. It's a small town. I used to work for Saturn Psychiatric Center quite a few years ago as an orderly. From what I can remember, the kid you're asking about is Timothy Cole. That kid needed more help than any of the staff at the center could give him. No matter how hard they tried. I remember his father bringing him in the first day. He fought tooth and nail to escape. Even as a kid, he threatened to kill his father for bringing him to Saturn. He was smart, though."

"Smart? How do you mean?"

"He knew enough to sway the doctors into thinking he was getting better. That was after they gave him shock treatments. Barbaric, those treatments, if you ask me. His family would take him out occasionally to see if he could behave in public. The trips out of Saturn were getting longer and longer. I'm guessing he put on quite an act to convince them to let him go on vacation with them."

"Why do you believe he wasn't getting better?" Reese asked.

"I saw firsthand the terrible things he had done to a few of the other patients. He broke arms, twisted legs in ways you could not imagine. One day I walked in and found him hanging a young boy from the bars on the windows. He had made a noose from the kid's own tee shirt. Luckily, I got to the kid in time. I reported all of this, but I never heard of anyone doing anything about him. He certainly should not have been allowed to wander around. I seriously wondered if the doctors there were experimenting on him. That's all I could think of anyway."

Reese could not believe what she was hearing, or why this

stranger was telling her all of this in the dark parking lot of a motel.

"Sir, may I ask you where this place, this Saturn Center, is located?"

"You mean where it *was*, Detective. It burnt to the ground. I don't think the cause of the fire or who may have started it was ever settled. But I have a pretty good guess. Tim Cole. Most of the residents escaped the fire with help from the staff, but some did not. It was believed that Tim Cole died in the blaze, but I don't believe that."

"Why not?"

"Because, he started the fire. I saw him light the match before an explosion threw me backwards. That's all I have for you."

"Please come in to speak with us. We need your help to catch this guy. We just want to talk. I promise you we are here to help. If what you are saying is true, he could be a major suspect in the death of his entire family."

Reese did not know Lake was listening to the whole conversation from the side entrance to the motel. When she hadn't returned from her walk, he went to look for her. Seeing this man talking to Reese in the lot, he had drawn his weapon and listened carefully. Reese couldn't see the man clearly, but Emerson could. His face was completely deformed. Emerson guessed it was from the blast that hit him. Reese continued to plead with the stranger, but he was frightened off.

Trying to run after him in a dark parking lot that led to God knows where was not smart without back up. She sprinted back to the motel room and burst through the door, but Lake was nowhere to be found. As she was about to head back outside,

Lake suddenly appeared in the doorway grabbing onto the shirt sleeve of a man he had in tow, hands cuffed behind his back. The man's badly burned face startled Reese, but she quickly regained her composure.

"Sir, I am so sorry for what happened to you at the psych center. I am equally sorry that my partner decided to chase you like a criminal. Detective, remove those cuffs immediately. Would you please tell us your name?" she asked.

"Andrew Kelsey."

CHAPTER 47

At Cromwell Medical Center, there was another challenge: trying to keep Kei Lien in the hospital for observation. As worn out as she was, there was no way she was going to let a doctor, or even a nurse, touch her. She was done with that part of her life.

"Kei Lien, please let the them help you," Daniel begged. "Please let these nice people check to make sure you are not hurt inside."

A nurse walked in and announced she was there to take Kei Lien's vitals.

"No." She glared at the nurse and Daniel with eyes that could singe your soul.

"Please, Kei Lien. She won't hurt you. I promise."

Kei Lien nodded it was ok. Thank goodness temperatures were now taken by running a gadget across the forehead! She would have bit the thermometer in half.

"She's running a fever," the nurse said to Daniel. "It's not too high, but high enough to warrant concern and urgency to keep her for evaluation."

She turned to Kei Lien.

"Are you willing to answer a few questions dear?" she asked. "Your friend, I'm sorry what is your name again, young man?"

"Daniel."

"Daniel could stay with you if you want."

Kei Lien glanced over at Daniel. He gave her a nod as if to say "I'm right here. I will not let anyone hurt you again."

She hung her head, fear still overwhelming her, not knowing the right decision. Tears began to spill from her eyes. So tired and giving in to defeat.

"Okay, I'll try."

"When was the last time you had your menstrual cycle?" the nurse asked.

No answer.

"All right," she phrased the question another way. "When was your last period? Kei Lien, sweetie, do you know what period means or menstrual cycle?"

The nurse was very compassionate. Daniel was glad for that.

"No," Kei Lien whispered.

Kei Lien just stared at the nurse and then at Daniel.

"Nurse, would it be okay if I had a word with you in the hall? Kei Lien, I'll be right outside the door, okay?"

"May I ask your name?" he asked.

"Mary Elizabeth."

"I just want you to be aware of what this young woman has been through. What she has endured for many years I am guessing. Her mother died giving birth to a stillborn child. Kei Lien was never allowed to go to school after that. So, this type of questioning won't help. She has no idea what you are saying to her. She is scared and although her age and body are that of a woman, her mind is that of a child. A child that was abused by many. No one knows just how many."

Mary Elizabeth was furious. "Damn it! No one explained the situation to me. All they said was to go ask the standard rape victim questions. A certified sexual assault nurse examiner is supposed to administer the rape kit test. That's not going to happen. No amount of coaxing is ever going to change this young woman's mind. I remember all the steps involved with the rape kit from maybe eight or ten years ago when I attended the classes. Don't even know if my certification still exists. I have not done one since. I know I could get into trouble for this, lots of trouble, for even thinking I could or should do it, but what the hell would they do, fire me? Who cares? Put me in jail? I doubt it. This may be the last good deed I do for this place before I am forced into retirement, so, screw it."

She apologized to Daniel. "I just came on duty. I've been away for a few days. I did not know this young woman's situation. Let's see if there is another way to approach the questioning sir. Would you be willing to stay for a while to help her with all of this?"

"Absolutely, if that's what she wants."

The nurse was no doubt older than most on the unit. Daniel surmised that she wanted to work, not had to. She was a rare breed you might say, someone who cares more about the patient than the bottom line.

This time the nurse went over to Kei Lien's bed fluffed her pillows and straightened the sheets, so they weren't all bunched up while she was sitting in an elevated position. She then made sure Kei Lien was completely covered with the sheets and blankets and tucked in tightly. Only her arms remained out.

"There. Now does that feel better? Are you okay? How about I get you a glass of orange juice to drink?"

She went to a small break room down the hallway nearly in tears fumbling to get the juice. Taking a napkin to wipe the moisture from her own eyes, Mary Elizabeth returned to the room.

Kei Lien looked over at Daniel once again, not knowing if this was a safe place. Daniel reassured her.

"It's fine, Kei Lien. This nice lady just wants to help you." Daniel took a chance and finished his sentence with, "Just like your mom would if she were here."

The nurse and Daniel saw the slight release of Kei Lien's fears as tears began to well up in her eyes again. She wanted her mom. Hopefully this nurse would be a substitute for a short while at least.

"Sweetheart, can you show me where your father and the others hurt you?" the nurse asked. "Just point with your finger. I won't touch you."

Kei Lien slowly picked up her hand and placed it over her vaginal area and then leaned to the side and placed her hand on her bottom. She then touched her mouth. Daniel was ready to vomit just imagining the torture she must have endured.

The nurse moved to the edge of the bed and asked, "May I hold your hand? By the way my name is Mary Elizabeth."

She then placed her own hand at Kei Lien's side on top of the blankets and waited for her to make the next important move. Kei Lien cautiously did.

"Did my mom send you?" she whispered.

"I don't know, Kei Lien. But I sure do like the way that sounds. Please trust me. I need to look at places on your body to see if you are hurt badly. If you want, Daniel can stay. Or if you prefer, he can wait outside. Just tell me if I hurt you in any way and I will stop. I promise."

Kei Lien didn't say a word at first. She just drank her juice, which made her feel better. When she was finished, she closed her eyes and whispered, "Yes."

Daniel told her he would be right outside the door. If she needed him to just call his name.

"Mary Elizabeth, you are an angel for sure," he said quietly as he left the room.

The exam was going to be difficult. There were no other attendants to help position this poor girl. And Mary Elizabeth wondered if Kei Lien would allow a speculum to be placed inside her, yet alone stay still long enough to obtain pictures and tissue samples. All she could do was try. When the nurse removed the sheets and blankets and gently moved Kei Lien's legs, she was horrified. Her skin was raw and mutilated. She explained to Kei Lien that she would need to take a few photos and asked if that was okay with her. It took a few minutes to describe what she was doing each time she touched her. Kei Lien flinched a little, but did not tell her to stop. Mary Elizabeth was grateful for that. She also had anal tearing and upon examining her further discovered the possibility of a pregnancy at some point.

When the exam was finished, Mary Elizabeth cleaned Kei Lien off with sterile solution, which she was sure stung, and tucked this brave girl back into a more comfortable position in her bed.

"Have a sip of water, Kei Lien, I will get you some lunch. Is there anything special you would like, dear?"

"Someone to love me like my mom did."

The only thing Nurse Mary Elizabeth could say without falling to pieces was, "She still does, sweetheart. She still does."

CHAPTER 48

"Did you say Andrew *Kelsey*?" Lake asked.

"Yes." Andrew replied.

"Reese, what are the odds of that name popping up here? I'm starting to think our town really didn't know anything about our beloved Sergeant."

"What name? Sergeant who? What are you talking about?"

"Andrew," Reese paused. "May we ask you a personal question?"

"I guess so."

"Who's your father?"

"What does that have to do with anything? Listen, I came here to help you with your case, not play *This is Your Life*. Now, am I being detained for something? If not, I'm out of here."

"No, you're not in any trouble Andy. May I call you Andy?" Lake asked. "It just seemed odd to me that the Sergeant in our town happens to have the same last name as you."

Andrew furrowed his brow. "A Sergeant? Really? Wouldn't that be a kick in the balls?"

"I don't follow you, Andy."

"I have no idea who my father is. My mother got knocked

up and lover boy took off on her. She tried to get him to pay child support, but she was too poor to afford a lawyer. She had to work three jobs just to keep our heads above water. When I was old enough, I got a job at the Center to help pay the bills. That's when this happened to me." Andrew motioned toward his deformed face. "The medical bills started to pile up and I guess it was all just too much for her. She committed suicide a few years ago. To be honest, I thought about doing the same thing, but either I was a coward or somewhere deep down I believe I have a chance to make something of myself in this world."

"You made the right choice," Reese smiled.

"Where is this Sergeant? If he is my father, I'd like to meet him and thank him for abandoning us. Tell him he's the reason my mom killed herself. That son of a bitch!"

"Whoa, hold on a second Andy. We don't even know if this man was your father or if this is just a coincidence."

"What do you mean *was*? He's dead, isn't he? I hope he is that asshole!"

"Andrew, we don't know anything yet. If you want, you could get a DNA test to see if there's a match, but that's all we can help you with right now. And yes, the Sergeant was murdered."

Lake touched Andrew's shoulder and gave it a soft shake. "Andrew, why don't we take your contact info and get in touch with you in the morning? Here's my card. We'll be in town through tomorrow at least. If you can think of anything else that might help our case, call me immediately. Day or night."

Reese was touched by this rare moment of compassion Lake was displaying.

She moved closer toward Andrew. "I'm so sorry for the loss

of your Mom. I bet she was a great woman. Suicide is such a difficult thing to grasp."

Andrew nodded his head. He gave the detectives his address and phone number and left.

Reese pushed the door closed, leaned with her back up against it and let out a big sigh. "What do you make of all of that?"

"I hate to say it, but it's starting to look like Martin Kelsey, our home town Sergeant, was a real prick."

Reese dropped her face into her hands. "You know, sometimes I hate the oath I took. Seeing the worst of humanity. I'd rather be soaking in a hot tub full of bubbles with a glass of wine in my hand instead of a gun."

Lake put his hand under her chin and raised her face gently. He stared deep into her eyes and for a moment allowed his feelings for her to rush over him. "This cheap motel has no tub, but why don't you go and take a nice long, hot shower. I'll go find us some wine and some snacks. Maybe some cheese and crackers? We can relax for the rest of the evening just watching mindless TV and put this case and our jobs out of our minds for a little while. Is that okay with you?"

Reese kissed him hard and then hugged him tight. "Thank you for actually listening to me. Now go get us that wine and cheese. I'm starving," she grinned.

As he turned to leave, she gave him a playful smack on the ass.

"Detective, I believe that would be considered sexual harassment," Lake winked as he slipped out the door.

Emerson Lake knew this was going to be a never-ending week. It seemed there were so many different directions to follow. So many what ifs and so many new suspects, including

Andrew Kelsey. Although he hoped that wasn't the case. That man had enough tragedy in his life. An accusation of murder just didn't seem fair. Even so, he certainly had motive. Around every corner were more unanswered questions. He highly doubted a pin board would be big enough to handle all of this. How could we not see the evil in our own Sergeant? Why did no one see what was happening to Kei Lien, and if they did, why not report it? Too much blame to go around, including himself, for only seeing what he wanted to believe.

When he returned with the wine and snacks, he found Reese sound asleep on the bed bundled in her white satin robe. He didn't have the heart to wake her, so he grabbed a few pillows and made himself comfortable on the floor. He would rather have been lying next to her after a long night of making love. Instead, he opened the wine and poured some in a paper coffee cup. At this point, he didn't care if he had to drink straight out of the bottle. Sleep came about twenty minutes later.

They were both jarred awake by a knock at the door. Almost simultaneously they grabbed for their weapons and practically vaulted themselves to their feet. Reese tiptoed to one side of the door while Emerson asked, "Who is it?"

"Detective Lake, you have a phone call at the front desk. Says it's important and they couldn't reach your cell."

That's odd, thought Reese. No one knew where they were staying. Not even the precinct knew they were at this particular motel. She motioned to Lake, shaking her head no back and forth.

"I'll be right down. Thank you. What did you say your name was?"

No answer. It was a trap. Reese crawled on her stomach across the floor until she was directly under the window. She gently pulled the curtains apart. A sliver of light pierced across the dark room from the exterior motel lights. She could see a large figure near the door. As she stretched her head a little further to get a better look, the man spun toward the window, raised a gun and shot through the glass. The bullet zoomed just a foot from Reese's head.

"Stay down!"

Bang! Another round fired. Closer this time. Emerson yanked the door open, reached his arm around the door jamb and touched off a few rounds. No shots fired back, so he carefully stuck his head out and heard a thud. The guy jumped the railing, hit the pavement and took off. Emerson made sure Reese was okay and then hopped the railing himself in hot pursuit, but he lost sight of him quickly in the poorly lit parking lot.

He was at a disadvantage not being able to see, but he kept running across the street and into darkness, hoping he would get lucky. The grass and twigs crunched under his bare feet with every step as he raced across the field. He could hear the sirens in the distance. Reese had called it in. He kept going and his eyes finally starting to adjust. There was no one in front of him. It was useless. He had lost him. Lake slowed to a jog and eventually stopped. He bent over, leaning on his knees, huffing and puffing trying to catch his breath. By the time he made it back to the motel, the local police were already on the scene, searching the perimeter of the motel.

Reese saw Lake emerge from the field and cross the street into the parking lot. She grabbed the hotel manager and one of the officers to greet him. "What the hell do you think that was about?"

"Besides us snooping around looking for a serial killer?" he scoffed. "What I want to know is how the hell that guy got away so fast. He was like a giant. Heavy and tall. Surprised he didn't break a leg when he jumped over the railing. We need to refocus on everything in this town. At daylight, we'll call Andrew and start fresh. In the meantime, we need somewhere else to stay. Officer, how big is your holding cell? Mind if we crash there until morning?

"Sure, no problem," said the officer.

Lake turned to the motel manager.

"We are going to need full access to your computers and surveillance footage from this motel, if there is any."

"There is," replied the motel manager. "I'll pull it right away."

"I'll go with him," said Reese. "I'll meet you back at the station."

"Really? How the hell are you going to get there without the car?"

"I'm taking the car," she yelled to him. "You ride with the local black and whites."

Lake turned to the officer. "Looks like I'm going with you."

The officer laughed, "Well I guess so."

CHAPTER 49

Now that Cromwell Police knew the family name of the six bodies found at the Bradford Theater, the most troubling part was knowing they were not a family of six, but of seven. Where was this other family member? Here in Cromwell? Was this person dead and just buried somewhere else? That scenario didn't seem logical. Was he alive and hiding out of fear for his own life? Or was he hiding because he murdered his family?

In the squad room, while all available officers were looking through files and once again going over the evidence they had, Captain Brown got in on the conversation. "Crime scene photos and files just aren't cutting it. What the hell is the motive here?" Also, there is no concrete evidence that this seventh family member is dead or alive.

"All of this is somehow connected to the murder of the Sergeant and the murder of Kei Lien's father, don't you think?" said one of the police officers to Manning.

"It has to be," Manning replied. "Two town residents murdered on the same night. Same way. And then a dead family shows up at the theater with the Dad wrapped in Christmas paper. Too coincidental."

"What the hell are we are missing besides the missing family member?"

"Another question unanswered. This had to be orchestrated by more than one person."

The Captain's cell phone rang. "Yeah?"

It was Detective Clayton.

"The hospital just notified me about what had happened to Kei Lien," she reported. "It appears she was assaulted. Bruises, abrasions, vaginal and anal tearing. In other words, Captain, she was raped. Unfortunately, she bathed in the lake. No body fluids or DNA to test, but I would venture a guess it was the father."

"And I would venture to guess our Sergeant, as well. Why else would they both be wrapped and stabbed the same way?" asked the Captain.

"You're probably right," Clayton said. "And who knows if there were more."

"How's it going in Jade?"

"We have some leads to chase down. As soon as I have something, I'll be in touch."

The call ended and the Captain headed back to her office.

A few moments later, Allen Manning's cell rang. He looked down at the caller ID and thought it was odd.

"Hey guys, I've got to grab this call. I'll be right back." He stepped outside and answered.

"Lake, what's going on? I know you both just spoke to the Captain."

'Listen, I didn't want to tell the Captain just yet, but I need you to do me a favor. It's got to stay quiet, though. Just between the two of us, understand?"

"Sure, no problem."

"Reese and I were ambushed at the motel tonight and we think our murder suspect could be in Jade."

"Holy shit, are you guys okay?"

"Yes, we're fine, but we need some information that we can't research here. I need you to run a name through the database. Andrew Kelsey."

"Who the hell is that?"

"Look, just run the name. Can you do that?"

"Got it, I'll see what I can find out and let you know."

"Also, Allen, Reese and I will be staying at the Jade County police department. Taking the safe way. No sense giving this guy any more free shots. We'll be seeing how the other half lives," he chuckled.

Allen took down the information and put it in his shirt pocket. When he hung up the phone, he waited for the precinct to quiet down a little and change shifts before starting his search for Andrew Kelsey. There was no warrant out on this guy. Why did Lake want him to do this search in the first place?

An officer walked by, "Staying an extra shift, Manning?"

"No, just catching up on some paperwork. You in tomorrow?"

"Yeah, I'm guessing there will be no days off for a while."

"Probably not."

He continued his search before deleting the program and shutting down the computer. He contacted the detective from his car.

"Lake, what connection does this person have to the Sergeant? I ran the search, but so far, the only thing that did pop up was

Martin Kelsey. His driver's license came up with information on address, social security number, and date of birth. He apparently lived in Jade at some point, but what does this have to do with this person named Andrew? What the hell was the search supposed to find? It didn't reveal anything we didn't already have on file apart, from Sergeant Kelsey living in Jade. That's not a crime to my knowledge."

"It's just a hunch we had about a possible illegitimate birth that could have involved Sergeant Kelsey."

"What the hell? Did we know this guy at all?"

"Still don't know if it has any merit or not. When we get back, I'll fill you in on why. Right now, it's still between you and me."

"Sure. When are you coming back?"

"First we have to find out who we pissed off enough to try and kill us. Oh, and by the way, Officer, I'll make this up to you. Promise. I know you were only trying to do the right thing by sending Teresa Kelsey to the hospital that day. No hard feelings."

Lake hung up leaving Allen speechless. When the hell did Emerson Lake turn into? A human being?

CHAPTER 50

Daniel returned home from the hospital to a waiting and anxious father. Kei Lien was heavily sedated after the ordeal she just went through with the examination. She definitely needed uninterrupted sleep. Daniel needed the same, although for different reasons. He was beginning to wonder how he got so involved in this mess so quickly. His father appeared in the living room and sat down in the oversized, overstuffed recliner.

"Sit down, Daniel. We need to talk a bit about recent events." His dad seemed so formal all of a sudden. His voice was strong, but low. It was the same tone he used when Daniel decided not to return to med school, but he certainly knew the reason behind that decision.

"Dad, can this wait until tomorrow? I'm exhausted."

"I think you know the answer to that. What is it you expect from this young lady? Do you think she will suddenly fall in love with you because you saved her from a dreadful life?"

"Dad, I really don't even know how all of this happened. All I wanted was a friend to talk to. You have always been there for me. I know I can talk to you about anything, but this is different. I just wanted a friend. Nothing else. When I heard what the Sergeant was doing to her, I had to see if I could help. I felt responsible for not climbing through the open window and kicking the crap out of the piece of shit that was hurting her. Really, I didn't know how this was going to turn out. Still don't. The guilt is horrible. I felt the same way when mom died. I couldn't help her either. So now I wait and try to be there for this tortured young woman because I wasn't there when she needed someone the most. I should have stopped the Sergeant no matter the consequences. Now I don't even know if she killed her own father or the Sergeant. Sorry Dad, but I hope the hell she did. What jury would convict her?"

"Unfortunately, Daniel, I don't believe that to be true. She would not have the strength to move those bodies let alone at two different houses. I seriously doubt she even knew where the Sergeant lived."

"I wish that made me feel better, but the truth is, if they weren't already dead, I would seriously consider doing it myself after seeing what they did to this poor girl. I don't think there are enough shrinks in the world that can mend her soul."

"So, what now?"

"For me or for her? I need to sleep. Can we take this up again in the morning? I'm going to shower, grab a peanut butter sand-wich and hit the sack."

"See you in the morning son. And Daniel…I love you."

"I know. Love you back."

CHAPTER 51

Both detectives decided to meet with Andrew Kelsey in the morning. Reese dialed his phone, but there was no answer. She tried a second time, still no answer. "Now why wouldn't he answer the phone? Maybe my fingers are faster than my brain."

"Reese, try it one more time before we go looking for this guy."

This time a machine picked up and started to spiel the recorded message and then Andrew answered. "What do you want?"

"Andrew, this is Detective Clayton. May we meet with you? Maybe over breakfast? We could meet at the diner."

"Detective, did you happen to notice anything about me when we met yesterday? The last thing people want to see while having their breakfast is someone who looks like the bacon on their plate. Now what can I do for you?"

"I apologize, really I do. Can we meet somewhere else? We really need to talk to you more about Tim Cole. Anything you have would be a huge help to us. A description, age, where the family lived. Please. We will meet you anywhere you wish. It's time you help us find him and take him off the streets for what he did to you and the others."

Andrew, still a little cautious of what all of this would do to his life, decided to help. "Why not? What else could this maniac do to destroy my life any more than he already has?"

CHAPTER 52

On top of a hill, looking out over the town, feeling the breeze, and soaking up the sun, a very large man tried to understand just what to do next. He was exhausted from running, but knew this break would be short lived.

I have to find a way to take back control of what's happening, he thought. Who else knows where I am? How did these detectives manage to track me down? Unless it's someone trying to destroy me back in Cromwell. His thoughts started to swell. Maybe the Boss or? His mind started to race and his hands contorted into tight fists. "I'm getting really tired of killing people," he muttered through gritted teeth. "I know it's wrong, but I will find out who is setting me up and they will pay! Just like those two who were hurting my friend. They were doing really bad things to her. I told her I would take care of them. I did, too! They can't hurt her anymore." His lips turned upward into a sideways grin.

His clenched hands began to loosen and he started to pace. His thoughts racing, "Could the Boss have sent me away to get rid of me? Or, was the Boss afraid I'd get caught? That taxi driver was taking me to a place I didn't know." He crossed his arms around his own torso sat down on the grass and began to rock. "Somewhere I wouldn't know anyone? I asked that taxi driver nicely if he could take me back to where I used to live a long time ago instead. At least I would know my way around there. But no, that stupid driver had to give me shit."

His arms dropped to his sides and his body stiffened. "I don't like to be told what to do! He didn't like it when I grabbed his throat from behind and told him to drive me to Jade." He giggled to himself remembering how fun it was Also, listening to him choke and gag. "He did as he was told after that and drove me here. And he would've been okay too if he just let me out of the car just outside of town when I asked instead of speeding up." His body softened as he noticed a squirrel sitting at the base of the nearby tree.

"Why did he speed up, Mr. Squirrel?" he asked in a soothing voice. "Stupid driver was yanking the steering wheel back and forth and hitting his brakes real hard. He was trying to hurt me. So, I had to do something. We went for quite a ride after that, Mr. Squirrel! Veering this way and that. And then suddenly it was like we were floating in midair and then THUD!" he yelled startling the squirrel part way up the tree trunk. His tail flickering nervously. "It was like a crazy roller coaster ride," he snorted. "People are stupid." He gazed at the squirrel, "Gee, I hope the squirrel I killed when I was younger wasn't your brother?" The squirrel scurried up the tree further.

"I really don't know why I would want to come back here. It was my home. Well, at least for a while, anyway. Until those doctors decided I needed to be put away. Mom and Dad didn't know what those doctors would do to me or else they wouldn't have sent me there. I love my mom. I told them both many times I didn't like it there. I begged them to take me with them on vacation. I told them I would be good and not get into trouble. I was never going back to that place. Yet, here I am sitting on a hill looking out at the very site I burned to the ground. That awful, awful place. I don't regret it at all. I think I'll stay on this hill for a while and take a little nap. Don't you worry one bit, Mr. squirrel. I won't hurt you."

CHAPTER 53

Daniel called in sick to his park ranger job. He didn't know if he could ever view the park as anything other than a burial ground after all that had happened. He told his boss he would need a few days. His boss understood where he was coming from and told him to take whatever time he needed. The entire city was on high alert knowing there had been two home invasions and a creepy murderer on the loose.

Minh Nyung decided it would be best if he drove his son to the hospital to visit with Kei Lien. He wanted to see just what was happening and offer to help if needed. He was quite sure she had no medical insurance, so he was ready to take care of the cost. This girl was important to his son. He couldn't fathom watching him go through another tragedy. Minh knew the stress of losing his own wife. Money was never going to change what had happened to this poor girl, but it made Minh feel like he was helping to heal the wound in his son's soul.

They arrived to find doctors all around Kei Lien's bed. She was awake and seemingly calm while they spoke with her about her ordeal.

"Dad, she looks so frail. It's not fair what she's had to go through. I should have done more. I should have stopped the Sergeant."

"This young woman was abused long before you even met her, Son. She is mentally torn and I'm not sure she can recover."

Daniel waited for the doctor and his students to come out of the room before asking questions so as not to alarm her. "What have you found out so far? Her condition? How bad are her injuries?"

The doctor was surrounded by, what appeared to be, residents. Future doctors. Although Daniel knew that some of them would never make it that far. He knew from his own experience. His own attempt at a medical career. Apparently, this doctor thought he should make an example out of Daniel. A lesson for these students in short white coats.

"Young man, certainly you are aware of a thing called a HIPAA law," he said condescendingly. "It states that no one has the right to patient information – no test results, no diagnosis, no prognosis - without consent from said patient or if you have court-appointed guardianship." He motioned to one of his white coat students, "You should be writing this down."

The students glanced at Daniel and then buried their heads in their clipboards furiously writing. This guy was a prick to say the least, thought Daniel.

"I got the message," Daniel sneered. "And apparently so did everyone else."

"I can't give answers where there are none, young man."

He wanted to punch him square in the mouth for treating him like a child just to make himself look important in front of his students. He had seen this kind of lesson before in med school.

"Arrogance, caused by a white coat," he declared as he pushed past all of them into Kei Lien's room.

Minh stayed in the hallway so Daniel could see for himself how his friend was doing. She appeared to be extremely calm and he knew why. Heavy drugs. No one gave them permission to do this, a mild sedative maybe, but not this much. One thing Daniel knew for sure was they just didn't want her to be trouble in their hospital, especially with all the media in the area. He approached her carefully. He didn't want to frighten her any more than she probably already was.

"Hi," he whispered. "Do you remember me?"

"Yes."

"Can I get you anything? Juice? More pillows? Anything at all?"

"I do like orange juice. Maybe some of that."

Daniel opened the door and asked his dad to get her some orange juice.

"Are you even sure she can have it?"

"Dad, she is so medicated she doesn't know her right foot from her left. She needs something to bring her back into focus. I don't trust what's going on here. Why is she on so much medication when a low dose anxiety drug like alprazolam would probably do?"

"I will ask the nurse out here if juice is okay. In the meantime, you need to settle down a bit. Not all doctors are alike. Not all doctors try to take advantage of their status. They probably want to make sure she doesn't feel threatened. So, the quieter she is, the better she will feel. She has had a very stressful time. You know that and you also know how quickly she can change into a scared little girl and run. Am I right? Now I will see about the juice."

"I know. I'm sorry."

Minh just nodded his head at his son.

"Is there anything you can tell me or want to tell me about all of this?"

"All of what? Did I do something wrong?" She sat up on her elbows in the bed. "Why am I here? What day is it? I want to go home. Who are you?"

"It's okay, Kei Lien. I'm Daniel. I came to visit you. I'm your new friend. Remember me?"

"Yes," she replied and lay back down.

Daniel's theory was correct. Too much medication. She was becoming agitated for sure. Her mind was going in all directions. He went to the nurse's station to get help, but they were already on their way. Bending her arms to sit up in bed had disturbed the wires she was attached to and set off the alarms. Daniel backed away while they hooked them back up. He decided it was probably better to leave and let her rest. He met his father in the hall and told him what happened.

"Daniel, drink the juice. It might help you instead of her. Let's go home."

CHAPTER 54

"Mrs. Kelsey, this is Sara Hunter. Your husband's body is ready to be released. Which funeral home would you like him sent to?"

Sara had all the information she could get from his remains.

"Well it's about damn time, don't you think?" Teresa Kelsey snapped. "The whole town has been waiting to pay their respects at my Martin's funeral. Now I have to make all these arrangements that should have been done a week ago."

Teresa continued with her bitch-fest, rambling on and on. "I need people to speak at Church and decide who should be the pall bearers. I'll need to get his nice suit ready for the viewing. Or maybe I should get out his dress police uniform."

Sara stopped her there. "Mrs. Kelsey, do what you need to do. I have another body here to tend to. Contact my assistant, he will have your husband ready for the funeral home of your choice. Thank you for your patience and I'm sorry for your loss."

Sara wanted to tell her what she really thought of *her Martin*, but decided that probably wasn't a good idea.

CHAPTER 55

Lying in his bed, Andrew Kelsey decided before his meeting with the detectives he would do a little investigating on his own. He wanted to know more about this guy with the same last name as him. He wondered if this guy could possibly be his father. Where did he come from and why didn't he stay with his mother when she got pregnant? What kind of a coward does that?

He decided to jump on his computer to search for news on a murder in Cromwell, South Dakota. Turned out it wasn't hard to find. The media had it all right there in front of him. At least their version of it. Andrew remembered how the media got it all wrong about the fire that destroyed his face and his life. Trust was not in his vocabulary. What he did trust though were the photos of the two victims. One was possibly his father.

I'm going to get that DNA test like the detective mentioned. And when it comes back positive, I'll be sure the whole town of Cromwell, heck the whole state of South Dakota, knows he ruined our lives when he left us. Martin Kelsey may have already paid the price for some other terrible things he did in his life, but that's not good enough for me. He stared long and hard at Martin Kelsey's photo until the screen timed out and went black.

He was looking to see if there might be a resemblance of some sort. Of course, there wouldn't be now, with his face so badly burned. He jiggled his mouse and the photo reappeared. Andrew saved the photo to his computer and continued to investigate this man's life. Where he came from. How long he had been a Sergeant. Where he had lived. If there were any children. Pretty much a complete bio on him. The only thing missing was a mention of Andrew's mother and his illegitimate son. Andrew grew more and more sure that this guy was his biological father. No proof yet, but in his gut he knew. He would have that DNA done.

After spending so much time on the computer, Andrew needed some fresh air. He decided to pay his mom a visit. He stopped at the local florist and purchased a bouquet of assorted flowers. He then walked to the cemetery where she was buried. He cried for a few moments at the gravesite and made a promise to her that he would once and for all find the truth. Get the answers he so desperately needed and then he laid the flowers on top of her headstone.

As he was leaving the cemetery, he crested the top of a knoll and saw a man on the adjacent hill lying in the sun.

"God help me," he whispered, the hairs on the back of his neck bristling. "I know who that is. It's him. He's much heavier now than I remember, but it's definitely him."

Andrew turned slightly and continued walking away, pretending not to notice this guy. He kept his head down, as if he was mourning a loved one, keeping a handkerchief over his face. If this was Tim Cole, he didn't want him to see his face, for sure. When he got back to the town line, he contacted the detectives.

"I know it's him!" Andrew shouted into the phone. He is a lot heavier now, but it's him. Why is he here?"

Andrew paused.

"Detective Lake," his voice trembling, "I left flowers on my mother's grave. If this nut goes to see who's in that grave, he'll know it's me who left them."

"Take it easy. Let's not make hasty assumptions about someone that was just getting some sun. How far away was this guy when you saw him?"

"I'm sure it was him! He was near the top of the hill, but I know it's that prick. I saw that devilish smirk and the evil in his eyes as he lit that match. I won't ever forget him, fat or not."

"We'll inform the local authorities about your sighting and have them check it out."

The entire Jade force was on the lookout for this guy after Andrew gave them a description, as best he could anyway. It had been a long time since the fire.

"We need to act quickly, but cautiously," ordered Reese. "All we have is Andrew Kelsey's accusation that this Tim Cole lit the match that caused the fire at the mental facility. There is no real proof of that fire being arson. The building is no longer there. We need concrete evidence before we can go after this guy for that fire." Not going to be easy considering he was presumed dead.

"I know, but if we can get him on taking the shots at us," Emerson said, "then we got him. That's if it is the same person."

Reese agreed. "Let's start by looking at the files for this institution case and see what we can piece together. Of course, that will take some digging through a warehouse full of old files. I'm sure the records weren't stored on a computer that long ago.

"I would like to detain Andrew, Emerson. I'm afraid he is a loose cannon right now and would not think twice about putting a bullet in this Tim Cole."

"I get it, but we have nothing to hold him on. What I can do is have an officer stay with him as protection since he's a possible witness to this suspected arson case. He won't like it, but we have no other choice right now. Agree?"

"Agreed."

CHAPTER 56

Minh Nyung hired an attorney. Not to protect his son, but to see if he could obtain documents to become legal guardian for Kei Lien. Someone had to look out for her. Minh figured if there were other relatives alive then someone would have stepped in to help her by now. Or, perhaps they didn't even know about her. The Chandlers adopted her or maybe this was not a legal adoption. Who knows where she was from originally? His attorney jotted down the details, informed Minh of the required documents needed to present a request such as this to a judge and told him he would be in touch. Minh decided it was best to not say anything to his son in case the judge turned them down.

"May I speak to someone in charge of the murder case for Adam Chandler? My name is Denton Hollingsworth. I'm the attorney for Mr. Minh Nyung." He handed the officer at the desk his business card.

"The two lead detectives, Reese Clayton and Emerson Lake, are out of town on a case right now, can I help?"

"Is there a number where I may reach them? It is very

NOW SAY YOU'RE SORRY

important that I speak with them."

The officer offered to send the detectives his information and have one of them contact him as soon as possible.

Emerson's phone rang about 2:30 pm startling him again. "Jeez! I have to get a new ringtone on that thing."

He answered, "Detective Lake."

The officer on desk proceeded to inform him of the attorney visit and gave Lake the number. "He said it was very important that he speak to one of you soon."

"Thanks, I'll follow up."

Puzzled, Lake hung up. What next? Why would Minh Nyung need to lawyer up? After filling Reese in on the call from the office, he dialed the number.

"Denton Hollingsworth."

"Yes, Mr. Hollingsworth, this is Detective Emerson Lake. You wanted to speak to my partner and me about the murder of Adam Chandler?"

"Mr. Nyung has asked me to file for guardianship of Kei Lien Chandler on his behalf. He claims she is under hospital care with no one to speak for her and unable to do so herself. Although she is an adult, he claims her mind is that of a child. An abused one at that."

"The murder of her father is an ongoing investigation. As far as this young woman not being able to speak for herself, well, that isn't up to us. I think you need to speak with the hospital staff and have a psychiatrist evaluate her."

"I know, Detective Lake, I'm merely asking you if Mr. Nyung is a threat to her or in some way involved in this investigation."

"Mr. Hollingsworth, I'm sure you're very aware that everyone is a suspect in an open case...until they're ruled out. Now, if there are no more questions, we really need to get back to work."

"Thank you, Detective. I left my card with the officer at the Cromwell Police Station. If there is anything you can think of that may help with this matter, please contact me."

As Lake hung up, he turned to Reese, "What do you make of this new twist?"

"I think he probably just wants to make sure Minh wasn't a suspect."

"I suppose, but what did he think we would say about an ongoing investigation? Yes, I think Mr. Nyung is a safe bet to care for her, but I can't rule out anyone either."

"I know, but he had to try to get some info, I guess. Either that or his stuffy sounding name doesn't match his degree." They both chuckled for a second.

"Seriously, someone does need to take care of that young girl. She is a mess for sure."

Denton Hollingsworth made arrangements for Kei Lien to be evaluated right away. The hospital assured him their findings would reach his office within 24 hours. He also reminded them that he needed a full report on her physical condition as well as mental to take to the judge. He already had a court date set up for Wednesday at 3pm. They had two days. The hospital staff agreed to have all of it ready. The last thing any hospital needs is a lawyer on their doorstep, especially with reporters all over the place. Hollingsworth hoped this would go smoothly and not turn into a pissing contest between him and the hospital administrators.

CHAPTER 57

Teresa Kelsey had gone to great lengths to give her husband the sendoff she wanted, not the one he deserved. Arrangements were made for the viewing to take place from 4-8pm at the funeral home with a full U.S. Army color guard at his side. She thought that would be a nice touch. He was a veteran after all. An American flag would be draped over his coffin and sprays of red white and blue flowers would surround him. Mrs. Kelsey, grieving wife of the beloved Sergeant, dressed to perfection, including a black veil to cover her face. She loved pomp and circumstance. An overstuffed, high-backed armchair with blue satin fabric would be easily accessible if she felt faint. She had asked the funeral director to place Sergeant Kelsey's obituary online so no one could say they didn't see it. It was a long and over the top listing of his accomplishments.

Mrs. Kelsey arrived at the funeral home in high fashion. Limousine and all. One thing she did not count on was no one showing up to pay their respects. Word had spread throughout the city that the Sergeant was suspected as one of the men that raped a young woman, even if there was no real proof yet.

"How did this happen?" she yelled at the funeral director. "Why is no one here?"

He didn't know how to answer except to say, "Maybe they will show up a little bit later. It is very early, Mrs. Kelsey. Some people work and like to eat dinner before they attend these things."

She didn't say a word. Just strode over to her throne-like blue satin chair and sat down with a huff. Lace hankie at the ready. She nodded to the soldier standing at her husband's side. There wasn't much else she could do. Around 5:30pm a few people walked into the funeral home, mostly to catch a glimpse of the show going on rather than paying respects. Teresa Kelsey was gracious as they walked past his casket and offered her their condolences. They were mostly patrons of the hotel and café.

When calling hours concluded, Teresa exited the funeral home to find a crowd of about twenty people waiting for her outside. For a brief moment she thought they came in honor of her Martin. How wrong she was. It was mostly reporters throwing questions at her fast and furious. The rest were angry Cromwell residents that wanted answers about his involvement with Adam Chandler's daughter. They encircled her. Vehement questions shot at her like bullets from a gun. She was scared and enraged all at the same time. She felt as if she were suffocating. She became dizzy and tipped slightly to the right, grabbed the handrail, and slumped down onto the funeral home steps.

"Please leave me alone!" she pleaded.

Sitting there on the cold stone step, all she could think was this is the thanks I get? All the hard work I put in to give him a proper sendoff was for naught. No accolades. Just berated by the press.

Buoyed by her fury, she boosted herself up, directed the funeral director to close the doors and pushed through the crowd. She hopped into the back of her limo and it sped away. When she arrived at her hotel, she told Randall she didn't want to be disturbed. She took the elevator to her suite, kicked off her shoes, grabbed a bottle of Scotch and a few pills from the bar cart.

CHAPTER 58

Andrew Kelsey was worried for his life. What little there was of his life anyway. He became increasingly aware he needed to do whatever the detectives wanted him to do. He started with giving the sketch artist at the police station a description of the man he saw at the cemetery. He told them approximate age, his height and guessed at his weight. He remembered the color of his eyes. A very pale green. A color he had never seen before. They were sunken deep into his skull. "You could see the evil in those eyes. That's something you can't draw on paper."

As Andrew was continuing his description of Tim Cole, he heard one of the Jade police officers talking about a report of an accident. A taxi was found flipped over on Old Route 19. The driver was dead. His throat had been cut. No one else was found in the vehicle. Andrew's skin began to crawl. He knew who did this. He could feel it.

"Detectives," yelled the officer. "You're not going to believe this, but the taxi cab was registered to a company in Cromwell. We have the I.D. on the driver from his license. We're checking now to see who his last fare was and where the pick-up point was located."

"Holy shit," exclaimed Lake. "Okay, I want every available law enforcement on this guy. We have a description. Let's get it out there! It looks like this guy is on a roll. Nine murders so far." As he was barking orders, a flood of anxiety washed over him, and he began to sweat. His breaths were becoming shorter. He was pacing the squad room wringing his hands. Reese grabbed him and pulled him into the men's room when everyone else scattered.

She first checked to be sure no one was in the two stalls. She sat him on a wooden bench and looked straight into his eyes.

"You need to breathe, damnit, or you're going to have a heart attack. Your blood pressure must be through the roof. I think you should see a doctor."

"Not now, Reese, I'm fine. Really, I am. Just too much caffeine causing me to shake a bit. You know how that goes. Law enforcement go-to and I go to it too often. I can't believe all of this is happening so fast. We now have nine bodies. Nine! It could've been eleven if you count the two of us. What is this guy's problem?"

"Besides being a lunatic? Now drink some water. No more coffee today, damn it, or I'll shoot you myself. Got it? Also grab a protein bar or something of nutritional value. Jesus, I don't have time to babysit you."

Reese had no clue that the love of her life was having anxiety attacks. The case, no sleep and having his ex-girlfriend covering the story; it was all a dangerous combination.

Reese contacted Allen Manning to fill him in on the latest. "I want all officers on alert."

Allen filled her in on the commotion at the Sergeant's funeral.

"Shit. One of us should have been at the service."

"I was, but it wasn't pretty. I was just headed over to the hotel to check on Teresa when you called. I'll let her know you were thinking of her."

"You do that and thank you, Allen. Try not to let her know you're lying."

Allen wanted to laugh out loud but restrained himself. "Will do."

Allen left for the hotel not really knowing how to approach Teresa Kelsey. He almost felt sorry for her, but on the other hand she really was a pain in the ass with her 'I'm better than everyone else' attitude. He pulled into the hotel garage and drove to the second level before finding a spot to park. That wasn't all he found. An ambulance with no plates was sitting semi-hidden in a corner. A light blue minivan blocked the one side. The garage wall the other. Allen was puzzled. That isn't one of our ambulances. Why would it be here in the hotel parking garage? There was no city or county name on the sides. Just the word ambulance. After snapping a photo of the vehicle, he walked down to the first level and into the hotel entrance where he saw Randall working the front desk. At that moment, it hit Allen like a bolt of lightning. He knew where he recognized Randall.

The night he sent Teresa to the hospital with the paramedics, Randall was one of those paramedics. Allen hadn't paid much attention at the time, but it was all coming back to him now. It was definitely Randall. Trying to remain calm, Allen approached the desk.

"Hi Randall. How are you? Is Teresa doing better?" He was doing his best not to sound any different than usual. He needed this guy to trust him.

Randall replied, "I'm very sorry ,Officer Manning, but Mrs. Kelsey is resting and asked not to be disturbed. She gave me strict orders. Is there something I can help you with?"

"No. Just tell her I was checking in on her and if she needs anything to just call. She was pretty upset after the viewing. Oh, and by the way, has anyone tried to bother her? More reporters? Anyone?"

"No, I've been trying to keep an eye out for her."

"Thanks Randall, I'll be in touch."

Allen was on the phone with Detective Lake before he even got out of the parking garage.

CHAPTER 59

Minh Nyung was trying to be helpful to his son and the young woman lying in a hospital bed. It wasn't easy, for sure. His main goal right now was to see to it that Kei Lien was well represented in this case. Her care would be dealt with very soon. He hoped anyway. There was not much conversation between Minh and Daniel throughout this entire scenario. Only when needed.

Today was needed.

"I feel like a lost soul sometimes. What am I supposed to do next? I really don't know what I should do for her. Or, if there is anything, I can do for her? How the hell did I get so mixed up in this girl? Woman? Whatever you want to call her."

"Daniel, do not worry. I have hired an attorney. Supposedly the best in his field. His name is Denton Hollingsworth."

Daniel immediately lashed out at his father. "Do you honestly think I had anything to do with the murders of Mr. Chandler and the Sergeant?"

"No, I do not. I hired him to look into having Kei Lien evaluated. When the mental health practitioners are finished questioning her, we will get this attorney to convince the judge to give us legal guardianship. Deal?"

Minh's son took a deep breath and choked back a few tears before responding. "Deal." It had been many years since he and his Dad did a fist bump, but now was the time for one.

Minh's phone rang just at that moment.

"Mr. Nyung? Denton Hollingsworth here."

Minh wished this guy would just say its Denton and not sound like an overpaid jerk.

"I've set up a time for the judge to hear reasons for this guardianship request. I will be at the courthouse around 2:30pm on Wednesday. I will meet you there. Hopefully he will be able to decide quickly. I can pick up the evaluation papers at the hospital on Wednesday morning. They assured me they would be ready."

Minh thanked him for calling and said he would be there.

"Dad, what are we getting ourselves into? We don't even know this girl. How do we know she isn't the one who killed her father? Or anyone else for that matter?"

"Daniel, I don't know the answers to much of anything, but there are two things I am certain of. One...this poor girl, woman, has been badly abused for most of her life. That much I know. And two...I know she lived a short distance from our own home, and we did nothing to help her. The entire town did nothing to help her. Someone should have stepped in when they heard her repeatedly sobbing, but no, we all looked the other way. The school system should also have intervened when she stopped going to classes. So, even if she did kill her father, we are all guilty of something."

CHAPTER 60

Tim Cole had taken a short nap on the hill that overlooked the cemetery. It was quiet. Slight breeze. Blue sky. For a short period of time, he felt like a normal human being and part of this town that he used to call home. Why, he thought, did my own family think I needed to be put in that awful place? The place where they wired your head and then flipped a switch to give you pain in your brain. Pain in your brain. That's funny sounding, he thought. It rhymes. It was time to go. As he stood up and gazed around ,he noticed flowers on a headstone at the bottom of the hill.

"I wonder who those flowers were for? I saw that guy put them on a stone, but didn't get a good look to see if I knew him."

Tim liked talking to himself. Why wouldn't he? There was no one else to talk to that would understand anyway.

"I'll head down to see. My family could have been buried here if they just would listen to me."

He walked down the hill, carefully looking around to make sure he wasn't being followed. "How is this possible?" he wondered as he reached the grave with the flowers. Tim Cole didn't know whether to laugh or be afraid. He stood there with his mouth open re-reading the name on the stone. "Huh? The woman buried here has the same last name as the Sergeant we just killed. How is that possible? I don't understand."

Fear began to take over. The twitch he developed after shock therapy all those years ago returned. This time with a vengeance. He quickly reached in his pocket to look for his phone. He wanted to call the Boss to find out what to do next. The phone wasn't anywhere on his body. The top of the hill he thought. I'll bet it fell out of my pocket when I took a nap. He turned around to head back up the hill as a man in a trench coat with a woman at his side approached him.

"Tim Cole? My name is Detective Lake. Cromwell Police Department. This is my partner Detective Clayton."

"I know who you are, detectives." Tim didn't know what else to say. He just stared at the two of them.

"We would like to have a few words with you."

"About what?"

"About where you were on June 9."

"I think you already know that I live in Cromwell. That's where I was until yesterday. I came here for a visit. I used to live here years ago. I think you already know that as well. Am I right?" he growled.

His eyes were now focused on the pretty detective. Eyeing her up and down. He gave Reese a huge grin, baring all his teeth. His twitch getting worse the more he spoke. He loved using his eerie voice on people. He would talk like this to the staff at the psych center once in a while. It was fun to watch them squirm.

Reese was un-nerved by this guy and kept her hand close to her gun.

"Is there something you think I did? Are you accusing me of something? Am I under arrest for something or are you just on a fishing expedition?"

"No," Lake chimed in. "You are not under arrest. We would however, like you to come to the police station to ask you a few questions."

"Really?" Tim was starting to enjoy this little back and forth stuff. He didn't really have many conversations with people. At least not with ones that were alive. So, this was fun for him.

"I can meet you there in a few hours. I need to find a ride. I have no car."

"No car?" asked Reese. "How did you get here from Cromwell?"

"I took a cab." Tim Cole never even thought that he might have just implicated himself.

"We can drive you, Mr. Cole. When we are through with our talk, we will have someone take you wherever you want to go. Is that all right with you?"

Reese was being extra polite. More flies with honey and all that.

"Okay, I guess." He was a little shyer now instead of arrogant. He stood firmly in place, but his hands were showing signs of sweat as he started to sway back and forth.

"Reese, you drive, I will sit in back with Mr. Cole."

"Why do I have to do the driving?" Reese knew the routine.

"Because I said so, that's why. Women." he scoffed. "They can be such a pain in the ass at times."

Tim Cole responded with a snort that came from the back of his throat. "I know. They want to be the ones giving orders all the time."

Once at the police station, Tim Cole was placed in a room with no windows, just a mirror. He could feel himself being closed in like so many times before. Detective Lake came in and had asked him if he would like something to drink.

"Coffee would be good."

"You know I could use a cup as well. Let's see what happens when I ask my partner to fetch us two coffees? How do you like yours, Mr. Cole?"

"Delivered by a woman," he remarked. "Cream. One sugar."

"You got it." Emerson opened the door and ordered Reese to get them both coffees.

When she came into the room, she had the look of a pissed off wife.

"Here's your coffee," she snarled slamming the mugs down on the table in front of them.

"Thank you, ma'am," said Cole.

"At least someone has manners in here. And it isn't you, jerk!"

Both men were laughing as she closed the door behind her.

Tim took a gulp from the mug. "At least she knows how to make a good cup of java."

Reese was in the room on the other side of the mirror listening to every word.

"Can we get started now?"

"Sure. What's this about anyway?"

"Your name is Timothy Cole. Is that right?"

"Yes."

"Do you understand that you do not have to tell us anything you don't want to and that you are entitled to have an attorney present while being questioned? Do you understand you are not under arrest?" Lake proceeded to recite the rest of the Miranda rights. "Mr. Cole, do you understand everything I just said?"

"If I'm not under arrest then why did you have to read me my rights?"

"So that you would understand your rights while we are questioning you. Now let's get Reese to get these cups out of our way. Are you finished with your coffee, Tim?"

"Yeah, you do know she is going to throw that cup at your head, if you keep pushing her buttons."

"Nah! She'll get over it. She likes me."

Reese came in and took the mugs. Tim's, of course, went straight to the lab for fingerprints.

"Mr. Cole, is it true you come from a family of seven counting yourself?"

"Yes," he replied. "Two brothers. Two sisters. Dad and Mom. I love my mom." He hung his head and stared at the table.

"Do you know where they are at this time?" He was trying not to frighten his suspect.

Tim Cole was getting a glazed look in his eyes. Almost like a trance. He was going to a place deep inside his mind. Much like a man with personality disorder.

"Mr. Cole, do you understand the question? Mr. Cole?"

Tim Cole stood up from the table, glared at the detective and then looked straight into the mirror. "I need a lawyer. Now!" he shouted. He was smarter than Lake or Clayton thought.

"I also need my phone," he demanded.

"Where is your phone? I didn't see you with one."

"I need to go back to the cemetery. You said you would take me anywhere I wanted to go after our talk."

"Okay. One of us will drive you back there."

Reese immediately sent one of the officers to the cemetery to look for the phone. She instructed them to look on top of the hill. Emerson, in order to buy some time, told Tim that he had to fill out some papers to get him a court-appointed attorney.

"We really can't arrest him on what we think he did. And those prints on the coffee mug are going to take time to see if they are a match with those on the taxi."

Reese agreed with her partner. "Emerson, let me go in and chat with him while you stay out of sight behind the mirror. Maybe he'll say something to me."

He agreed, but told her to stay alert. "This guy can turn on a dime. I think he has multiple personalities along with definite mommy issues."

"I know. I heard that little scenario on mom when I was behind the mirror."

Reese proceeded into the interrogation room. "Mr. Cole, do you mind if I sit with you while the detective gets your paper-work ready?"

Tim wasn't sure what was happening. This was new for him and he did not like being in this small, closed-off room. His heart was beating faster. He was sweating and a little light-headed too. His breathing was short and labored.

"Mr. Cole, are you all right?"

Emerson was in the room in seconds, afraid this was a ploy on Cole's part. A ruse to get out of there any way he could.

Cole sat in the chair staring off into space. His complexion was turning from red to blue.

"Get an ambulance!" yelled Reese from the doorway of the room.

"Mr. Cole. It's Detective Lake. Can you take a few deep breaths for me?"

Cole looked directly at him, terrified. His eyes widened. His pupils looked like sunken pools of death. He slumped over the corner of the desk and then slipped to the floor. He stopped breathing. Lake immediately started compressions on him and yelled to an officer to get the mask. Emerson was grateful they had these kits for emergency situations. He cringed at the thought of placing his bare lips on this crusty mouth that had not seen a dentist or toothbrush in years. EMT's arrived and took over the CPR. He was alive, but they were instructed to take him to the hospital in Jade. Reese rode with him in the ambulance, Lake soon followed after he brushed and gargled. Mask or no mask, that mouth was polluted.

CHAPTER 61

"Mr. Nyung, I have acquired the necessary paperwork needed for the guardianship."

"Thank you, Mr. Hollingsworth. What exactly did the judge have to say?"

"The Department of Mental Health determined that Kei Lien is not capable of making decisions regarding her health. Her medical records will be accessible to her guardian when needed. The judge agreed to allow you to become her guardian instead of a ward of the state, on the basis that this young woman needs special care that you can afford to provide. He said after investigating your personal life, you are an upstanding citizen, no issues with background checks and as your attorney, I made the point that this woman had been through unbelievable torture in her life and needed more medical, psychological and personal care than the state could provide."

Minh, now becoming emotional, something he rarely allowed himself to do. "I am very grateful for your help in this matter."

"The judge agreed to the terms until such time when Kei Lien could be re-evaluated. Do you understand the meaning of all of this, Mr. Nyung?"

"Yes, I do."

Daniel was happy with the decision. He no longer had to worry about what would happen to her. It was out of his hands, but in the hands of his dad, which Daniel felt was the right choice.

Minh Nyung arrived at the hospital with his paperwork in hand, ready to speak to the doctors and other staff on duty. He approached the nurse at the desk. "I would like to see Miss Chandler's medical records," he insisted pointing to the papers.

The nursed grasped the papers and shuffled through them. "Okay. We need to make a copy. I will let her doctors know you are here."

"Thank you, that will be fine." Minh recognized the nurse immediately. "Oh, Mary Elizabeth, it is so nice to see you again. I'm sorry, but I don't think I ever got your last name."

"It's Hollingsworth, Mr. Nyung. And yes, your attorney is my son."

"Well now I know how the paperwork was acquired so quickly. Thank you for your help, Mrs. Hollingsworth. May I still call you Mary Elizabeth?"

"Yes, you may. My husband passed many years ago so it's rare that anyone calls me Mrs. Anymore. But thank you for asking."

Minh recognized the attending physician approaching the desk. He expected this was going to be another round of I'm better than you, but Minh stayed cool-headed. "Doctor Hart, may I see Kei Lien's medical records now?"

"Of course. Let's go into my office so I can go over everything with you."

Minh couldn't believe how polite he was. Was this the same doctor who was so rude earlier this week? A bit of legal paperwork seemed to change his attitude drastically, but of course, he didn't have an audience this time either. Minh followed him to an office down the hall and took a seat in front of the large oak desk.

"Mr. Nyung, Miss Chandler is suffering from many physical injuries as you can probably imagine. She has been sexually abused, I assume for many years, and this torture has affected her mentally as well. She is on heavy doses of I.V. antibiotics to combat the infections she contracted via the unprotected sexual encounters. The lining of her uterus has also been severely damaged. I assume it was someone's attempt at an illegal abortion. She will never be able to conceive. She also has sustained a tremendous amount of damage to her rectum plus her bowel has been torn. Her own feces are quite literally poisoning her. She needs surgery to repair that damage as soon as possible. If it's not done in the next couple of days, she will die. As with any surgery there is always a risk. Even if she makes it through surgery, the recovery will be very difficult. She would need to stay hospitalized for at least a week. I am concerned how the anesthesia will affect her. This is a long surgery and she'll be under for quite a long time. She is already quite fragile."

Minh chimed in, "Doctor, her mental state, will her mind ever be free if she happens to make it through this ordeal?"

"Unfortunately, I can't give you that answer, Mr. Nyung. Please know we are trying to help her. Even though your son made it quite clear the other day that he doesn't see it that way."

"With all due respect, doctor, it was pretty clear to me that you were making an example of my son in front of your residents. For your information, he does know about HIPAA. You unnecessarily embarrassed my son during your teaching moment. For that, I could easily file charges on you for your unprofessional conduct. You don't even know my son. He is a very caring, smart young man. He too wanted to be a doctor. He even went to med school before his mother took ill with breast cancer. He dropped out to help care for her and never went back. I tried to convince him to return to school. I do still think it's his path, but that is up to him. I just want what's best for him. We both loved his mother very much."

"I'm very sorry for your loss. I apologize. To you and your son. You're right. I was out of line to treat your son in that manner."

Minh nodded with acceptance. "Thank you for all of the information about Kei Lien. It seems I have some decisions to make. May I see Kei Lien?"

"Yes, of course."

Minh walked into the room where his son's new friend lay quiet. She was heavily sedated. Minh now knew the reason why. She looked peaceful. No longer scared and ready to run. What anguish this young woman must have felt all these years. The fear. The pain. The loneliness. She was robbed of her childhood. He leaned in close to her. "Kei Lien," he whispered. "I am so sorry you had to endure this life. I'm sorry your neighbors, your educators did nothing to spare you from this life of torture. Your community has let you down. Please forgive us."

Daniel was standing in the doorway listening to his father's plea. "Dad, what did you find out from the doctors?"

Minh sat Daniel down in the chair and explained everything to him knowing he likely understood it all much more than he did. "What is your opinion? I want what's best for her and for you. Do you believe she has a chance with the surgery?"

"Dad, it's not the surgery I am worried about. Despite everything she's gone through, I think she is a strong woman physically. How else could she endure this nightmare? My concern is after surgery. Do you think with the right help she will be able to find peace? Happiness? Will she live a full life? What if she was involved in her father's murder? Will she end up in a mental institution for the rest of her life? Is that what's best for her? What kind of life is that? A life locked away being drugged and God knows what else for the rest of her life. Is that fair?"

"Daniel, like I said, I don't think she was strong enough to kill her father and wrap the son-of-a-bitch up in Christmas paper."

"You're right. I know. Let's get her into surgery. It's the right thing to do. And then we'll make sure she gets the right help. This is going to be a long road. Do you think we can handle it?"

Minh placed his hand on his son's shoulder. "I'm not at all sure, but somebody has to try to right the wrongs done to her. We need to find the peace in our own hearts as well. I'll tell the doctor to go ahead and schedule the surgery."

CHAPTER 62

A team of doctors and nurses met the ambulance at the Jade Hospital ER entrance. Lights still flashing, everyone went into full life saving mode. Two attendants slid the gurney out of the ambulance onto the pavement and through the sliding doorway. The wheels of the gurney clicking on the tile floors as it sped to the first open bay. A sound that meant another patient was being brought in. Someone checked vitals again, even though they were done in the ambulance. Doctors shouted orders on what tests needed to be done. Someone on the ER team ushered Reese past the curtain. "We got it from here, detective. You can wait outside in the hall." Reese was hesitant about leaving him behind curtains in a room she did not have full view of. "You don't understand. This guy is a loose cannon. You could be in danger. I can't leave."

Suddenly, Tim Cole bolted upright. The staff stepped back, one of the nurses shrieked. For a man that had been unconscious a minute ago, he looked as if nothing happened.

"What are you doing to me? Who are all of you?"

"Mr. Cole," a nurse approached his side, "you were brought in because you passed out in the police station. Detective Clayton thought you were having a stroke or heart attack."

"Yes," Reese chimed in, "while my partner Detective Lake and I were questioning you. Don't you remember Mr. Cole?"

"No, I don't." He laid back down on the gurney knowing full well he needed to be admitted to this hospital. Not for medical reasons, but he knew it was the only way he could make a plan to escape. I can't escape from jail, but I know what to do in here.

The doctors told Reese she needed to wait outside while they did their job. She assured them that she would be right outside the door. Tim allowed the hospital to hook him to a heart monitor. They ordered lab work and x-rays. Tim liked the idea of all these special tests. It was his chance to disappear without being caught. He had done this before at the Saturn Psych Center. These people have no idea who they're dealing with. No idea at all.

Emerson met Reese at the hospital. She gave him the update on what the doctors needed to do. "Where is he now?"

"Right this way."

They approached the curtained room, but it was empty.

Reese was furious. She stormed up to nurse's station slamming her fist on the desk. "Where did they take Mr. Cole and why was I not told where they were going? Where is the security guard I told to stand by the door? I specifically told you I needed to be notified of everything going on and that he was not to be left unattended."

"Detective, there is no need to shout at me. I think your guard went to the men's room. Mr. Cole was taken to X-ray while you were talking to the other officer. He'll be back shortly."

"Call security and lock this hospital down now! Damn it, now! Hopefully he hasn't gone too far. Where's the X-ray department?"

"Bottom floor. Take a left at the elevator midway down that hallway on your left."

Transport wheeled Tim Cole's bed down to X-ray where he was met by a technician. The tech asked if he was able to get himself onto the table, but Tim said he needed help. The tech walked closer to the gurney. In an instant, Tim's hands were wrapped around the technician's neck raising him up off the ground. His eyes bulged with fear and his legs kicked wildly. Tim cocked his head slightly and stared curiously into the tech's eyes. He wondered what he might be thinking as Tim's thick fingers squeezed tighter like a boa constrictor. The thought was fleeting though. With a flick of his wrists, he cracked his neck. The technician went limp. He dragged his body up onto the table, covered him with a sheet, and slipped silently out the door through the basement back exit.

When the elevator doors opened, Reese raced up to the desk. "Tim Cole," she stuttered through shallow breaths, "which room is he in? He was just brought down for X-rays."

"He's either in room #3 or #8 depending on what test is being done." The girl was just a transport. She had no idea why Reese was yelling at her. She escorted them both to room #8. Nothing. She opened the door to room #3. "Now why would a corpse have been left in this room?"

Lake and Clayton glanced at one another, hands hovering over their holsters. Lake cautiously moved toward the body and carefully lifted the sheet.

The young girl let out a blood-curdling scream.

"Son-of-a-bitch," Reese muttered.

"He got away! Put out a BOLO on this guy! I want him arrested for the murder of a hospital employee. And tell them, try not to kill him when they find him. I want that pleasure myself. At least I want to be there to watch him fry."

While Emerson was on the phone Reese was barking orders at hospital security. "You need to lock this place down and check every nook and cranny in case he's still hiding in here."

"They found the security guard, knocked out in a linen closet. At least he didn't kill him." said Lake.

She turned to her partner, "The cemetery, Lake. He might go back to look for his phone."

"I'll call it in."

The officer at the desk told Detective Lake the phone had already been recovered at the cemetery and was on its way back to the station. "I could have my men turn back to see if this guy shows up."

"My partner and I will go. This guy can't be that far ahead of us so maybe we can find him there."

"Got it."

When they got close to the cemetery, he told Reese to circle around to the back entrance while he came in the front. "Maybe we can see him near the top of the hill. But Reese, watch your back. This guy is quick. We don't need any more surprises."

Near the top of the ridge, where you could see the entire south side of the cemetery, Tim Cole was on his hands and knees searching the grass. Reese spotted him first. "Lake," she whispered into her radio. "I see him. Head straight up the hill. I'm right in front of him about 20 feet away."

"I see him." Lake didn't wait. He removed his revolver aimed it right at Cole's head.

"Put your hands on your head and stay down on your knees. You are under arrest for the murder of a Jade Hospital employee."

Reese came up behind, grabbed his wrists, slapped the cuffs on and once again read him his rights. This time for real.

"Women," Cole muttered. "They always have to be in control."

"You're damn right! Now get on your feet!"

Detective Lake never took his eyes off Tim Cole and kept his gun pointed right at his head. "Give me a reason to shoot you, I'll be happy to oblige."

They put him in the back of the car. Emerson jumped in the back seat; Reese slid into the driver's seat.

"Oh, I see you're still taking orders from your man. How about that little lady?"

Like a wild cat, Reese launched halfway over the seat and punched him in the face. Blood poured out of his nose over his lips and dribbled down his chin.

"You can't do that, bitch!" Cole snarled.

"Detective, did you see how Mr. Cole just slammed his head into the door trying to get out?"

"I sure did, Detective Clayton. Why do you suppose he would try to do something like that?"

"I think he was trying to escape."

"I would advise you to not mess with Detective Clayton again. I hear she is one hell of a good shot with that gun."

"I want a lawyer."

"Well," Reese said, "I hope you can afford a good one because you're going to need it. Oh, and by the way, we already have your phone."

CHAPTER 63

"Kei Lien, I'm Doctor Hart. Are you ready to go to the operating room for surgery?"

Kei Lien looked at Daniel then at Minh and nodded yes, not really understanding what the word surgery meant. But if it was okay with Daniel, it was okay for her. As they were wheeling her to the operating room, she panicked.

"Where am I going? What are you doing?"

Doctor Hart told the nurse to give her a little more of the sedative through the I.V. to calm her down.

"One thing is for sure, she is strong willed," said one of the nurses, as they continued to wheel her toward the operating room.

The nurse was surprised how she could still be awake, let alone talking, with that much sedative in her. She should have been in la-la land by now.

Minh and Daniel decided to go to the chapel to say a prayer for their new friend. They both figured she could use all the help she could get. Minh said an extra one for his son.

It was a few hours before the news came. Doctor Hart approached the waiting room with sadness in his eyes. This was the hard part of being a surgeon.

"She's out of surgery and in the recovery room. You may see her when she comes out of the anesthesia."

Daniel was first to ask, "What did you find? Something is wrong. I know it."

"Mr. Nyung, Daniel, I'm afraid your friend had a lot more damage than we expected. We repaired the tear in her bowel, but Miss Chandler has a tremendous amount of tissue damage. It's far beyond what we thought from the original tests. The result of years of untreated sexually transmitted diseases alone. It's ravaged her body. I'm sure you understand Daniel, having been to medical school."

Daniel was surprised at the change in the doctor's attitude, but also cautious.

"The sexual abuse and recurring infections appear to have taken their toll. We have no way of knowing what all of this has done to her state of mind. We really know nothing of her background. For all we know she may have been mentally impaired from birth. My recommendation at this point is to keep her on high doses of antibiotics and hope she has enough fight left in her to battle the infections and recover. It's all a waiting game now. One of our very qualified nurses, Mary Elizabeth Hollingsworth, has volunteered her time to stay with Kei Lien round the clock if necessary."

"She is a wonderful nurse," Minh agreed. "She has a huge heart."

"When Kei Lien begins to wake-up, please do not stay too long. She needs all the rest she can get right now. We will notify you if anything changes."

"Thank you, Doctor."

A few more hours passed, and they were finally told they could see Kei Lien, but only for a few minutes. As they approached her bedside, she lifted her head and opened her eyes. Just part way, but the look she shot at Minh and Daniel was not the sweet, doe-eyed demeanor they had come to know. It was a piercing, rage-filled stare from a deep dark place. No one thought about how she would feel coming out of surgery. The incredible pain from surgery was reminiscent of the pain she felt after each encounter with her father and the rest of the Santa gifts.

"What did you do to me?" she growled.

Coming out of the anesthesia had her in a psychotic state, at least that's what her recovery room nurses assumed.

"You said you were not a gift from Santa! What did you do?" she screamed. "I thought you were my friend."

Daniel began to tear up as he watched Kei Lien fill with anger and fear.

"I didn't touch you," he said. "I promise I didn't do anything to you and neither did anyone else in this hospital. All of us, including the doctors want you to get better. Please believe me. Kei Lien, I am your friend."

Minh noticed Mary Elizabeth coming down the hall near the nurse's station. He met her before she entered the room. "Can you and I talk?" she asked. "Somewhere private please?"

"Of course."

She led him to a break room near Kei Lien's recovery room. "This room is not used anymore. It just collects everybody's junk."

She had already been briefed on the surgery and possible outcome.

"Minh, I fear for your son. I believe he cares about what happens to Kei Lien for reasons he doesn't even understand. I'm glad you decided to move forward as Kei Lien's guardian. Your son can now concentrate on being her friend like he said and not have to make tough choices."

"Thank you, Mary Elizabeth. It is certainly an unexpected journey."

After their chat, Mary Elizabeth approached Kei Lien's bed, straightened her sheets, fluffed her pillow, and patted her hand.

"There now. All better. Daniel, I think you and your father need to go home for a while and let Kei Lien get some rest. I'll let you know if anything changes. Promise. She's not thinking straight right at this moment and you're too emotional to handle the things she's saying to you."

"But…"

"No. Not another word. Go home, please." She nodded to Minh to take him home.

The ride back was quiet.

"You must be hungry. Let's stop to pick up take-out. I don't know about you, but I'm not in the mood to cook."

Daniel nodded. He was afraid to speak for fear of breaking down into tears.

CHAPTER 64

Officer Manning informed the precinct of what happened in Jade along with the suspect's name, Tim Cole.

"So how does this Cole guy tie into the murders of the Sergeant and Adam Chandler?" asked Officer Sorenson.

"I'll take this," Captain Brown said.

Officer Manning stepped aside to allow the captain to take over.

"Timothy Cole is a resident here in Cromwell and a former resident of Jade. He lived in a mental institution there at some point. They're going over the DNA and other evidence to be sure, but they believe he is the missing brother of that family found at the theater. Possibly a suspect in their murder. They arrested him for the murder of an X-ray tech at a hospital where he was being treated in Jade. Detectives Lake and Clayton will be tied up for a while processing this guy. He has already lawyered up; they are waiting to meet with them. In the meantime, I want all of you to go over anything tying Cole to this family."

"That still doesn't help us find the murderers of Kelsey and Chandler. And how they are connected, if at all, to this Cole character."

"Officer Sorenson, I get what you're saying, and I agree, but there's someone else in Jade that might have more info on this guy."

"Really? Then why aren't they giving us that info as well?"

"I don't know yet, but there has to be a connection, otherwise Clayton and Lake wouldn't be so adamant about this. Okay, you have your assignments. Now let's get everything we can on this guy. Dismissed."

Ken's assignment was to contact Teresa Kelsey since Allen Manning didn't appear to be getting anywhere with her. She was either busy, not feeling well or just didn't want to be disturbed every time he paid her a visit. Ken entered the hotel around 10:30am. He logged it into his journal. No problem getting into the hotel because he had been there a lot in recent months. In fact, he had lived at the hotel before, during and after his academy training. Before he applied for this job. He was only staying at the hotel until he could find his own apartment. One he could afford. He finally did find one, but by then Teresa Kelsey had him by the balls.

"Is she taking visitors today?"

Randall smiled, "Let me call her and let her know you're here."

"Thanks, my friend. I owe you one."

Teresa was waiting patiently at the door when Ken got off the elevator.

"Well, it took you long enough to come by and pay your respects. Where the hell have you been? I've been sitting in this suite with booze and a bottle of pills waiting for you to service me and believe me I need servicing. Now get over here and let me help you out of that uniform. Oh, how I love a man in uniform," she crooned, "but I love them even more when they take it off."

She giggled like a little schoolgirl.

It wasn't difficult to satisfy her needs today. It had been a long time since he had been in her suite. Just too much stuff going on and he didn't want the connection to her to go public so he waited as long as he could for things to quiet down before he approached her. Ken was only with her for about an hour. He told her he had to return to the precinct.

"I have to go, but I will come by soon. Promise. Right now, I need to figure out what to put on my report. Seeing how I'm supposed to be interviewing you about your husband's demise."

"You could start by telling them that I'm wonderful in bed, but my husband wouldn't take the time to satisfy my wants and my needs. He couldn't see how good that would have been for us both. He just wanted a quick piece of ass. Apparently raping young girls was the only way for him to get off."

"Calm down, I got this. And yes, you certainly are wonderful in bed." He leaned in and kissed her.

She shoved two crisp one hundred-dollar bills in his uniform pocket for services rendered and walked him to the door. "Thank you, Ken."

As soon as the door clicked shut, she floated over to her bottle of booze and headed off to take yet another one of her lengthy baths.

Ken stopped to talk with Randall before he headed back to the precinct.

"Randall," he whispered looking around the lobby. "We've got a problem. Cole is in custody. We need to distance ourselves from him. He obviously didn't stay out of sight like he was supposed to. I don't want anyone knowing I recommended him to work for Teresa. He supposedly killed the cab driver that Teresa hired to take him out of the area."

"That idiot killed Donald?"

"You know him?"

"He's the guy I hired to help me to pick up Teresa in the ambulance. He's just an old acquaintance. He had nothing else going on that night, so I met him in a club. He's an okay guy. Or was. I told him the ambulance gig was just for that one night. He was fine with it. I paid him cash. Teresa hired him again to take Cole out of town."

"I have no idea what happened, but I assume Cole is the one who murdered him before going to Jade. We need a new plan. I just don't want any loose ends. My career and my life are at stake here. What a fucking mess."

"You're right. Let me know when you sort it out. Cole is a loose cannon for sure."

Ken nodded and headed back to work.

CHAPTER 65

Teresa was second-guessing her choices while soaking in her rather extravagant tub. Wondering if she should have made Ken her primary focus all along.

"He would make a terrific Sergeant and a great politician one day," she muttered out loud. "I should show him how to climb that ladder. At least he knows who to dedicate his loyalty to. He treats me like a princess when I see him. That's exactly what I wanted from Martin. How could that prick do this to me? He made me into a sad, terrified woman."

Her thoughts suddenly drifted to Kei Lien. I can't imagine how terrified that young girl must have been. All those years being abused by Chandler and others, including my unfaithful louse of a husband. Then to top it off, that piece of shit made her say I'm sorry. It was awful when Cole revealed that to her.

"I should have killed him. I should have done it long ago."

Now totally high on her prescription meds and a half bottle of White Label, Teresa managed to crawl out of the tub, her feet sliding on the tile floors. Her attempt at standing straight up was a losing battle. She slumped down and sat on the bathmat for a moment until she could regain her balance. Nothing but a bath towel to partially cover her wet, naked body.

"What have I done? What have I done?" She placed her hands over her face and sobbed. When she had enough of feeling sorry for herself, she laid her head down next to the tub. Sleep soon followed, along with the nightmares spurred by alcohol, drugs, and a guilty conscious.

CHAPTER 66

She owned him right from their first meeting.

While in a grocery store buying a few items and finding he didn't have quite enough cash, he asked the store owner if he could do some work around the store to pay the rest of his bill. Having overheard the conversation, she signaled the owner of the small store that she would pay for his groceries.

"Hello," putting on her most professional sounding voice that most found more obnoxious than professional. "I overheard you say you were looking for work. Can you do landscaping? You know, mowing lawns, trimming shrubs, that kind of work?"

"I can."

He felt like asking her who the hell she thought she was for making him sound like a poor homeless person. Even though that's exactly what he was at the time.

"Do you have a place to stay?"

"Not yet," making a mental note of the diamonds on her fingers.

"Well I do believe I can help with that, too."

She was the first person he met when he arrived in Cromwell.

"What is your name?" she asked, giving him her hand.

"Ken Sorenson. And you are?"

"Teresa Kelsey."

It didn't take long for him to find out that she wanted a pool boy all along, just without the pool.

She rented him a room at the Stratford when he needed housing, at a discount of course. Gave him a job. And encouraged her husband to get him into the police academy and eventually on the force. He eventually found an apartment of his own, but was still at her beckon call. After all, she was the reason he had this career. He felt like a marionette, built by the sergeant, but his wife operated the strings.

New to the job and trying to make a good name for himself in Cromwell, Ken took any overtime he could get. Night shifts, patrolling the city, anything that would make him look good to the department. One night, he came across a drunk hanging around the park near the playground equipment muttering to himself, but not making any sense at all. He looked homeless, but seemed harmless. Just lost. He could have hauled him in for loitering around the children's playground or for being intoxicated in the park. Instead he felt bad for the guy and just told him to move along. He warned him about this not being a good place to hang out and asked if he was hungry. He nodded his head yes. Ken went to his car and pulled out a small, insulated lunch bag and handed him the contents. He questioned whether he had a job. He didn't. He took his name and told him if he heard of anyone looking for help, he would let him know.

He saw Cole a few more times in the area, making a mental

note of where he was sleeping each time. He was never any trouble. He felt sorry for him and told him he wouldn't say anything about where he was sleeping at night as a favor. That favor was collected when he hired Tim to be Teresa's private investigator. Her husband was fooling around on her, and although she was doing the same, she wanted to get even. Ken knew there wasn't much he could do about Tim's appearance, but he did buy him a few new clothes and arranged a shower and shave a local motel room. He paid for his lunch and sent him off to Teresa. He never questioned Tim about anything. He just knew he had to deliver when Teresa made the request. He feared Teresa and for good reason.

The thing Ken could never have imagined though was that Tim Cole would eventually be wanted for murder. The fear started washing over him. His mind raced as he recalled every detail that led to this daytime nightmare. Had Teresa actually hired Tim Cole to kill her husband? He was the one that had set it all in motion by getting Cole the job. He could be implicated. He had to find Tim Cole before anyone else did.

CHAPTER 67

Timothy Cole sat in a cell at the Jade police Department, waiting for his lawyer to arrive. Every few minutes he got up and paced the small area in deep thought about how he was going to get out of this mess and out of this jail cell. He wondered what it would be like to stay in a cell for a long time. Would it be like the Saturn facility?

"I doubt it," he thought to himself. "I don't think they can hook you to wires in a jail. I'm strong. I can handle anyone that comes near me. It might be nice to have a place to sleep every night and food every day that I wouldn't have to steal. Of course, I wouldn't be able to wander like I did at the Saturn. I'm quite sure of that."

Public defender Raymond L. Schmidt, a young man possibly early thirties, arrived at the jail with his brand-new brief case in hand. Detective Lake saw him coming in the door.

"I'll bet you fifty bucks, a gift from his old man for graduating law school and passing the bar exam. Either that or mommy made him a big lunch. Either way, I'd say there's a few dollars in that family."

Reese elbowed him in the side. "Shut up."

"Good afternoon, my name is Raymond Schmidt, I'm the attorney representing Timothy Cole. I'd like to speak with my client."

"I'll bet you would," Lake mumbled under his breath. "Until you meet him."

"What's that? I'm sorry I couldn't hear you."

"Nothing important. Right this way. Anything you need, just ask."

"Well, right now I'd like my client removed from that cell and placed in a room where we can speak in private."

There's nothing private at a police precinct, Reese thought.

She led him to Tim Cole's cell where he introduced himself. The two were brought into an interrogation room. Tim in handcuffs and leg restraints. An officer was placed outside the door.

"As your court appointed attorney, I have to ask you a few questions. Were you read your Miranda Rights, when you were arrested?"

"Yes." No sense lying about that, he thought.

"Sir, do you understand the charges being brought against you?"

"Not really. They say I killed a guy in the hospital. I don't remember that. I was in there because they brought me in, saying I had some sort of an attack. I just decided I didn't want to be tested again so I got off the exam table and left the hospital. Nobody told me not to leave."

"What do you mean, tested again? When were you tested and where? Most important for what were you tested?"

"A long time ago. Right here in Jade. A place called Saturn

Center or something like that."

"Mr. Cole, do you have family or anyone that I may contact for you?"

"No."

"You have no family?"

"I said no. They're all gone." Tim was beginning to feel the heat rise to his face again.

"I'm just trying to get to know more about you," the lawyer said.

"My rights said I had a right to remain silent. Isn't that true?"

"Yes, it is, but I'm your lawyer and if I'm going to represent you in court, I need to know the answers to these questions. Do you understand what I am saying?"

"Yes. I have a right to remain silent and I am."

With that Tim made the motion of zipping his lip, like a child being told not to tell a secret.

Raymond L Schmidt walked out of the interrogation room shaking his head. Tim was taken back to his cell.

"How'd that go, Mr. Schmidt?" Clayton asked.

"I would like to speak to the District Attorney."

"I'll arrange the meeting to be held here at the precinct. Is that all?"

"No! I mean now." He was getting a little hot headed with her.

"Look, Counselor, we'll call right now," Lake interjected. "But no promises that she is available on such short notice. Got it? And in the future, be a bit more respectful of my partner or you and I are going to have a problem."

"Is that a threat? Because it sure sounded like one."

"Not a threat. A promise. Now here is the number for the D.A. If she doesn't answer our call now, then you can try to contact her yourself later. Are we on the same page, Schmidt?"

"Yes. And I apologize for being rude." He put out his hand for Emerson to shake and then did the same with Reese. He told them he needed coffee and would be right back.

"I almost feel sorry for that kid," Lake said. "He has no idea what he's doing and this could be a very complex case - even for the big guns. He might as well hit that pretty briefcase with a hammer now because by the time he is done with Tim Cole's case, it will be banged up from hitting the table out of total frustration anyway."

Reese nodded in agreement as she dialed the D.A.

"District Attorney Dawson's office, how may I help you?"

"Yes, this is Detective Reese Clayton, Cromwell Police Department. Is Ms. Dawson available?" It felt strange to pick up a regular, old-fashioned telephone. The whole planet it seemed uses cell phones.

"One moment, please."

"This is Eve Dawson. Aren't you a bit out of your jurisdiction?"

"Yes, my partner, Detective Emerson Lake, and I are following a lead in a murder investigation. The suspect is in the Jade lock-up as we speak. His name is Timothy Cole. His attorney, Raymond Schmidt, asked us to see if you are available to come to the precinct to meet with him and his client. Is this possible sometime today?"

"Forward me his contact information. I will speak with him myself. Will you be at the precinct?"

"Yes, we will be here for the rest of the day."

"Who is the victim? I am assuming it has to do with what's going on in Cromwell. Is that correct?"

"So far, one victim from here and a possible connection to the murders of his entire family and two others in Cromwell."

"Seems like a lot going on, Detective. I'll contact Mr. Schmidt and the judge as well."

"Thank you, Ms. Dawson. Talk soon."

Reese hung up the phone. "Well, it appears Ms. Dawson will be here this evening. Let's get something to eat before the madness."

"I have a better idea."

"No, you don't. I'm quite sure about that."

CHAPTER 68

D.A. Eve Dawson met with the accused and his attorney and the detectives at the Jade precinct at 6pm.

"Now, Mr. Cole, you have been accused of murder of an X-ray technician. One Jeremy Boyle," she said looking at her paperwork.

"My client has no recollection of this incident, Ms. Dawson. Nor does he have any recollection of why he was brought into the hospital in the first place. Yes, he admits to walking out of the Jade hospital, because he didn't understand why he was there. He claims he felt fine. So, he left."

"Is that true, Mr. Cole?"

No answer.

"Detectives, why was my client detained at the Jade precinct? Was he under arrest for something else? Detective Lake, you first."

"He was not under arrest at the time. He was brought in for questioning on a tip we had from a third party about a murdered taxi driver found between here and Cromwell. His throat was slit. Cab was found turned over on the edge of the road leading into Jade. While we were questioning Tim, he had some sort of medical problem. He turned blue, fell over and wasn't breathing. We started CPR on him until the paramedics arrived. As you have already read in the report. There have been eight murders in Cromwell and we recently determined Tim Cole is a suspect. Dental records show that the six bodies discovered in our local theater are the parents and siblings of Timothy Cole."

"And yet there is no real proof that my client murdered anyone. Is that correct?"

Emerson was furious. "He is also a suspect in the murder of the technician. He was the last person to see him in X-ray according to the transport girl. Mr. Cole is also suspected of firing a weapon at my partner and I at our motel the other night."

"Detective, did you actually see my client take shots at you? And furthermore, did you get a sworn statement from this transport person?"

"To answer your first question, no. Just the outline of a very large man that jumped over the railing. Second question, yes. We did get a statement saying she recognized this man as the person she brought to X-ray."

Detective Lake's phone rang. "Excuse me. I need to take this."

Lake turned his back on the group and accepted the call.

"Emerson Lake here. Yes. What did you find out? Okay, thank you very much."

Lake turned toward Cole. "That was the lab. Timothy Cole, you are under arrest for the murder of the taxi driver found along the road near the Jade County line. Your fingerprints were all over the knife and the cab as well. You have the right..."

Tim began to laugh. An uncontrollable laugh. He knew this was the only way. The way to get transferred into a mental hospital. He had done it many times before. He rocked back and forth in his seat and began to sing "Rock a bye baby, in the tree top. Where's my mommy? I love my mommy."

Raymond Schmidt was in total disbelief at his client's behavior.

"I believe this meeting is over for now," he boomed. "I will be asking for the judge to have my client Timothy Cole evaluated by a mental health professional."

Eve totally agreed. "A mental work-up will need to be done before we can move forward. Mr. Schmidt, see to it that you make those arrangements with the judge's full knowledge as quickly as possible. And remember, I am entitled to receive a copy of the diagnosis when the tests are complete. Understood?"

"Ms. Dawson, you will treat me with the same respect that you would apply to any other attorney. Is that understood, Ms. Dawson?"

"Shit, where did those balls come from?" Reese thought.

Emerson was about to step in to put the fire out, but, she had already extended her hand out to make amends. "I apologize. Are we good?"

Schmidt nodded and left, motioning to the officers to escort his client back to jail.

"Son-of-a-bitch," growled Lake. "This is the same way he acted at the hospital and the same trick at the station. He played us."

"Of course, he did," Reese shouted. "But there is more to this story. More to this killing spree. A whole lot more and I for one am determined to find out the truth. Pull yourself up by the bootstraps partner. We need to find out who else is involved in this. It must be more than just Timothy Cole. He may be smart, but not that smart."

CHAPTER 69

Mary Elizabeth Hollingsworth called Minh Nyung with a heavy heart. It wasn't a call she wanted to make, but knew she must. She thought it would be nice to be friends with him one day. He was such a kind man. Maybe even a little bit more than friends. She had been alone for a very long time. Maybe it was time for a new direction. Her thoughts were interrupted when Minh picked up the phone. He answered with a pleasant-sounding voice. Soft, yet manly. One of his many nice traits. Something she really liked about him.

"This is Mary Elizabeth. I think you should come down to the hospital to have a conversation with the doctors about Kei Lien and what's next. You should bring Daniel as well."

"Something is wrong. Am I correct?"

"Please. It would be wrong for me to try and answer that. I'm not her doctor, but I do care about what's happening to her. Can I expect you soon?"

"Of course. I will try to reach Daniel so we may come together."

When Daniel received the call from his father he was on his daily walk in the woods. His first thought was to run deeper into the woods. To hide. To forget all of this. But he ran deeper into his soul instead and ran most of the way home. He prayed that the worst would not happen to this girl he now considered his friend. Although, he thought, what could be worse than what had already happened in her life? As he approached his house a strange calm ran over his body.

"Dad, am I wrong to wish for her peace and the possibility of once again being re-united with her Mom? Is it wrong for me to even say these things? I feel that is the only answer for this woman...well...child. What possible good could come from her being subjected to months, maybe even years, of questions? She will never recover her childhood. She will never be able to do all the things that children do nor the things that adults do either. Could she ever allow a first kiss without running away? Would therapy even be an option? Physical or mental? Dad, I know it's not up to me to say when. I'm just trying to be as level-headed as I can when it comes to her care, now and later. Yes, there is an emotional bond between us. Mostly me because of what I allowed to happen to her that day under her window."

"Daniel, please stop now. This is a difficult time for all of us. Guilt is never pretty, no matter the situation. The time will come far too soon to bear the feelings of regret when it comes to this young lady. Now it is time to leave. Go. Get cleaned up. Maybe grab a healthy snack. Something with a lot of protein to help your state of mind. I do not need two of you in hospital beds or on the proverbial couch, so to speak."

As much as Minh loved his stepson and felt everything that his son was feeling, he had to stay focused on the task at hand. Getting the best care for Kei Lien. Minh paced up and down the driveway waiting for what seemed like forever for Daniel to come out of the house. He was deep in his own thoughts about starting a new life for himself. Although he was anxious to get to the hospital, he was secretly excited to see Mary Elizabeth again. It would be nice to have someone, a companion, in his life again. He had been alone far too long and missed the connection of a woman lying beside him. I'm too young, he thought, to let my life pass me by. One day Daniel will be gone, and I will be alone if I don't think of myself. The calm, soft-spoken man, who always tried to be the level-headed one, suddenly was overwhelmed knowing Kei Lien's life was in his hands. It was his decision. A decision that should be in God's hands. A decision that would be a little bit more comforting if he had a shoulder to cry on. A female shoulder.

Daniel appeared on the scene. Peanut butter sandwich in one hand and one wrapped for his father in the other. Minh smiled at the thoughtfulness of his son.

CHAPTER 70

Tim Cole was sitting in a warm room full of framed photographs of someone's distant memories. Memories of happy times, maybe vacation times, he thought.

"This will be fun," he snickered.

A rather large recliner sat on one side of the room with a sofa nearby and a mahogany desk with all the essentials on top to complete the picture-perfect décor. A fine place to tell your life story to a total stranger. Tim was in full manipulation mode as he waited for the questioning to begin. He knew he had to play this right for him to be committed to a facility. A facility he knew he could control. He had done it before.

"Tim… may I call you Tim? We are here to determine your mental status in connection to the charges against you. Do you understand?"

Tim shrugged his shoulders. "I guess you can call me Tim."

"My name is Doctor Carl Brickman. Do you understand why you are here?" the doctor repeated.

Tim gently nodded his head staring directly into his eyes and deep into his soul. He was already unnerving the psychiatrist even though there were armed guards outside the door to his office.

"Let's begin. You live in Cromwell, South Dakota. Is that correct, Tim? Could you tell me a little bit about your family? How many siblings do you have? What are your parents like?"

Tim sat quiet, continuing his piercing stare.

"Mr. Cole, please answer the questions the best that you can? I'm just trying to get to know a little bit about you."

"I like the sound of Mr. Cole," Tim grunted. "Yeah, that's a better way to ask me something. My family, well, I have two sisters, two brothers, mom, and dad. They're gone now, though."

"Where have they gone, Mr. Cole?"

"I lived in a place for a long time. I was sixteen years old. Every now and again my father would take me home, but he'd eventually bring me back to that place. That place is bad. You get wires hooked to your head and then your head buzzes and burns and really hurts. Do you know the kind of place I mean?"

"Do you remember the name of the place where you stayed? Was it near here?"

"Saturn. Not here anymore. I took care of that. I took a match to it a long time ago."

Dr. Brickman was surprised at how quickly Tim admitted to the arson. "Why did you do that, Mr. Cole?"

"Wouldn't you?"

"Can you tell me what happened?"

"My dad took me out of there so I could go on a trip with him and mom. I love my mom. We went to the cabin in the woods with my sisters and brothers. After that, I went back to Saturn because I had no place to go. So, I hitched a ride. I just walked in. Nobody asked me how I got in, but then they wanted to put those wires on me again. So, I burned the place down and ran away to Cromwell again. Not in the woods though. Just anywhere I could find."

"Why didn't you have anywhere to go? Where were your parents? Mr. Cole?"

Tim seemed to be impressed with himself just hearing those words…Mr. Cole.

"Can you tell me why your father didn't go with you back to Saturn?"

"He just couldn't."

"Is there anything you'd like to share with me? I'm here to listen. That's what I do. I listen to the stories people want to talk about. Sometimes those stories are about their families. Do you want to tell me about your home life? What was it like growing up with two sisters and two brothers?"

Tim's face began to turn a fiery red, his breathing labored, his chest rising and falling at a quick pace. He abruptly stood up and stomped around the room. His shackled ankles tangled caused him to trip, knocking over a Tiffany lamp next to the sofa. Immediately, the office door sprang open. The two officers in the doorway with guns drawn.

"Everything okay, Dr. Brickman?"

"Yes, everything is okay. Mr. Cole just bumped into my lamp and it fell to the floor. Thank you though for your concern."

"We're just on the other side of this door if you need us."

With that the officer holstered his gun and closed the door behind him.

"Now let's continue. Mr. Cole? You were about to tell me about your home life. Do you need a drink of water before we begin?"

Tim's face returned to its normal coloring; he was now breathing easier. He sat down in the recliner this time and put his feet up. He liked the feel of this leather monster of a chair. He knew exactly the right thing to say to this shrink because the truth will set you free. The corners of his mouth turning up slightly into a distorted smile. "When I was sixteen, I was taken out of Saturn by my father as a trial-run at freedom."

"Freedom from what, Mr. Cole?"

"Freedom from that shithole where they injected my arms with stuff that would give me bad dreams. Freedom from that machine they put on my head. You know, the one that had wires. I didn't like that machine. I didn't like my brothers and sisters, either. They got all the attention from mom. I told mom I would be good if they let me go on vacation with them. It was a place in the woods, a camp I guess."

Doctor Brickman listened very carefully to how Tim told his story. The way he spoke, his movements, his eyes, as well.

"Dad insisted we have fun scouring the woods and learning how to survive with very little. I always liked the squirrels the best. It didn't take much to kill them."

Tim saw the doctor take a deep breath and heard the creak of the leather as he shifted slightly in his desk chair. He continued.

"Then I would wrap them up and put them under a pine tree for my brothers and sisters to find. Dad got so mad at me. He yelled at me for being so mean. He said he was going to punish me so I would learn a lesson."

Tim pulled his knees into his chest and started rocking. Eyes focused on the floor. His voice sputtering like a scared child.

"He took me out…out back, stripped me naked and…and…

rubbed dirt from around the outhouse all over my body. And then shoved the dead…dead…squirrel so close to my face. I could feel the fur…fur on my cheek. I threw up and then he told me to say I'm sorry to my brothers and sisters."

The doctor feared he had a Dissociative Identity Disorder case on his hands, but he let Tim continue. It was too soon to tell.

"I told my mom what Dad did to me. She was mad at my Dad, but even more at me. She slapped me across the face, sent me out to the pump to wash off and then to bed."

Tim scrunched up his face and took a long pause, as though the memory was too hard to handle. His face eventually relaxed, and he continued.

"Later that night I crept down to the kitchen. I was hungry. I didn't get supper. I wasn't sure I could keep it down. When I got close to the doorway, I heard my parents talking about sending me away. Somewhere I wouldn't hurt anyone or anything again. Mom was crying. I know she loved me. I just know it. I killed all of them that night with a butcher knife and then buried them in the yard. Even my mom. I love her."

Doctor Brickman stiffened, trying to keep a poker face despite the bile creeping into his throat. He had his report for the attorneys and the judge.

"What about the cab driver, Mr. Cole? And the X-ray technician?"

"That was different."

"How so, Mr. Cole?"

"They were trying to hurt me. Well, maybe not the kid, but the other guy."

"Can you tell me a little about your life in Cromwell?"

"What do you want to know?"

"Did you have a job there and what kind of job?"

"I watched people."

Dr. Brickman thought for a moment and decided to jump right to it.

"Mr. Cole, did you kill Adam Chandler and Sergeant Martin Kelsey?"

"No, at least I don't think so. I didn't kill Kelsey. I wanted to for what he was doing to that girl for so long, but Chandler…"

He paused for a moment.

"Mr. Cole, are you alright?"

"I don't think I killed him. I just pushed the knife in a little bit more."

Tim gave the good doctor a slanted grin, bearing all his rotting teeth, knowing he did what he set out to do.

Doctor Brickman went to the door and motioned for the officers to take Tim back to jail. He was thankful for the cuffs and leg restraints. For the first time in his life as a psychiatrist he was afraid of a patient.

CHAPTER 71

Detectives Lake and Clayton asked Dr. Brickman to join them for lunch at a diner nearby while waiting for the judge to arrive in court. Reese was theorizing how she thought this would play out in the courtroom.

"Timothy Cole will be put away for the rest of his life," she proclaimed swallowing a half-chewed bite of her sandwich. "Schmidt will certainly recommend he be placed in an institution. I'm sure he will try to make a plea deal on the grounds that Mr. Cole doesn't have the mental capacity to understand the difference between right and wrong."

"A life gone horribly wrong," Dr. Brickman remarked, a hint of compassion in his voice. "Whatever the reason, this guy will certainly be a hot topic at medical seminars and among law enforcement for years to come."

"One thing is for sure, we won't get any answers about how he got to be this way now," Reese interjected. "His entire family was murdered."

"After speaking with us, the D.A just might want to go for life in prison or the death penalty." Lake stated.

"Well, regardless, Emerson, Cole will be put away for the rest of his life. That much is certain. The only question is where?"

Dr. Brickman's phone beeped with a message to head to the courthouse. The judge wanted a preliminary meeting to discuss the request to have Cole questioned again. Reese went to the counter to pay as Lake pulled cash out of his wallet to leave for a tip.

Jade County Court House was equipped with the usual security check-in area with very high ceilings so that sound echoed through the vast area of stone columns and marble tile floors. Inside the court room, wood visitor benches lined the room in rows much like pews in a church. In the front of the room, the judge's bench. To the left, the jury box. And facing the bench were the tables for attorneys and their clients. The use of very high windows and perfectly placed lighting allowed for the appearance of natural light to fill the room without allowing sunlight to interfere with anyone's view. The room was neat and clean, much nicer looking than one would expect for a small-town court room.

Once all parties arrived at the courthouse, Judge John Orrick turned to the detectives.

"Detective Clayton, it's my understanding that you and your partner would like to question Mr. Cole again. Mr. Cole is already facing Class A felony charges for his actions. Why the unusual request?"

Standing up from his seat at the table, his hand still on top of his shiny new brief case, Raymond Schmidt spoke.

"Your Honor, that is exactly why I can see no reason for my client to be questioned again."

"Noted Mr. Schmidt, but the question was directed to the detectives. I am the judge, remember?"

"Yes, Your Honor."

"Detective Clayton?"

"Yes, Your Honor," Clayton replied as she stood. "Mr. Cole is a suspect in the murders of two Cromwell residents. Adam Chandler and our very own sergeant, Martin Kelsey. We have reason to believe Mr. Cole has pertinent information on who else may be involved in those cases. When we questioned Mr. Cole the first time, he told us the Boss was the one that told the cab driver to bring him here to Jade. We're hoping to find out who the Boss is, your Honor."

"Your Honor," Lake interjected, "we would also like to request that Mr. Cole be brought back to Cromwell for his sentencing procedure and allow us the time to file charges on his involvement in those two murders. We are hoping that in this process we can find all the guilty parties in this bizarre case. A case that has taken many lives and all but destroyed the life of a child."

Eve Dawson, now on her feet.

"Your Honor, I agree with the detectives. Mr. Cole should be transferred to Cromwell for his sentencing trial. On the grounds he has already admitted to killing his family and they were in Cromwell at the time of their deaths. His admission to murdering the cab driver is somehow connected to this person he calls the Boss."

"We would also like to request that Mr. Cole be placed on 24-hour surveillance, Your Honor," Lake added. "Until his questioning. That is, if you agree to it. He is quite the escape artist, Your Honor."

Judge Orrick shuffled through the paperwork in front of him.

"I will agree to the questioning of Mr. Cole with strict guidelines. The interview will be video recorded, both attorneys will be present, along with myself and Dr. Brickman. As far as surveillance, detectives, are you implying that our system cannot safely secure the accused in this matter?"

"No, I'm not Your Honor," replied Clayton. "I am just concerned for everyone's safety."

"Detectives, your request for surveillance and transfer is duly noted."

"Thank you, Your Honor."

The judge rose to his feet. "Date is set for Wednesday 11am."

He banged the gavel and swiftly exited through a door behind him.

CHAPTER 72

"Officer Sorenson, how may I help you?" Sorenson said into the phone.

"Sorenson, it's Lake. Is the Captain available?"

"No, she's not here right now."

"Ok, listen. Detective Clayton and I will be in Jade for a few more days. We have Timothy Cole in custody. The judge is going to decide on Wednesday whether or not to allow him to return to Cromwell in connection to the murders of Kelsey and Chandler. We're hoping for a miracle. And hoping to be back in Cromwell by Thursday afternoon."

"You got him? Wow, that's great news. Is there anything I can do here until you get back?"

"Contact the Captain. Give her the update and tell her we will call her when the judge makes his decision."

"Will do."

Ken Sorenson slowly hung up the phone. He feared for his life, his career. He could go to jail for his part in all of this. Most of all, he feared Tim Cole. What would that lunatic tell the judge?

CHAPTER 73

Once in the car, Minh and his son ate their peanut butter sand-wiches in peace. Soft, comforting music played on the radio. Minh knew the right time for quiet. He feared his son would soon come to a breaking point in all of this. The soft tones fill-ing the car on the ride to the hospital were a temporary solution to a maddening chain of events. Minh found a parking spot and the two of them walked slowly into the hospital. Not one word between them.

"Can I get you coffee or tea? Anything?"

"No, but thank you, Dr. Hart." Minh replied. "We really just want to talk to you about Kei Lien."

"We've been administering heavy doses of antibiotics since she arrived, but we're just not seeing any signs of improvement. Whether or not she is capable of surviving is now left up to her and her will to live. We can continue treating her infections for a time, but we cannot heal the damage done to her mind here. She doesn't trust anyone except for the two of you and her nurse. She needs additional help to work through the trauma she has endured. We are suggesting she be placed in a behavioral health facility. We have some of the finest institutions around. I can give you a list of the ones we recommend. Other than that, there is nothing more we can do for her. We need the space for those we can help. I'm so very sorry. She can stay with us for a few more days while you make other arrangements."

"Dad, no! Please not a mental facility. Don't do it!"

"Daniel, collect yourself, NOW!"

Minh politely inquired "Doctor, will she still get the treatments for the infection if she is transferred?"

"Once she leaves our hospital, we can prescribe antibiotics on an outpatient basis. However, it will no longer be at the expense of the hospital."

Dr. Hart began to tear up and came around the front of the table sitting on the edge.

"I'm so sorry, but I have to answer to corporate. And the way they see it is we need the space. Her medications will have to be paid for by outside means. It sounds cold, I know, but hospitals have a bottom line to adhere to. Or there would be no hospitals. She has no insurance. Well, none that we are aware of anyway. And inpatient care costs a lot of money. Not to mention the cost of the drugs. So far, her care has been pro bono because of the bizarre circumstances. Our nurse will also need to return to her regular duties around the hospital. I don't know how else to make this any easier for all of you."

"How long could Kei Lien survive without these antibiotics?"

"I can't say, Mr. Nyung. She has lived with all of this for a very long time. I don't think it is up to us to determine her life expectancy. Based on my own personal religious beliefs, which I know I'm not supposed to share, this young lady's fate is to be determined by a higher power and I'm not referring to my Board of Directors."

"Thank you, Doctor Hart. My son and I will be in touch."

Daniel wanted to see Kei Lien immediately, so he headed in the direction of her room only to be stopped by Mary Elizabeth Hollingsworth.

"Please wait, Daniel. I'd like to speak to you and your father. I'm guessing you have met with Dr. Hart. Now I have an idea."

She led them into an old empty waiting room.

"This decision," she whispered, "will be yours, of course. But if you say yes to my proposal, it will mean so very much to me. I am coming to the end of my career here at this hospital. I've been told that if I don't return to my normal duties the hospital will terminate me, but I truly believe Kei Lien needs me. I would be willing to retire and take on the task of caring for her at no charge to you. Only thing I require is a place to sleep and food. My home is paid off and between social security and my pension I can manage my bills. Unless, of course, you would agree to allow Kei Lien to stay with me instead. It might be more comfortable for both of you and for her. I know how to obtain a hospital bed and needed supplies for her care. Almost like a hospice homecare situation. Now that I think about it, that might be the better idea. As a hospice nurse, I could obtain the right medications to keep her comfortable without risking her rights or yours. Or my pension for that matter. What do you think?"

Minh was baffled at how far this woman would go to help someone she barely knew. An angel, to say the least.

"You don't have to make a decision right this minute. My

lunch break is coming up at 1:30. Let's talk more about my proposal then. I'll meet you in the cafeteria and you can buy me lunch," she smiled, "Okay?"

Minh and Daniel both nodded.

"Great! Now let's get you to Kei Lien."

Mary Elizabeth guided Daniel by the arm down the hall to her room entrance.

"She'll be glad you came to see her. Even if she is unaware of her visitors."

CHAPTER 74

Sara Hunter and Bill Oosterhout finished with all the evidence, taking particular care with each body that came to them, keeping everything documented.

"Now I need some down time. I'll bring the report up to Officer Manning after I get something to eat."

Sara left the morgue and headed to the cafeteria for some much-needed breakfast, even though it was two in the afternoon. A ham and egg sandwich with a sweet cinnamon bun on the side and a large cup of coffee sounded terrific. Comfort food. It was time for Sara to relax and feel more in control now that her autopsy reports were finished. She sat quietly eating until Ken Sorenson appeared at her table.

"May I?" he asked, pointing to the chair across the table from her.

"Sure." Although she really wanted to tell him to get lost, but she didn't have the heart to tell him to leave again. Ken was really being sweet, but she needed her down time.

"How's the autopsy going?"

"It's finished, finally. I just have to drop it off to Officer

Manning. Detective Lake and Detective Clayton are still in Jade." Her cell phone rang. "Oh, excuse me. I need to take this call."

She stood up and walked away from the table. It was her doctor telling her that all her tests were normal. She had nothing seriously wrong with her other than needing a good night's sleep and a vacation wouldn't hurt. She returned to the table to find Ken had already left.

She finished her meal thinking to herself that maybe now that her medical worries were put at ease maybe it wouldn't hurt to allow friends back into her life. Ken seemed like an okay guy. I should give him a little more wiggle room. I can't believe he gave it another try to sit with me. Sara had to laugh at that one. She picked up her tray, wiped down the table and picked up her sweater and bag, but there was no envelope under her purse. The envelope that contained the results of the autopsies she and Bill had worked so hard to complete was gone. She panicked and started frantically looking under the table and chairs. She even checked the trash. Phew! There it was covered in coffee. How did it get in the trash? I know I put it right under my purse when I sat down. She fished the large yellow envelope out of the trash can, hoping to salvage it. The envelope seemed wet, but not soaked. She wiped off what she could and decided to go back to her office to repair any damage to it.

The damage was far worse than she thought. Some of the pages were missing. "Ken, that son-of-a-bitch, he took it! How could I be so stupid to leave it when I took the phone call?"

She immediately phoned her colleague Bill explaining what happened and asked him to grab the videotape and his copy of the report and meet her in her office ASAP.

"I have it!" he said bursting in and helping himself to a chair and a bottle of water. "What the hell is going on?"

"I have no idea. It had to be that new cop, Ken Sorenson. I left him at my table. He asked if he could sit down with me. My cell rang and I had to take the call. So, not even thinking, I just got up and went out to the lobby area for privacy. He was gone when I got back to the table. I asked everyone left in the cafeteria if they saw Ken leave and if he was carrying anything when he left. Someone told me they saw him leave with a cup of coffee. He could have just folded the papers and slipped them into his pocket. You know what? I'm going to call him."

She dialed Ken's cell. He picked it up.

"Hey, I didn't think you were coming back anytime soon, so I left," he said. "I ran into Teresa Kelsey on the way out and chatted for a minute. She's looking for Allen. Said he wanted to speak with her. I just said I hadn't seen him. What do you think that's about?"

Ignoring his question, she took a deep breath. "Did you happen to see a yellow business envelope under my sweater on the chair?"

"No, I didn't. Honestly, I don't really remember seeing your sweater, either. Observant right?"

An uncomfortable silence settled over the call.

"Wait, Sara, do you think I took your envelope?"

"To be honest, it crossed my mind."

"Why? What the hell was in it that I would steal?"

"Let's talk about it later. I have to go."

"Sara, really?"

Click.

CHAPTER 75

"Is she taking visitors today?" Allen Manning asked Randall, trying one more time to speak with Teresa Kelsey.

"I don't believe she is in. Do you want me to give her a message for you?"

Allen had enough of her trying to avoid him.

"Please tell Mrs. Kelsey that Officer Manning is here to speak with her on official business pertaining to her husband's death. If she doesn't comply with my request then perhaps I should make this an awkward official visit. Do you understand what I am saying? Now ring her and tell her I am here."

Randall lifted the handset and pushed the button to Teresa's suite. "Uh, Mrs. Kelsey? Officer Allen Manning is here to see you. He said it's official business."

"I see. Tell him I will be down in a few minutes. I need to get dressed."

Allen took a seat in the lobby to wait for her appearance. What a pain in the ass, he thought. She really thinks she is something special and doesn't have to abide by any law except her own. He was furious that he had to give her an ultimatum.

After twenty minutes, still no Teresa. Allen was fuming. He stormed up to the desk.

"Dial her suite, I will speak with her myself this time. This is bullshit."

Randall let the phone ring several times then dialed her again. Still no answer.

"Randall, I want to see her immediately. Show me to her suite."

"I can't just let you into her apartment. Not without good reason."

"The reason is called obstruction. Now do I get a warrant for her arrest? Maybe I should get one for you as well. Am I making myself clear?"

Randall escorted Allen to the suite. No answer. Another knock, same results.

"Open the door."

"I can't do that."

"Then I will break it down. She might be in trouble. Maybe she fell. That's probable cause. Open the damn door!"

Teresa Kelsey was nowhere to be found. She obviously left through the back entrance.

"You knew she left, didn't you?"

Randall kept quiet.

"I will deal with you later. You can bet on it!"

Allen contacted Detective Clayton and let her know that Teresa gave him the slip.

"I think she knows something about her husband's murder. I'm going to Judge Canton for a warrant."

"Good. I think she knows more about it, too. Hopefully we'll be back by Thursday. Until then, anything you find, call one of us."

CHAPTER 76

The cameras were set up in different areas of the court room to record the continued questioning from all different angles. Court officials, including Judge Orrick, Dr. Brickman, both detectives, both attorneys and the accused Timothy Cole, were all present.

Reese began, "Mr. Cole, did you murder your entire family? Two sisters, two brothers, your mom and your dad?"

"Yes, I did."

"Why?"

Tim was sitting in a chair across the table from Reese. He was handcuffed with his legs shackled. He began playing with each one of his fingers. First licking them and then curling them up as if he was holding a gun and pointing in the direction of Reese. He noticed a pen lying on the table. He knew if he could reach it, he could put the tip right into the detective's eyeball and push it right through to her brain. Just like he pushed the knife through the hearts of his family. Watching them gasp, blood trickling at the corner of the mouth, eyes as wide open as they could get. Feeling sexually satisfied when he finished killing them all. He then flashed Detective Clayton a huge smile, baring his rotting teeth and red, swollen gums. "I don't really like this orange color suit, do you?"

"Just answer my question, Mr. Cole."

"They were mean to me and wanted to send me back to that place. Mom loved me though."

He was trying for the same reaction he always got when he mentioned his family, insanity.

"I see. Did you also kill Donald White in his own taxi?"

"He wanted to take me somewhere I didn't want to go. I asked him to leave me in Jade. I know my way around here. He tried to stop me from getting out of the car by turning the wheel fast and hitting the brakes hard. I put my knife to his neck and sliced through it. He won't be doing that again."

Tim's eyes started to glaze over.

"Now, Mr. Cole, what about the Saturn mental facility? Did you burn that down as well?"

"Your Honor," interjected Mr. Schmidt, "my client already admitted to these crimes. Does Detective Clayton plan to continue to waste our time with this line of questioning? My client has been evaluated by a psychiatrist and we are requesting Mr. Cole be placed in a secure mental institution for the rest of his life."

"Mr. Schmidt, you are here to observe the questioning by the detectives," Judge Orrick reprimanded. "You'll have ample time to defend your client."

"But Your Honor, I feel my client's rights are being abused now."

"What might those rights be? He has admitted to these crimes, yes. But we are looking for confirmation on other charges in Cromwell. Continue, detective, and get to the point."

NOW SAY YOU'RE SORRY

"Detective Lake, would you take over the conversation, please?" asked Reese.

"Mr. Cole, you reside in Cromwell, South Dakota is that right?" Lake asked.

"Y... Ye...Yes." Tim stuttered.

"Then why were you coming back to Jade?"

"I wasn't. I told you the cab driver wanted to take me someplace else."

"And why would a cab driver want to take you somewhere you didn't want to go?"

Tim was becoming agitated. His legs were restless rattling the chains that shackled his ankles. His wrists were twisting to try to release the cuffs.

"Because, he was told to."

"Tim, who told him to do this to you? And why would a cab driver want to take you somewhere you didn't want to go?"

"I don't remember, I guess."

"Did you know it was wrong for this cab driver to take you somewhere you didn't want to go? Is that why you killed him?"

"Yes!"

Tim started banging his cuffed hands on the table, standing up and then sitting back down, knowing there was no where he could go. As soon as he stood, there were police ready to stop him.

Eve Dawson stood in front of the judge. "Your Honor, if I may. The accused has just admitted he knows right from wrong. That makes him capable to stand trial."

"I hear you, Ms. Dawson. Detective Lake, please continue."

"Thank you, Your Honor," Lake said before turning to address

Cole again. "Timothy Cole, who hired that cab driver to take you where you didn't want to go?"

"The Boss! I don't want to talk anymore. I'm tired. I need a shower."

"Mr. Cole, you just had a shower before we came here."

"I need a nap. I need to speak to my mom. I love my mom, you know."

"Your Honor, just a few more questions. Mr. Cole, do you know the name of the person you call the Boss?"

Tim put his cuffed hands to his lips and made a zipping motion.

"Your Honor," Schmidt stood up. "Clearly, my client is upset and in need of rest. How much longer will this questioning go on?"

"Not long at all, Mr. Schmidt. Mr. Cole will be remanded to jail without bail until such time as arrangements can be made for me to oversee his sentencing in Cromwell, South Dakota. Transfer granted. 24/7 surveillance granted. Guards, remove Mr. Cole from this hearing room. I will want copies of this entire video sent to my office at once. Copies should be sent to both attorneys as well."

He stood up from his chair. Everyone else stood in response. Except for Tim Cole. He sat stone-faced in his chair glaring at the judge with a look that sent shivers down his spine. He wrapped his robes around himself holding it tight as he exited the chambers.

Reese slumped down into her chair.

"Well, we didn't get much out of that did we?" she mumbled to Lake.

"We need to get a look at Cole's cell phone," Lake whispered back. "Whoever the Boss is could certainly be listed in the contacts."

After securing Cole back in the Jade lockup, Reese retrieved his phone from the evidence locker. Signed out. By the book. No mistakes. She handed it to her partner, who started scrolling through the recent call history.

"Holy crap! This phone certainly does have numbers in it. This is going to shock you."

"Why? Do we know these people?"

"More than know them. Look."

Reese leaned in over his arm and glanced down at the screen. "Oh shit!"

"We have to report this to the captain. Set things in motion back in Cromwell."

He gave Reese a half smile and made the call.

"Captain, we will be back in Cromwell soon, in the meantime we need warrants."

He then explained why and who.

Captain Brown paused for a second to grasp the gravity of the situation.

"Not a problem, detective. They will be waiting when you arrive. Watch your backs extraditing him here." After hanging up, she thought this may very well be the biggest case they ever had. And all of it happened right under their noses, starting with the rape of a young woman who was basically held hostage for most of her life. She never knew she could or should walk away and get help. One for the books.

It took two days to coordinate Cole's transport back to

Cromwell. As he was being led to the armored police van fitted with heavy mesh and metal bars, Cole saw Reese and let out a loud, "Ha! Well little lady, I see you're not driving this time. Just along for the ride, Honey? Did you bring some hot coffee for us? Did ya?"

"No, darlin. But I do have a gun. A big one." Reese sneered.

The Jade police officer shoved Cole in the back of the van and slammed the double doors. Reese sat in front with an officer while Emerson sat in the seat behind with his weapon on his hip. Prepared for whatever this sick bastard might try. Leading the procession was a police cruiser escort and in the rear were two-armed officers driving the detectives' vehicle. Tim had planned on getting rid of his escorts with one squeeze of their necks, but he did not plan on having this many people guarding him. All he could do now was wait for a different opportunity to arise.

Once back in Cromwell, they were greeted by the media and members of the community, all wanting to get a look at Tim Cole. A large WDC 23 news van with its satellite antenna extended to the fullest sat outside of the Cromwell police station. As soon as the procession pulled up, reporters swarmed the armored vehicle, their microphones at the ready for any answers they could get. Flashes from cameras popped. Everyone was talking at once. This was indeed the biggest thing to happen in Cromwell ever. And right there in the thick of the frenzy was Brenda Charles.

The officers threw open the back doors of the van revealing Cole in his bright orange jumpsuit, hands cuffed and ankles still shackled. It was the perfect scene. Flashes from cameras and the bright lights of the video cameras illuminated the street. Tim began playing his role as an abused victim.

"I didn't know what I was doing," he wailed. "I want to see my mom. I love her. I didn't mean to kill her. I know she loved me. I just know it."

Reporters were writing as fast as he was speaking. The detectives pushed him through the crowd as quickly as they could, never letting go of him for an instant. Brenda managed to get close and began to rattle off her questions to the accused, not getting anything but the same rant. Brenda then shoved the microphone into a detective's face, but immediately regretted that move.

"Emerson," she gasped pulling the microphone away.

Shocked to see her, Lake's eyes met hers for a brief second, but he instantly returned his attention back to the prisoner. There was not nearly enough police presence to break up the crowd, but they managed to get Cole into the station. The media stayed outside for hours waiting for just one comment or one more photo, with the exception of one. Brenda entered the news van and left the gaggle of reporters behind.

The captain and the other officers were gathered inside to watch as Cole was escorted back into the station. Once in his cell, Cole spotted Ken Sorenson.

"It was him!" Cole shouted. "He knows I didn't mean to hurt anybody. You...you know me. You helped me. Am I right?"

Ken spun around and glared at Tim in disbelief.

Detective Lake grabbed the cell phone in his pocket and, sure enough, near the bottom of the list was a number with just the name Ken. Lake never once thought of connecting the two.

"Detective Clayton, would you escort Officer Sorenson into the interrogation room please?" Lake asked. "Officer Sorenson, please hand over your badge and your weapon to Detective Clayton until we straighten this out."

"Are you kidding me?" Sorenson yelled. "Are you accusing me of something, Detective?"

"An admitted murderer suddenly recognizes you and claims you helped him. What do you think?"

"Just wait a minute," Ken pleaded. "I do know him and I did help him, but not with a murder. I saw him sleeping on a bench in the park near the playground. He said he was homeless. I kept an eye out for him now and then and saw where he would sleep and as long as he wasn't bothering anybody, I left him alone."

"Why wouldn't you bring him in? Can you explain that to me?" Lake was furious. His cheeks reddening with each passing moment.

"Why would I? He wasn't breaking any laws. He was just sleeping. I asked him to leave the playground and he did. He was homeless and I could relate. I was homeless once, but I made it through because of two people that saw the good I could do. Teresa and Martin Kelsey. They helped me, so I decided to pay it forward. Now, unless you think I am guilty of anything more than being a human being, then I have reports to file. Otherwise, arrest me!"

"Officer, your name and number are in this man's cell phone. Do you care to explain?"

"I gave him my number when I met him. In case he needed help. And, yes, Detective, I felt sorry for him. It appears you don't believe my side of the story."

Captain Brown stepped in, "Officer Sorenson, I suggest you stop talking and get yourself representation. Do you understand what I am telling you?"

"Yes Captain," Ken replied with a nod. He handed Reese his badge and removed his gun from its holster. But instead of handing it over, he put his finger on the trigger. Immediately, six different cops drew their weapons and aimed right at Ken.

"Nice way to ruin a person's career," he said, staring directly at Lake. "Fuck all of you."

He lifted the gun to his head and pulled the trigger.

CHAPTER 77

Sitting in his cell, Tim Cole looked solemn. A little tearful even. He began talking to himself to get the attention of Detective Clayton. He began to cry real tears yelling, "What have I done? What have I done?"

Reese told the officer guarding Cole's cell to take a coffee break. "I'll keep an eye on him until you get back. 15 minutes, got it?"

Tim was now sobbing uncontrollably. Then it was like turning the gas off on the stove. He began to laugh hysterically, staring directly at Reese. Deciding to ignore him, she just sat and waited for the officer to return.

"You guys are no better than me," Tim said through the laughter. "No better than me for sure."

"What the hell is your problem?" Reese snapped back. "Sit on your cot and shut-up!"

"You just don't want to hear the truth do you, Detective?"

"And just what might that truth be?" she asked, holding her hand on her firearm.

"You and your partner just allowed a man to kill himself for doing nothing." Tim let out a sinister laugh. "That cop was telling you the truth. He did nothing, but try to help me. First time ever anybody gave a shit about what happened to me. Everything he said was true. He even said if he heard of anybody looking to hire some help, he would let me know. That's why the phone number. If you look in his phone, mine is there."

"And did he find you a job?"

"Yeah, sort of. Some lady wanted me to follow her old man around to see if he was cheating. You know take pictures and all that."

"Can you tell me the name of this person that hired you? Or the name of the person you were following?"

"What's in it for me? Why should I help you when you are the reason the only person who treated me right killed himself?"

"I want to help you. I just don't know what to do or what's going on in that head of yours."

The officer on watch was back from his break right on time, which gave Reese the opportunity to leave Tim thinking a bit. She hoped, anyway.

"Detective, when you come back, I'd like a nice hot cup of coffee. You know how I like it. Hot and delivered by a woman. Remember?"

Reese had all she could do to keep from shooting this bastard. She just waved her hand in the air as if to say 'sure thing.' She had enough to worry about with the sudden death of Ken Sorenson.

It was going to be a nightmare for everyone that watched Ken commit suicide. There would be countless interviews, statements from every witness, evidence to be logged, samples sent to the lab and Ken's body transported to Sara Hunter for an autopsy. Not to mention the cleanup of the bloody mess left behind. They would all need counseling. Ken was a friend, a colleague, someone they all cared for. They would all feel some sense of responsibility for not giving their friend the benefit of the doubt. And no one would feel that heavy blanket of guilt more than Detective Lake.

CHAPTER 78

Adam Chandler was buried in the town cemetery in a wooden box, nothing expensive. The only people that were there were the gravesite custodians to lower him into the ground. There wasn't even a headstone. Only a small, flat slab placed on the ground marking where he was buried. There didn't appear to be any relatives to give him a sendoff. His only child, the one he abused for so many years, lay in a hospital bed fighting for her life. She was still wishing for someone to love her, like she begged for in her letters to Santa. If she could find that person, her life may change in an instant. A will was never found, nor an insurance policy, so the estate would go directly to his only known surviving relative, Kei Lien.

CHAPTER 79

Sara Hunter, now frantic at the thought of someone stealing part of her files, managed to find Allen Manning in the grocery store that morning.

"Allen, did Bill reach you about the autopsy files on Chandler and the Sergeant?"

"No. You find something new?"

"It's not what's in the report. It's the report itself. Pages of it are missing."

"Who do you think would take it?"

"That's the thing. I feel terrible. I had been with Ken Sorenson when I noticed they were gone. I called Ken and practically accused him of taking the pages. He claimed he didn't even notice the report and left the table to get back to work when I took a business call. Strange thing though, he mentioned he ran into Teresa Kelsey on his way out. Said she was looking for you, Allen. Seemed like an odd thing to share with me. Anyway, I just feel awful how I treated Ken. He was really offended. I need to apologize to him, but we also need to find out who took those pages."

"Sara, I gather you haven't been to the morgue yet today. Did Detectives Lake or Clayton get in touch with you last night or this morning?"

"No, not yet. Why?"

"Ken Sorenson committed suicide."

Sara gasped clasping her hand over her mouth and started to cry. "Oh my God," was all she could get out.

"He was being questioned by Lake and Clayton when it happened. Luckily the swarm of reporters had dispersed before it happened."

"Oh my God!" she repeated blowing her nose on the handkerchief Allen had handed to her to wipe the tears running down her cheeks. "You know, I might be ready for a whole new career. I certainly didn't help matters by blaming Ken for my missing papers. Then to have Detective Lake assume the worst of his latest recruit. He must have felt like a cornered rat. I feel awful."

"Sara, knock it off. Don't do this. You need to focus on the missing pages of your report. They are important to the case against Tim Cole. And we need to know if he had help."

Allen knew now was not the time for him to bandage her wounds.

Sara snapped out of it quickly and agreed.

"Time," she said, "time to get this guy off the streets."

CHAPTER 80

Minh Nyung signed the necessary papers, officially releasing Kei Lien from the hospital into his custody. The arrangements to send her to Mary Elizabeth Hollingsworth's home for in home hospice care were set as well. Mary Elizabeth planned to do everything in her power to help Kei Lien with whatever her destiny may be.

"This will not be easy," Minh said. "Just trying to get her into an ambulance to be transported to your home is sure to be a task."

Mary Elizabeth took a deep breath and took Minh and Daniel by the hands. "I have been working with life and death situations my entire career. Kei Lien will be safe and in good hands. I promise."

Daniel begged, "Please, Kei Lien, do not fight the paramedics on the ambulance ride home. We are here to help you. We are your friends."

"Friends...friends...friends." she repeated. "My friend...I think he is in trouble."

"Who, Kei Lien?"

"Tim. He's my friend, right? Did I get that right? I got that right, I know it."

Daniel looked at his father and shrugged his shoulders.

Minh leaned closer and whispered, "What do you say we worry about you for now? Daniel and I will help Tim after you are settled in at Mary Elizabeth's lovely home. She has a very nice room for you, Kei Lien. It has a beautiful closet with all new clothes for you and a bathroom of your own. It has a real pretty bed with pink flowers on the spread and all kinds of stuffed toys on top. Just like your mom would have for you. Will that be okay with you?"

Kei Lien's eyes opened a little wider and a faint hint of a smile appeared on her face. A single tear ran slowly down her cheek. It was like a glimmer of hope. And for the first time, Kei Lien wasn't afraid.

The ambulance ride went off without a hitch. Mary Elizabeth rode with her, just in case she tried to escape again. The whole ordeal of the past few days had exhausted Kei Lien. She spiked a fever on the way to Mary Elizabeth's house, but she was very excited to see the familiar stuffed toys on her new bed. Mary Elizabeth gave her some meds to reduce the fever and she also gave her a little something to relax her so they could more easily get her into bed. Kei Lien was a child once again, surrounded with stuffed toys. Sleep would be her medicine now.

CHAPTER 81

Nothing would or could change the morale at the Cromwell police station. One of their own had just committed suicide at the barracks in front of most of the department. A mess to clean up on all levels. Lake felt the weight of the world on his shoulders. He knew the blame would be placed squarely on him unless he could find out the truth about Ken Sorenson.

"Reese, can we go somewhere to talk?" he asked his partner. "Somewhere I'm not going to be judged before the facts come out."

"Sure. I'll meet you tonight at your place. Say around 8pm?"

Even Reese, his longtime partner, his longtime lover, was cool toward him. He needed to find answers. Answers that would not likely be found at Sorenson's desk.

Emerson entered the morgue, seeking answers from Sara. She couldn't give him any, not yet anyway.

"Detective, I need to speak with you about some of my files. They were stolen while I was at lunch with Ken."

"I know," Lake said. "Allen filled me in on what happened. Who do you suspect now, if not Ken?"

"I remembered something that Ken said after I jumped on

him about taking my files. Maybe just an idea, but I want to run it by you. It seems Ken was very quick to mention he had run into Teresa as he was leaving the cafeteria. Do you suppose she took them? Maybe he knew Teresa took them, but that was his way of sharing the info with me without directly saying it was her."

"It's possible. She really is a pain in the ass when it comes to *her Martin*. From what Allen told us, she was livid when barely anyone showed up for his huge send-off into heaven. I think the bastard went to hell. But that's just my opinion."

"What do you think she thought she would find in those files, Emerson? Maybe something that would clear his good name? Something that would say her husband didn't rape that young girl? I'm guessing he was responsible for a whole lot more than what he did to that helpless child. You know, Ken seemed like a nice guy, just a little pushy. He went out of his way to try and sit with me in the cafeteria on several occasions. And to be truthful, I was thinking of giving the guy a second look some-day, if you know what I mean?"

"I'm sorry," a statement Lake rarely made, "Sorry for what happened. I'll do a little digging into Teresa Kelsey and why she might be interested in your report. I'll keep you informed. I have to run, but will catch up with you soon. Are you all right? Are *we* all right?"

"Yes, we are."

CHAPTER 82

Judge Orrick announced the court date for sentencing Timothy Cole in Cromwell. It was far enough out so the detectives could establish who else was involved in the murders of Sergeant Kelsey and Adam Chandler and if Timothy Cole did, in fact, take part in those murders. Eve Dawson and Raymond Schmidt would go to Cromwell as well for Cole's sentencing. Judge Canton, the sitting judge for Cromwell, would handle all other trials for anyone else who participated in these crimes.

This was the very first time Detective Clayton had a case with an admitted killer involved. This guy made her skin crawl. His eyes were vivid pools of darkness. His hair, recently washed, still had a greasy sheen as if someone poured baby oil over his head. His fingernails were long and filthy. He had a habit of biting and picking at his rough yellow cuticles. Just the tone of his voice made the little hairs on the back of her neck stand up. "Hopefully, when this animal is sent to prison, he will be scrubbed down and not gently," she thought to herself. "Then again, I wouldn't want that job."

She headed into the station, passing Cole's cell.

"How is the jury selection going, Detective?" Tim taunted her. "Do you think they can actually find a jury of my peers?"

He knew there would be no jury. He also knew he wouldn't be left alone for a second and certainly not out of sight. They had him locked up in the visible holding cell so he could say anything he wanted to anybody that walked in the station.

Reese groaned, "This is going to be a long, few weeks."

Cole was furious with that news. "Weeks? What am I supposed to do for the next few weeks? No one told me I'd be stuck here that long! Hey, I'm talking to you bitch," he growled.

A huge grin formed across Reese's face.

"Well, it would seem, Mr. Cole, that your attorney should have mentioned that to you. Furthermore, that's Detective Bitch to you, asshole! Now shut up!"

CHAPTER 83

Detectives Clayton and Lake were thrilled to have warrant in hand as they entered the Strasburg Hotel.

"Randall Cummings, you are under arrest for impersonating a paramedic and for obstructing justice in the death of Martin Kelsey. Please place your hands behind your back. You have the right to remain silent," Reese recited while Lake cuffed him.

"I have no idea what you're talking about. I didn't do anything wrong!"

"We have it on good authority that you were one of the paramedics in the ambulance at the scene of Sergeant Kelsey's murder. Now is Princess Teresa in the building?"

"I don't know."

"Well, that is interesting. I guess we will find out for ourselves," Clayton said. "Tell me where the key is to her suite. Now!"

Randall didn't have much choice and had no way of warning Teresa since he was cuffed and couldn't push the silent alarm. An officer was waiting outside to take Randall in.

Lake and Clayton approached Teresa's suite with caution. This was going to be a knock and shock arrest. Lake knocked on the door, covering the peephole with his hand. Teresa opened the door.

"What the hell is—," Teresa stopped mid-sentence.

Taken a back, she cleared her throat and continued.

"Detectives, I didn't know you were here. Randall didn't announce I had company."

"Teresa Kelsey, you are under arrest in connection with the murder of your husband Sergeant Martin Kelsey. You have the right to remain silent."

Clayton continued to read her rights, while Lake handcuffed her.

"We have a warrant to search your apartment for files that were stolen from the Medical Examiner. Files relating to your husband's autopsy."

It didn't take long to find them. They were sitting on her ottoman nice and tidy.

"Guess you really weren't expecting company, were you?" Lake was enjoying this part.

"I didn't take those," Teresa insisted. "They were given to me by Officer Sorenson. He'll tell you I'm sure. Call him."

"I'm afraid that's not possible." Lake continued. "He killed himself."

Teresa fell backward, Lake catching her.

"No!" she wailed, "I loved him! He treated me like a princess. He took care of all my needs when Martin wouldn't."

The tears, real this time, streamed down her cheeks.

"It can't be true," she sobbed. "I loved him. I loved him. Why would he do such a thing?"

"We are looking into that," Clayton replied.

"Where is Randall? I need to speak to him."

"We had a warrant for his arrest as well," Lake coldly replied. "Now, where are your shoes? We're taking you in."

They escorted Teresa out of the suite and into the elevator riding down in silence. When they reached the lobby, the doors opened revealing a small crowd forming. Clayton grabbed hold of Teresa's arm. Lake held the other as they moved her forward past the onlookers.

"Wow, an audience all for you, Teresa," Lake taunted. "This must really make your day."

Teresa spit venom. "Screw you!"

"Aw...now is that any way for a lady to talk? Especially in front of her hotel guests?"

Once back at the precinct, Teresa was placed in an interrogation room. Randall in another.

"Which one should we start with?" Clayton asked Lake, giving him the choice.

"I think Randall. Let her sit and stew for a while."

Clayton started the questioning.

"What role did you play in the murders of Martin Kelsey and Adam Chandler?"

Before he could give an answer, Lake threw another one at him.

"Where did you get the ambulance that's hidden in the hotel parking garage with no plates? What did you use it for? Do you understand it is a violation to impersonate an EMT?"

"I wasn't impersonating anybody," Randall replied, starting to sweat.

He couldn't believe they found the ambulance.

"Mrs. Kelsey asked if I could find one and drive it to pick her up whenever she might need it. So, I found an old one not in use anymore and had a guy paint AMBULANCE on the side. Mrs. Kelsey gets what she wants."

"You're right about one thing," Clayton said. "That ambulance won't be used for anything anymore except as evidence in this case. We'll need that so-called artist's name."

She was dumbfounded at the measures Randall would take to keep his job.

"Now," Lake continued, "why do you suppose your boss would want an ambulance? If she just wanted a vehicle for you to pick her up in, she could have requested a limousine. Did she need an ambulance because she planned on taking her husband's body somewhere after you killed him?"

"What? Wait a minute," Randall's heart was pounding. "I did not kill the Sergeant. That's the truth! I want a lawyer."

Lake and Clayton left the interrogation room and closed the door behind them.

"What do you think?" Lake asked. "Did he have a part in this or not?"

"I think he played some kind of role, but I'm not sure it was murder. We still have enough to hold him, though. Too bad he lawyered up. I wanted to ask him how well he knew Ken."

Teresa was still unnerved about Ken Sorenson's death. When the two detectives walked in to question her, she was still crying.

Lake broke the sentimental moment. "Mrs. Kelsey, did you kill your husband?"

Clayton shot him a disapproving glance.

Teresa held the tissue to her nose, collected her thoughts.

"I would like my lawyer. Now."

Clayton was not happy her partner went for the jugular right away. She was hoping they could lead Teresa down a path that would reveal more information, but she lawyered up after Lake's accusation. Freaking Lake! Sometimes he just didn't know when to take it slow and steady.

CHAPTER 84

Reese needed a break from all the chaos at the station.

"Lake, I'm going to pay a visit to Kei Lien."

"Good idea, I'll go with you."

"If you don't mind, I'd prefer to go alone. She doesn't really trust men."

"Makes sense."

Reese stopped at a florist on the way to Mary Elizabeth's house. She picked out a nice vase of pink and white roses. She was hoping Kei Lien would be awake enough to see them and maybe a little more aware of what happened to her and her father.

"I wish that jerk I'm in love with would bring me roses once in a while," she thought.

When she arrived at Mary Elizabeth's home, Reese wasn't surprised at how beautiful Kei Lien's new room was decorated. It was adorned with love. Like something a grandmother would do for their granddaughter. Stuffed animals in pretty colors surrounded Kei Lien's beautiful face. She seemed much less stressed than before. Her straight, chin-length black hair and thick, full bangs gracefully framed the face of this tortured woman.

"Thank you for bringing her flowers," Mary Elizabeth said. "That was very kind of you. I know you want to ask Kei Lien questions, but I'm not sure she can answer them. Have a cup of tea with me. We'll let her rest a little while longer. I made some cranberry muffins. They're still warm."

"Sounds great to me. If you don't mind, I would like it if you are in the room when I do ask Kei Lien questions. Just in case we need your testimony at trial."

"What have you found out, Detective? Do you have a suspect?"

"A few, matter of fact. Please, call me Reese."

The two sat in the kitchen enjoying tea and muffins for over an hour. Reese really missed this kind of home life growing up. But that's the way some families are. Not everything can be perfect all the time.

CHAPTER 85

Tim Cole, sitting in his holding cell, laughed maniacally when he caught sight of Teresa and Randall being escorted into the station in handcuffs. It was what she deserved, he thought. Only now, he would have to wait until they finished interrogating her before he figured out his own plan. It all depended on how much she told the detectives. He didn't have to wait long. Randall and Teresa were led into the cells next to his by Detective Lake.

"Guess they finished with you already. Get a lawyer, did you?" he teased.

"Just shut your mouth, you idiot," Teresa snapped. "Got it? Not another word or else!"

"You know this man?" Lake asked. "Anything you would like to share? Anything at all?"

"Yes, Detective, there is. But it's sign language," she said, extending her middle finger.

"Now is that any way for a lady to behave?" Lake said with a wink.

When Teresa's attorney arrived, she was polite, but direct.

"My name is Alexis Wade. I am the attorney for Teresa Kelsey. May I speak with her? In private, please."

The lawyer and her client were both escorted into an interrogation room. It was about twenty minutes later when Alexis Wade reappeared in the squad room.

"My client has something she would like to say, but I see Detective Clayton is not here. Would you rather we wait for her to return?"

"No, that's not necessary." Lake answered.

The interrogation room was rather small. One wall mirrored, double-sided of course. Neat and clean. Walls more of a jail cell gray tone. An iron bar ran across the metal table, about four or five inches from the top for handcuffing purposes. Lighting was a little bit bright, but not that bad. The chairs, straight backed and purposefully uncomfortable.

"What is it you would like to share, Teresa?" Lake asked.

"First of all, Detective, those files you saw in my hotel room were the ones taken from Sara Hunter. I will admit to that. I needed to know if my late husband was responsible for raping that young woman. I was mortified to think he would do such a thing. I knew he was cheating on me, but I had no idea with who he was having an affair. The pages I took told me nothing of what he did or didn't do. As a matter of fact, I really didn't understand any of it."

"You do know that whatever you say to us will be used in court?" Lake asked.

Alexis Wade stepped in.

"Yes, I have informed her of her rights, but she insists on telling you what she knows. She's aware this whole conversation is being recorded. She is trying to be of help, Detective."

Lake knew better. Cooperation was not in Teresa Kelsey's vocabulary. But he went along with the charade, asking Teresa another question.

"Mrs. Kelsey, did you hire someone to spy on your husband?"

"Yes, I did, but I am not proud of that. His name is Timothy Cole."

He continued with the questioning, but wondered why Teresa was telling him all of this.

"Where did you find Mr. Cole? The yellow pages?"

"Detective," said her lawyer.

Teresa's body stiffened. She wanted to tell him off, but her attorney squeezed her leg under the metal table. Just the thought of sitting in this dull gray, cold, poor excuse for a room nauseated her. Did the suspects placed in this room seriously believe that was a mirror on the wall? The table felt ice cold on her elbows. She knew she had to keep calm, for a while at least.

"Ken Sorenson recommended Mr. Cole to me," she answered.

"Teresa, how well did you know Ken Sorenson?"

Her face reddened.

"What are you implying, Detective?" inquired her attorney.

"Well, we already know that Teresa gave him a place to stay while he went to the academy. We also know from Randall Cummings that Officer Sorenson made frequent visits to Teresa's suite, even though he had moved out and rented his own apartment. Would you care to tell us why he stopped by so often?"

Teresa was livid. She turned to her attorney

"I'm done here."

"Oh. One more question, Mrs. Kelsey," Lake said, savoring

the moment. "On two separate occasions you made a casual statement to my partner and to me. Would you like to explain how you knew the knife plunged into your beloved husband's heart was a ten-inch butcher knife?"

Teresa's face froze. The fiery red color in her cheeks washed to a whiter shade of pale.

"Why you son of a bitch! Who do you think you are talking to?"

Lake stood and opened the door to leave the room.

"See you in court, Mrs. Kelsey. Officer, please escort Mrs. Kelsey to her cell to await her bail hearing."

CHAPTER 86

Reese knew that a conversation with Kei Lien was going to be difficult. She set up her recorder and then thought she probably shouldn't question her without her attorney present. Does she even have one? Does she even know what an attorney is? She could speak with her, but Reese knew nothing she said would technically hold up in court.

"Mrs. Hollingsworth, does Kei Lien have an attorney?"

"Well, my son represented her guardianship hearing for Minh Nyung. I don't know if it is possible for him to represent her in court for this, though. By the way, what exactly is this?"

"Her father was murdered. It's a possibility that Kei Lien either knew his killer or maybe was his killer. I would have killed the bastard long ago if he was my father."

"I think you're right. We need to be sure this young lady is well-represented with an attorney before she answers or tries to answer anything."

"Let's just agree that Kei Lien was unable to speak when I was here."

"Deal. I'll show you out. And, detective, thank you."

"Thank you for the wonderful muffins and conversation. Maybe next time she will be awake," Reese said with a wink.

Reese reported back to the station and gave Lake a quick update on her visit with Kei Lien and that she couldn't speak with her.

"It's probably for the best," Lake replied. "She probably should be represented. This whole case is getting to be a cluster…"

"Don't say it."

"I spoke with Teresa and her lawyer while you were gone. Teresa admitted to taking Sara's files. She claims she just wanted to see if her husband was a rapist. She claims she didn't understand the report at all. She also admitted that she hired Tim Cole to spy on Sergeant Kelsey, not kill him. I asked her to explain the relationship between her and Ken. She flipped out and stopped the conversation."

"Damn it, Emerson! What about the knife? That's what I would have thrown at her."

"Ye of little faith. I loved the expression on her lawyer's face when I asked how Teresa knew it was a ten-inch blade. It was priceless."

"You're a good boy, Mr. Lake," she mocked.

"That's Detective Lake. Your partner, remember?"

"Touché, you pain in the ass."

"You are cute when you get ticked off," he teased.

"Then I must be cute a lot."

CHAPTER 87

"This case is going to be a nightmare for the judge and jury," Clayton said.

She was reviewing the case with Lake and pacing back and forth as she thought out loud.

"It's so complex. Tim Cole has already confessed to so much, but we need to prove his involvement in the murders of the Sergeant and Chandler. He must have had help. That would have been a lot of work to clean up the blood, destroy their clothing and gift wrapping them. Not to mention sewing a dog tag into someone's head. He couldn't have done all of that alone. I think we still need to try and get some answers from Kei Lien. She might have the missing pieces of this puzzle. Her attorney is Mr. Hollingsworth. He needs to be there when we question her."

"Got it," Lake said. "Do you want to start with Cole first? His attorney and the not-so-new looking briefcase are speaking with him now. I'll get him back in here to see what else we can find about his client's confessions."

Reese chuckled a little. "That poor guy had no clue what he was getting into. He seems very smart though, just pulled the wrong straw. I'm surprised he's still Tim's attorney, he could have asked to stay in Jade. Although this could put him on the map. Okay, partner, let's do this."

"I'll also get Randall and Teresa's statements signed. They have the same lawyer. Alexis Wade."

Lake really wanted another shot at Teresa. He also knew it was not likely going to happen.

"I just received a call from the D.A in Jade," Officer Manning said coming from the Captains office. "She'll be here for Cole's sentencing trial."

"She really does want Cole in jail for the rest of his life," said Reese. "Plus, this case has made national news. Looks good for her if this goes the way she wants it to."

First thing Reese did was contact Hollingsworth to set a time for the meeting with Kei Lien. Next was the task of questioning Tim and his lawyer. Reese somehow had to find out the name of the "Boss," although she had a pretty good idea it was Teresa.

Raymond Schmidt approached Reese.

"Detective, I hear you would like to question my client. Yet again. I don't know what more you could possibly ask Mr. Cole. What else is there to say?"

"We would like a few more answers," she answered.

"You do know that he will most likely be sentenced to life in a secure mental facility due to the findings of the psychiatrist? It's all in the reports."

"I am well aware of that. Why don't I join you two in the interrogation room?"

Tim raised his head out of his hands as they entered the room.

NOW SAY YOU'RE SORRY

"Mr. Cole did you see anyone else in the Chandler house when you were there?" Clayton asked.

Tim really liked the way *Mr. Cole* sounded coming from Detective Clayton.

"He hurt her," Tim replied.

"Who? Who did he hurt?"

Reese and Cole's attorney watched as Tim morphed from rabid criminal to a big brother protecting his little sister. His eyes and face softened and it sounded like he really did have a heart, instead of putting a knife through one.

"He hurt his little girl. He's no good because he did the same things to her as that no-good sergeant. And after they were done with her, they would make her say I'm sorry."

Tim sat very still for a few seconds feeling the pain of his friend. His new friend.

"Did you see anyone else while you were in his home, Mr. Cole?" Reese continued.

"The girl climbing out the window. Chandler's girl."

"By Chandler's girl, do you mean his daughter?" Reese asked.

Schmidt was just as disturbed as Detective Clayton with this new info. It seemed no matter how many times he advised his client not to answer, he completely disregarded his pleas. This was the kind of testimony you would expect in a courtroom.

"Tim, I would recommend that you keep silent at this point," Schmidt advised.

But Tim continued.

"I just made sure what needed to be done was done. Then I left. But I had to come back to put that dog tag in his head."

"Mr. Cole," Schmidt interrupted, growing agitated with his

client. "How am I supposed to help you if you are disregarding my advice to not say anything else?"

"Does it matter?" Tim shrugged. "I'm going back to one of those places anyway. Where they fill your head up with wires and give you drugs that make your head hurt."

Reese proceeded.

"Mr. Cole, why a dog tag that said Santa?"

"Because Chandler was Santa. He would tell his little girl that it was her fault these things happened to her because she wrote letters to Santa asking for someone to love her. So, I wanted all of you to know it was him that hurt her. Santa. And the others. Even the Sergeant."

"Mr. Cole, how did you know all these horrible things were happening to Kei Lien?" Reese asked. She was doing her best to keep the conversation running smoothly and not frighten him into silence. She was beginning to feel a little bad for this guy. It seemed he was trying to help this girl, right or wrong.

"I guess I felt bad for her. I watched her hang clothes on the line and cook food. Never seen anybody else. No girlfriends. No mom. Mom..." Tim's voice trailed off. "I love my mom. You know that, right?"

"I know," Reese said gently. "How long have you been going in Kei Lien's house to watch her?"

"I don't know."

"Mr. Cole, who is the person you call Boss?"

The conversation ended.

CHAPTER 88

Detectives Lake and Clayton arrived at the Hollingsworth home as scheduled. A houseful of people greeted them. Kei Lien's attorney, Denton Hollingsworth, along with Minh, Mary Elizabeth and Daniel were inside. Everyone in the room was advised the conversation was being recorded. Reese began by assuring everyone that she and Detective Lake were there to find out what happened on the night of Adam Chandler's murder and not to accuse anyone of anything. Reese thought it wise to start the questioning, seeing how her partner didn't have a great bedside manner. Mary Elizabeth held Kei Lien's hand to let her know she was safe during the conversation and not to be afraid.

Reese began.

"Could you tell me your name, please?"

"Kei Lien."

Reese was surprised she could speak at all, considering what she had been through. She glanced at Mary Elizabeth.

"It's fine," Mary Elizabeth said. "Kei Lien is having a good day today. No medications. We even shared a cranberry muffin this morning."

Reese smiled.

"Do you understand what Mr. Hollingsworth told you before we arrived, Kei Lien? You do not have to say anything to us that you do not want to. Do you understand that?"

Kei Lien nodded her head yes and her lawyer verbally acknowledged that Kei Lien understood so it would be on the record.

"Can you tell us what your father did to you and why he did it?" Reese asked.

Kei Lien stared blankly at the detective. Mary Elizabeth chimed in.

"Kei Lien, can you show the officers where your father and the other gifts from Santa hurt you?"

"My client is pointing to her mouth, her vagina and her anal area," Denton said, explaining Kei Lien's actions.

He was nauseated knowing this girl was tortured. Even though she was not the first rape victim any of them had been involved with, this was incest. And a very disturbing life for this woman.

Reese continued. "Kei Lien, can you tell me if you saw any other people in your house besides your father the day you ran away?"

"Yes."

"Do you know how many? Do you remember?"

"The gift from Santa, a woman and my friend Tim," she answered. "Is he in trouble?"

Kei Lien started to get anxious, Mary Elizabeth squeezed her hand tighter.

"No one will hurt you now," she reassured Kei Lien.

"My friend Tim said that to me."

"Said what?" asked Reese.

"No one will hurt me now."

Kei Lien's breathing was getting shallow, her legs were beginning to thrash. Reese knew she better wrap this up soon before this young lady needed another shot to quiet her. She held up a photo of Martin Kelsey.

"Is this the man you call Santa?"

"Yes, one of them."

"Did you stab your father with a knife?"

Denton interrupted. "She does not have to answer that question, you know that. Shut off the recorder now."

"This will be off the record," Reese shot back.

Kei Lien lifted her head slightly and answered.

"No."

Reese shared a photo of Teresa Kelsey.

"This is the last question I will ask today," Reese said, hoping to calm Kei Lien a bit. "Can you look at this photo? Was this lady in your house the night you ran away?"

"No."

Everyone in Kei Lien's room glanced at each other in silence. They thought they had this case wrapped up and certain Teresa Kelsey was the Boss.

Denton broke the silence.

"I think we should all leave now so she can get some rest."

Each one filed out of the room. Daniel was the last one left to leave. He stood in the doorway and gazed lovingly at Kei Lien.

Kei Lien raised her hand, smiled, and gently waved to Daniel.

"My new friend."

"Where do we go from here?" Lake asked once they were back in the car. "Is this back to square one? If so, I'm going to need a drink. A real drink. What the hell just happened to our case? There is something else we are missing, another piece to this, another person. Not that I don't think Teresa is involved. She sure as hell is, but there is more."

"Maybe we should have that so-called drink later tonight, Detective Lake," Reese answered. "That is if you behave yourself between now and then."

"Oh, Miss Clayton I do declare. I'm not sure if you call what we do behaving ourselves."

"Yeah, Yeah, Yeah. Back to work."

CHAPTER 89

Alexis Wade was trying her best to seek bail for her clients.

"Randall Cummings was arrested for impersonating an EMT," she stated. "He was doing what his employer asked. Nothing harmful to anyone. Teresa Kelsey was arrested for stealing a few documents from her husband's autopsy report. I believe she has the right to that information, Your Honor."

"Ms. Wade," Judge Canton replied, "Mrs. Kelsey may have had a right to her husband's records, but she did not have the right to steal them. She will be placed under house arrest. Bail is set at five hundred thousand dollars. I am requiring an ankle monitor to be worn until trial begins."

"What about Randall Cummings, Your Honor? I'm not aware of any other charges pending at this time."

"I will set bail for Mr. Cummings at two-hundred and fifty thousand dollars and placed under house arrest with ankle monitor until the outcome of the trial."

"Your Honor, that seems a little steep for driving an unmarked ambulance."

"Counselor, do not undermine my decisions. Would you

rather I hold both of your clients without bail?"

"No, Your Honor."

CHAPTER 90

"How on earth are we going to get Cole to rat out his Boss?" Lake asked. "We need to figure out what his ties are to the two victims. I thought for sure that crazy, stuffy Teresa had something to do with this. I'm still not convinced she didn't. After all, the Sergeant was fooling around on her. I wonder if he was keeping his encounters to just this young lady. Maybe he had others and one of them was angry enough to hire Cole?"

"Possible," Reese agreed. "Very possible. Although, we never saw him with anyone. Then again, we never saw him with Kei Lien, either. Obviously, someone did. But who?"

"Teresa hired Cole to follow her husband. She knew he was fooling around on her, but didn't know who with. Suppose, just suppose, Cole found out who that someone was and decided to take money from this person to kill the Sergeant. You know, like playing both sides against the middle. "Lake now fidgeting in his desk chair, my ass is sore, "we need new furniture in here."

"But what about Chandler? Reese said. Where did he come into the mix? Who hired Cole to kill him?"

"Maybe Cole did that on his own after seeing what was

happening to Kei Lien. Although, he did say Chandler was already stabbed, he just finished the job."

"Even if you are right, we still don't know who the Boss is. That's what we need. Let's try to speak to Cole again. He's admitted to so much already. It's hard to believe he would keep this person a secret much longer."

"Whoever this Boss is, they must have bigger and better plans for Cole."

CHAPTER 91

Reese decided to take it upon herself to approach Tim Cole one more time. He was sleeping in his cell when she banged on the cell bars.

"Mr. Cole, wake up."

Tim sat up, shook his head back and forth a few times, ran his filthy hands through his even dirtier hair and lifted one side of his buttocks and farted. He smiled to himself, cleared his throat and spit on the cell floor.

"Well, Detective, what brings you to my newly appointed housing development?"

"I brought you a cup of coffee. I can hand it to you through the bars if you like."

"Really? You remembered to bring me coffee, Detective?"

Tim liked this treatment.

Reese reached through the bars to hand him the small Styrofoam cup, which easily slid through the bars with a little squeeze. She had her other hand on her weapon, just in case he planned on grabbing her arm.

"Mr. Cole, I'm sorry we've been so hard on you. I do believe you were trying to protect that young girl from any more pain."

"My coffee tastes okay, but it's only half a cup. It's not very hot."

"I won't lie to you, Mr. Cole. It's not hot on purpose. I prefer it that way, in case inmates try to scald me with it. The cup is not full, so I could squeeze it through the bars."

Tim smiled at her honesty and liked that about her.

"You and I both know your fate. I wish it weren't true, but you are accused and frankly guilty, of murdering a lot of people. You must pay the price for that. But would it be possible for you to answer a few more questions for me?"

Tim retreated to his cot and sat down. Reese could see his face soften just a bit. She waited patiently for an answer.

"You can call me Tim."

"Thank you, Tim. We know you didn't plan this on your own. So why are you trying to protect whoever it was that helped you carry out these crimes? You said you heard Mr. Chandler's chest gurgling. You said you went over to finish the job by pushing the knife in further. Do you know the person who stabbed Chandler? Was that person still in the room with you?"

Tim began to get red in the face, like it always did when he was upset or nervous. This time Reese was on top of the situation.

"Take a few deep breaths and have a sip of your coffee."

Tim did as he was told. He rather liked someone caring about him. It was the first time ever, except for mom.

"I love my Mom," Tim said out loud.

"I know you do, Tim. I think she would want you to help us find out about these awful men that hurt your friend. Don't you?"

"Yes. Maybe. I'm not sure."

"What aren't you sure of, Tim? You've already been hurt,

many times I'm guessing. So why hide the person that made you do these things?"

"Because. She said she would light a fire and burn me alive."

"Who said that?"

"Detective Clayton, what do you think you are doing?" Raymond Schmidt interrupted.

Reese spun around to see Tim's attorney standing behind her.

"My client has nothing further to say to you. Do you understand me?"

"Yes, I do," Reese answered. "Tim and I were just having a little coffee that's all. Isn't that right?"

"Yes, we were," Tim agreed. "But it's not really hot enough. That's what I was just telling her."

Reese nodded her head at Timothy Cole to thank him for not ratting her out.

He would never tell her, but Raymond Schmidt was more concerned for Reese's safety than whatever information Tim was giving her. He knew this guy had tricks up his sleeve for every situation. He never let on to Reese his concerns. Which is the way it should be. He was Tim Cole's attorney and not supposed to be Detective Clayton's friend, confidant, or protector.

Reese, annoyed that it was another missed opportunity, left to go home. She called Emerson on his private cell.

"We need to talk now."

Emerson didn't often hear that tone of voice from Reese.

"I'm almost to your apartment anyway," he told her. "I'll meet you there."

CHAPTER 92

Daniel made it a point to visit Kei Lien at least every other day. His dad filled the other time slots. He knew his dad didn't mind going to visit because he could tell there was a connection between Mary Elizabeth and his dad. He didn't have any issues with that at all. It was just like Minh said, it's time for the living, not the dead. His mom would approve of this woman, for sure. When this scenario with Kei Lien was resolved, he was sure the two would become one.

"Good Morning, how are you feeling today?" Daniel said to Kei Lien. "Do you remember me?"

"Yes, you are my friend Daniel, right? Where is my other friend, Tim?"

Daniel did not know how to answer, so Mary Elizabeth jumped in.

"Sweetheart, Tim can't be here today, so Daniel is here instead."

"I know he can't be here if he is in trouble. I know he's in trouble. That lady yelled at him for a long time. Maybe she was yelling at my father or the gift from Santa. I don't know now."

"Do you know the lady?" Daniel asked calmly. "Do you know

301

her name by any chance? Has she been to your house before?"

"The day I ran away, she saw my Dad doing those things to me. I opened my eyes once and she was peeking through the door. I don't think my dad saw her. He just told me to close my eyes, like he always did. I heard the woman and my friend Tim talking later. Before I ran away."

This was the first time that Kei Lien had put more than one sentence together, yet alone a whole bunch of them. Maybe she *will* have a chance to recover, Daniel thought.

Kei Lien drifted off to sleep. Her breathing was easier today and she wasn't thrashing. Perhaps she needed to say these things, Daniel thought.

"This is so bizarre," Daniel told Mary Elizabeth. "What do you think we should do now? Should we call the detectives or your son? I'm at a loss."

"Me, too. I say let her rest. I will call my son in a little bit to tell him what just happened. I think too many people in the room make her agitated. So, let's leave her be for now."

"I will tell my father when he gets back tonight. He needs to know as well."

"Daniel, please be careful. We know nothing about this other woman. We certainly don't know what she is capable of, or even who it is. If she was seeing Kei Lien's father, then that is a motive. Oh jeez, listen to me. I've been hanging around my son too long. I'm beginning to sound just like him."

Daniel had to laugh. Even though the situation was very scary, he knew he needed to tell someone and that someone would be his dad. Daniel took one more peek into Kei Lien's room and softly whispered, "Sleep my friend. I'll be back tomorrow."

He glanced over at her wonderful, caring nurse and asked if he could give her a hug.

CHAPTER 93

When Reese arrived home, Emerson was sitting on her doorstep anxiously waiting to hear what happened to upset her so much. He helped her with her things and unlocked the door to her apartment. Once inside he put his arms around her.

"Whatever this is, we can fix it."

He kissed her cheek, never once trying to get her into bed.

"Sit down and I'll get you a drink before you tell me what's going on. What would you like?"

"I would like this case to be over with soon, but a beer will be fine for now."

"What the hell happened?" he said.

She proceeded to tell him what she had done. Interrogating Cole as he sat in his cell.

"Are you nuts? You know what a danger he is. What were you thinking?"

"I know...I know...but I had to take the chance. I was making headway too, until his attorney walked in."

"Oh my God! Reese, he could ruin this whole case for us if he thinks you were questioning him without counsel. What were you thinking?"

"Relax. I told him I was just bringing him some coffee. Believe it or not, he actually backed up my story and didn't throw me under the bus."

"Interesting. So, what did Tim tell you before he came in?"

"There is definitely another suspect involved and Cole is obviously too afraid to identify her."

"Her? It's a woman? How do you know that?"

"Because he said *she* told him she would light the fire and burn him alive."

"I don't know. Burn someone alive? That sounds more like something Cole would do. Are you sure he wasn't just making up a story to throw you off the trail? Or maybe Teresa or Randall put him up to spinning this tale. Remember when we first brought Teresa in? She was furious with Cole and ordered him not to say another word. She obviously has some kind of control over him."

"I'm going to trust my instincts on this one, Lake. Do I think the guy is a life-long serial killer? Yes, I do. But he also tried to protect Kei Lien and told her he was her friend. That's got to count for something. If there was another woman involved, could she have been having an affair with the Sergeant? Or maybe she was involved with Chandler and she found out what he was doing to his daughter?"

"Interesting theories. Let's talk to Teresa again to see if she knew anything about the person her husband was having an affair with. She could have a name or possibly even some photos, if Cole took any when he was doing surveillance for her. Teresa also said she thought Adam Chandler was running a whorehouse. Maybe Teresa could give us names of other men who frequented the Chandler home. Maybe it's another disgruntled wife?"

"Great idea!"

"One thing is for sure. You have to be the one to start that conversation. Teresa and I seem to have a love-hate relationship. We love to hate each other."

Reese laughed, picked up a decorative throw pillow off the couch and threw it at him. Emerson tried to dodge it, but it bounced right off his head tousling his hair.

"Hey! I'm just speaking the truth," Lake joked.

"Yeah, I know. I'll wait for her to make bail and approach her one-on-one."

"Enough shop talk for one night. I'm starving. Do you feel like going out for dinner or should we order in?"

"Wow! You're going to take me out in public? When we're not working? To an actual restaurant and not a fast-food joint?"

This time Lake picked up the pillow from the floor and tossed it at Reese. She batted it away with a flirty grin.

"Well, you are kind of hot in your work clothes, but maybe a dress would be nice for this evening."

"Oh my God. You called me hot."

"I'll call for a reservation at the burger joint down the street."

"You do that, you jerk, and I will not be inviting you back here for a *drink*."

"Come here," he grabbed her by the arm, pulling her close, and kissed her with amazing passion. "Now stop being a smart ass and get dressed. Or undressed. It's up to you."

"What am I going to do with you? Never mind. Do not

answer that question. I'll be ready in a few minutes. Go make those reservations."

Chez Don Wie, one of the finest restaurants in Cromwell, was nearly full. Reese didn't know how he managed to get a reservation so quickly, but glad he did.

"Good evening," the waiter said, on the top of his game. "Welcome. May I get you a nice bottle of wine this evening?"

He was holding a bottle wrapped in a white linen towel.

"I don't think so right now," Reese replied, "but I would like a cocktail."

"Very well. What may I interest you in this evening, miss?"

"How about a Manhattan?"

"I'll have the same," Emerson said. "Thank you."

"I'll be right back with your drinks."

He left the couple alone and Emerson smiled at Reese.

"Are you feeling a little more relaxed now that you are on personal time? By the way, you look beautiful this evening."

"Why, thank you," Reese said, flashing him a big smile. "I somehow don't think we are ever on personal time. And this is a lovely place, Detective. I hope you brought your wallet. If not, we will be doing private duty for a while."

She paused for a brief second. "Do you mind if I say something work related?"

"Do you think I'm dumb enough to say no? Especially when I know you are packing heat some place on that body of yours? What have you got? I'm all ears."

"What if Cole was being paid by two women at the same time?"

"Possible. I'm going to try and talk to Randall. He's the other cog in this wheel. I can ask questions even with his attorney in the room. Maybe I can get him to slip up a little."

"I've made arrangements with Mary Elizabeth to see Kei Lien tomorrow afternoon. Maybe she will be more helpful after a little rest. Hopefully we both have a bit of luck."

The rest of the evening was just about having good food and eventually a nice bottle of wine. Once back at Reese's apartment, she noticed how different her date was acting. He really seemed to care about her. He took his time undressing her, kissing her neck, her back and shoulders. Running his hands through her hair. He was always attentive to her needs, but tonight more so than ever. Every kiss, every touch, was sensual. His kisses went to her navel, where he lingered, driving her crazy with desire. He then climbed on top of her and whispered, "You have the most amazing body." He entered her with passion, making her wait for that release. When she was nearly ready, he took the long strokes like always, to heighten her orgasm. But this time he said to her, "I love your body, Reese. And I love you."

Reese was floored. He had never told her he loved her before.

"I love you," she said, nearly out of breath, having the best orgasm she could imagine.

She lay with him still inside of her, holding him, not wanting the moment to end. Tears began to glisten in her eyes. When he softened and slid out of her, he stared deep into her watery eyes.

"I mean it. I do love you."

CHAPTER 94

Teresa made bail by putting up the equity in the hotel as collateral. Not surprising. Randall, on the other hand, was left in jail, certainly not able to pay that amount of money. He was in shock that Teresa, the person he had tried to protect since he started working at the hotel, would not bail him out.

"I'm already paying for your attorney," she told him. "It won't hurt for you to stay in here for a little while longer."

Upon hearing this news, Officer Allen Manning saw an opportunity to start a long over-due talk with Randall Cummings. Detectives Lake and Clayton were not in the building, but he knew this was his chance to get Randall to come clean.

Randall wasn't really a threat, so he was placed in a holding cell in the back of the barracks. Allen took a walk and purposely did a double-take when he strode past Randall's cell.

"What are you still doing here? I thought you and Teresa were out on bail?"

"I couldn't come up with that kind of money."

"Why didn't Teresa post it for you? She's loaded, isn't she? I'd be a little pissed, considering all you do for her. What a lousy thing for her to do. Is she at least still paying for your attorney?"

"Yeah, but we have the same one, how much more money or work could that be for a lawyer? She is such a spoiled brat is all I can say."

"She is still your boss. You need the job, right?"

"I won't if I go to jail. Especially for something that's not my fault."

Allen had him right where he wanted him.

"Randall, do you want to tell me what happened? Maybe I can help."

"I wasn't part of this whole thing," Randall said, letting it all spill out. "All I did was drive an ambulance for her. She's the one that hired that Tim character to spy on the Sergeant. And she didn't like what he found out at all. Especially when she found out what he was doing to that girl. Calling himself Santa. What kind of fucking moron does that? And who does that to a young girl. Telling her to say she's sorry. For what? Sick bastard! And then, instead of my boss blaming her husband, she blamed the girl and her father. She's the one that told Cole she would pay him outrageous amounts of money to take care of him."

"Meaning?"

"You know. Finish him off. Cole even had a dog tag. A blank one that he hammered the word Santa into. He was going to put it where someone would see it. I have no idea where he would get a blank dog tag. All I did for her. I even kept Teresa's affair with Ken quiet. They are all lunatics if you ask me."

"Ken? Who is Ken?" Allen asked cautiously.

"You know, the cop that works here. Or, did work here. He is the one who told Teresa about Tim Cole. Got him the job. Not the killing part, I don't think."

Randall was beginning to lose it, choking up trying to clear his throat and rubbing his eyes to prevent himself from crying.

"I want to tell you something else, Officer."

"Do you want your lawyer here?" Allen asked.

He knew he had crossed a line and thought it better to cover his own ass.

"What's the point? She's just going to work to get Teresa off, certainly not me. Besides, I have another little secret."

"What?"

"I was with Tim when he murdered the Sergeant. I didn't do it. I swear! I don't know if Teresa told Tim to kill him. I thought she just wanted to scare her husband. I couldn't figure out why she wanted me to go with Tim. He is one creepy bastard. Afterward, I helped wrap Kelsey's body in the Christmas paper. I thought the paper was for Chandler, but I guess it was for both."

Randall took a deep breath, feeling relieved to finally let it all out.

"Then we went to Chandler's house. But he was already on the floor with a knife in his chest. He wasn't dead. Not until Cole pushed the knife in farther. The girl was in her room and she wasn't alone. I heard a woman's voice telling her to run. To climb out the window and run. Cole and I were scared of getting caught. Well, at least I was scared. Cole opened the bedroom door when the girl was halfway out the window. He told her no one would hurt her again. He told her he was her friend and not to be scared."

"What about the woman?" Allen asked.

"I caught a glimpse of her behind the door through the hinges.

Tim glared at her when she spoke to him. I think he was ready to finish her off. He's crazy, but knows exactly what he's doing. That guy needs to get the chair not another mental hospital, if you ask me. Anyway, this woman told Cole she would pay him a lot of money if he kept quiet and cleaned up the mess of Adam Chandler on the floor. She also said something like, I don't know, burning him or something. I just wanted out of there."

"Who was she?"

"Cole told me her name."

Allen turned to leave.

"Officer, you can't tell anyone what I told you."

"Are you nuts? Of course, I'm going to. I have a job to do. I will try to help you. Put in a good word, but that's all I can do."

"No, Officer Manning, if you say anything, I'm going to deny it. Plus, if you tell anyone about this, I'm going to tell the entire police department your little secret."

Allen froze.

"What secret is that?"

"I know you are gay," Randall answered.

Allen Manning slammed his hand against the bars ready to tear Randall apart.

"Who do you think you are? You little prick!"

"I'm guessing you haven't mentioned it to your colleagues or else you wouldn't be frequenting a gay bar in another town. I've seen you there myself, just didn't let you see me. I'm quite sure you're not going there for police surveillance. I know how cops feel about having a gay officer on the job. Maybe not so secure that you'd have their back. Am I right? And that, detective, is *my* little secret."

Allen left the jail cell, not only scared about his career, but also how was he going to tell Detectives Lake and Clayton how he got this information.

When they arrived back at the barracks, Allen was waiting. He knew what he had to do, regardless of his career. 'Don't ask, don't tell' may be the unwritten rule, but everyone knows that's not how it goes all the time.

"Did you find out anything else about Teresa?" asked Lake. "I know she made bail and was told to stay in town. Do you think she's a flight risk?"

"That's only one problem," Allen answered.

He took a deep breath before continuing.

"I have a verbal confession of what happened the night of the murders. Nothing in writing."

"From whom? Cole?" Lake asked.

"No. From Randall. He spilled his guts to me. Told me everything."

"Damn it, Allen! Did he say he would testify at least?"

"No. He just wanted me to know his part in all of this. I felt like a priest sitting on the other side of a confessional. He told me something else. He knows the name of the other woman in the Chandler house. It wasn't Teresa."

"Then who?" Reese urged.

"All he said was he knew her first name. You'll see in the interview. Not what I wanted to hear. I don't know guys. This just keeps getting worse. He did say he has seen her around before. That's all he said."

Allen took another deep breath.

"Detectives, I have something else I need to tell you both.

Randall threatened to reveal a personal secret of mine if I shared any of this info with you. I need to beat him to the punch, no matter the consequences. My first priority is and always will be this job and making sure these people go to jail for the rest of their lives. So, I'm just going to say it. I'm gay."

Emerson and Reese exchanged glances. Reese was first to speak.

"First of all, Allen, no one cares about that. I promise you. Now let's get these assholes put away where they belong."

"Wait. Are you saying everyone knows?"

Lake nodded yes.

"Of course," Lake confirmed. "Can we get back to work now?"

Allen stood silent for a minute.

"Um, yeah, sure."

Emerson asked one of the other officers to pull the video from Randall's jail cell.

"Thank goodness we have cameras in all of them. We need to go through the whole conversation you had with him. The bad part is a judge will probably say it's inadmissible in court because there were no lawyers present."

"Somewhere during the conversation, I asked him if he wanted his attorney there. I thought I better protect myself. He said no. It should be on the video."

It was.

CHAPTER 95

Reese thought it was time to have yet another talk with Teresa. This time, she took Officer Manning with her. First, they had to make sure she made bail. Judge Canton confirmed she had. Next was to show up at her hotel unannounced. There was some college-age kid on the desk who clearly was not aware of the circumstances of why they were there.

"I'm Detective Clayton, Cromwell Police Department. This is Officer Manning. We'd like to see Teresa Kelsey please."

"She's in Suite 1001. Top floor. Do you want me to tell her you are here?"

"No," Allen replied, "we'll find our way to her suite. But thank you."

As they headed for the elevator, he nudged Reese.

"That girl is definitely going to lose her new job as soon as we knock on Teresa's door."

Once they reached the suite, Allen covered the peephole while Reese knocked on the door.

"Who is it? Go away!" Teresa yelled from the other side of the door.

"It's Allen Manning. We need to talk."

She opened the door and saw it was both Allen and Reese.

"I have got to get someone to clean that peephole. What do you want now? Haven't you already ruined my life enough? Do you need to remove all my dignity?"

"I think you did that yourself by hiring Tim Cole to spy on your husband," Reese said. She was getting sick of Teresa's attitude.

"We just want to know if you had any idea of anyone your husband was seeing on the side," Manning said. "Did Cole tell you he saw anyone with him? Are there photos of any kind? We are trying to help you, Teresa."

"Shouldn't I have my attorney with me during this little visit?"

"You certainly can have her here," Reese answered. "It's up to you. We just want to know if Cole found your late husband with another woman. And if so, did he say who that was?"

Teresa was tired of this whole mess and wanted out of it as soon as possible.

"The only one he could find was Chandler's daughter. I really didn't know she was just a child, or at least acted like a child. Tim told me how Martin hurt her and how Adam did the same. Sick bastards. Both of them. And I don't know what I was thinking hiring that guy. I knew my husband was having an affair. Ken told me this guy needed a job. So, I hired him. He didn't say he was a lunatic."

"Meaning?"

"Meaning he wanted to hurt my husband for what he did to me and to that poor girl."

"How did he want to hurt him?"

"He said if I paid him extra, he would take care of it. I thought he was just going to beat him up or something like that."

"You want us to believe you didn't have any idea what Cole meant by, take care of it?" Manning asked, getting right in her face.

Teresa was now furious with the implication and wanted to spit in his face. She would have, except she knew she had to make her statement sound believable.

"And did you pay him?" Reese asked.

"I did," Teresa hung her head. "What good would it do to lie about that now? Are you going to arrest me again?"

"No," Reese answered. "But we would like you to give us your statement in writing. Of course, check with your attorney if you like."

Allen and Reese thought it best this way. They had enough evidence to arrest her on conspiracy to harm the Sergeant. But they were after bigger things. Teresa said she would make the statement after she got to see her attorney.

Outside of the hotel, Reese thought out loud.

"So, if Teresa only knew about Kei Lien then she must not know there was another woman at Chandler's house the night of the murders, correct?" Reese mused. "Do you think Cole might throw this other woman under the bus if he thought she was trying to blackmail him? I seriously don't think he would agree to kill either one of the victims without knowing who hired him. I suspect he would go for the highest bidder."

"He certainly is a crazy SOB, but he's also smarter than we think. We already know number one boss was Teresa. He has to know the name of number two."

"Allen, let's go back to the station to see how Emerson is making out with the video of the century."

Allen chuckled. He was feeling the weight of the world lifted from his shoulders, knowing his secret was no longer a deterrent to his career.

On the way back to the precinct, Reese noticed a familiar face coming out of the bank. She immediately pulled over.

"Reese, what are you doing? Why are we pulling over?" Allen asked before glancing down the sidewalk. "Whoa! What happened to that guy? Man, that's messed up."

Reese jumped out of the car and Allen followed.

"Andrew!" she yelled. "Wait up!"

But Andrew kept walking. Allen was trying to keep up with Reese's quick pace.

"Hey, is this the guy you told us about? The guy from Jade with the same last name as the Sergeant?"

"What gave you the first clue?"

"Uh, the burnt skin. Christ, what's wrong with you? One minute you're as nice as pie and the next you're a…"

Reese ignored him and finally caught up to Andrew.

"Andrew…Andrew Kelsey, do you remember who I am?"

"Of course, I do, Detective Clayton. I suppose you want to know why I'm here. First, I had the DNA test done myself. That prick, your Sergeant, is my father. Or should I say was? I have the paperwork right here."

Reese glanced at it briefly. "So, what are you doing in Cromwell?"

"I'm here to claim what is rightfully mine."

"Meaning?"

"He had a will when he lived in Jade. It was drafted many years ago. Probably when I was born. I went around town inquiring about Martin Kelsey after you left town. I talked to a few lawyers. Found one that had the copy of his last will and testament. It says he left all his worldly belongings to me, his illegitimate son, Andrew Kelsey. I confirmed the will was up to date. The lawyer said it was the only time he filed one in the town of Jade. He also suggested I travel to his last known address to speak with an attorney or a bank manager in town to see if he had a safe deposit box. The first one I went to had nothing. This one did, but I need to get a copy of his death certificate in order to open the box."

"I will see to it that you get those copies right away. Where are you staying?"

"The Strasburg hotel. It is mine now."

"I want you to feel comfortable. You do know who owns that hotel, don't you?"

"Yes, I do, Detective"

"Please reconsider your choice. There is a lot of investigation going on as you might suspect. So, I'm asking you to stay at a motel nearby, just until I get that death certificate for you."

"I thought you already found the killer. Tim Cole."

"He has admitted to several murders, but we think he had help. So please try not to complicate this investigation."

"Okay, but I still want those certificates so I can open his safe deposit box. I don't need to stay at the Strasburg, but want to know what is in that safety deposit box."

"I promise I will have the copies for you tomorrow. Would you like me to go with you then? To the bank, I mean?"

"That would be great. Call as soon as you get the copy for me. You have my cell correct? And, Detective, I am expecting you to do the right thing."

"I will, and yes, I have your number."

CHAPTER 96

The precinct was buzzing when Allen and Reese got back. By now, everyone had seen Randall's taped confession.

Emerson didn't even say hello when he saw the two of them coming down the hall. "Reese, locate the judge. Get him to issue another warrant."

"Can I at least ask for what? I'm guessing you found out who the female is?"

"I'm sorry, Lake," Manning intervened. "I thought it was better if you saw it for yourself on the video."

Allen wasn't quite sure how all of this was going to play out.

"Change in plans, Allen. Let Captain Brown know we need a warrant."

"Would someone please tell me what the hell is going on here?" Reese was ready to pounce on her partner for not giving her answers.

"Reese, you're with me. I'll fill you in on the way down to the morgue."

A deep, raspy voice interrupted them.

"She's going to burn me alive now. Isn't that right?"

Tim was standing with his face pressed between the bars of his cell.

"Burn me alive."

Lake ignored him.

"The rest of you keep an eye on both of our prisoners. Do not let them out of your sight or out of their cells. I don't care if they say they're dying. Do not open the doors to the cells. Everyone on board? Allen, as soon as you have that warrant in your hands call one of us. In the meantime, we will be down in the morgue to see if any other evidence has emerged."

Bill Oosterhout was in the middle of the autopsy on Ken Sorenson's body when the door swung back hitting the wall with a thundering bang. Bill was startled.

"So, Bill, is there anything else you can tell us about Ken Sorenson's body?" Emerson asked. "Did you find any kind of drugs or alcohol he may have taken that would cause him to do this?"

Emerson sounded angry, as if Bill had done something wrong.

"Can you give us any idea, William Oosterhout, M.E. for Cromwell?"

Bill was alarmed, Detective Lake never referred to him as William. Always Bill. He also never called him 'The M.E. for Cromwell.' Sara walked in behind the detectives.

"Sara, can you help me out here?" Bill asked.

"I don't think she can answer for you, Mr. Oosterhout," Reese said.

"What's going on?" Bill's voice was shaking.

Lake's cell phone rang. He never said a word to the person on the other end. He just put his phone in his coat pocket and removed the cuffs from his back pants pocket. Reese put her hand on her weapon.

"Sara Hunter, we have a warrant for your arrest. Anything you say or do can be used against you in a court of law. You are entitled to an attorney. If you cannot afford an attorney, one will be appointed for you."

Sara never said one word as two officers appeared and stood on either side of her. Lake had had them waiting in the hall, ready for his signal.

Lake and Clayton apologized to Bill for scaring him half to death.

"We had one thing right. You are, for now anyway, the M.E. of Cromwell."

"What did she do?" Bill asked.

"We'll go over all of that soon. But we will need your full cooperation."

Bill nodded his head.

The detectives and officers led Sara out of the autopsy room by way of the back elevator to an old interrogation room, keeping her clear of the jail cells that held Cole and Cummings. Once out of earshot of her coworker, Sara asked, "Why am I being arrested?"

"For the murder of Adam Chandler. What the hell were you thinking and why didn't you come to us before doing something like this?"

Sara said nothing.

She was placed in an interrogation room. About a half hour later, as soon as Allen had placed the warrant in Lake's hand, Reese said that she thought they were ready.

"Sara Hunter, has your attorney been contacted?" Reese asked.

"Yes, he should be here any minute."

"May we ask his name?"

"Denton Hollingsworth."

Emerson and Reese looked at her, shocked.

"Are you kidding? You're really going to use the same counsel as Kei Lien?" Reese asked.

"It's better this way. You'll see."

Emerson went around the back of Sara's chair and released the cuffs from her wrists.

"I don't think you are going to try anything, are you?"

Sara just smiled.

Even though Denton Hollingsworth was delayed for two hours, the detectives and Allen thought it best to keep Sara in interrogation, rather than placing her in a cell right away. They wanted to show her a little respect. Conversation was sparse. Nothing could be said concerning her arrest without her lawyer present.

"We know you can't tell us anything right now, Sara. But is this really who you are?" Reese questioned.

Lake put his hand on Reese's shoulder.

Sara just stared at Reese with eyes that were lost in her own soul.

When Denton Hollingsworth arrived, he asked Sara if she was all right. She confirmed that she was and he then wanted to know what she had said to the detectives before he arrived.

"I just asked why I was being arrested."

"Detective Lake?" Denton directed his attention to the detective.

"Suspicion of murder," Lake replied. "The murder of Adam

Chandler."

"Sara, you don't have to answer anything you don't want to," Denton advised. "I'll be with you through this whole conversation, advising you. You may begin, detectives."

"Sara, what is your connection to the victim Adam Chandler?" Lake asked. "Other than being the one to do his autopsy."

"Mr. Hollingsworth, I need to tell these people my story. They have been my friends since I became the Medical Examiner for this city. Just tell me when I should stop."

Denton nodded.

Sara was nervous and emotional as she began to tell her friends what happened between her and Adam Chandler.

"I met Adam about five months ago. He invited me out to dinner and I accepted. Eventually we had a few more dinners… movies…it was nice. About a month after I met him, he asked if he could come up to my apartment. I said yes. It had been a very long time since I had let anyone into my life. I felt like it was time to be with the living. I liked Adam. He made me feel like a woman again. He was kind and gentle. Well, at first anyway. The sex became a little bit more aggressive each time."

Reese and Emerson were glued to her voice like this was some romance story.

"I asked him to stop on this one particular encounter. He told me he was sorry. He told me that his wife liked it that way before she died during childbirth. I told him I wasn't his wife and I didn't like sex that aggressive. I asked him if the baby survived, but he said no. He never mentioned having an adopted daughter. After that, I cooled things off, but he asked me out again. Everything was much better this time. We always went out or spent time at my place.

"One late afternoon, things were slow at work so I decided to pick up some take-out and surprise Adam at his house. When I got closer, I saw the Sergeant leaving. I rode around the block a few times, just to think. I couldn't imagine why the Sergeant was at his house. I was trying to decide if I should go in or not. I finally decided to go in. I stopped the car and walked up the steps. I noticed that the door was slightly open. I touched it and it opened a little, I quietly called to Adam, but got no response. So, I went in anyway.

"As I walked into the house, I could hear someone. It sounded like crying. As I moved further into the house, I could tell it was more than that. It was a woman and she was sobbing in fear. When I walked through the house, I saw the door to the bedroom. There was Adam having sex, rough sex, with this young woman. The young lady opened her eyes and looked straight at me. As if to say 'help me.' He yelled at her to close her eyes tight and remember that this is what she asked for in her letter to Santa. Then he shouted, "Now, say you're sorry!" She did what she was told.

"I was mortified. I screamed at him to get the fuck off her. That's when I saw the bruising all over her. He was naked, of course. He jumped out of bed and lunged toward me. There was fury in his eyes. He grabbed my arm and pulled me into the living room, screaming at me, asking how I got in the house. I told him the door was open and when I saw the Sergeant leaving. I started to ask who the woman was, but he grabbed me by the hair and shoved me to the floor near the fireplace. He was like an animal. He pulled my skirt up, tore my panties off and raped me. I fought like hell, but he was just too strong. Next thing I saw was this woman… Kei Lien…walking toward us. A huge guy next to her handed her a butcher knife. I thought I was going to be killed."

Sara paused. "I need a drink of water. I feel like I'm going to vomit."

"Sara, take your time," Denton said quietly.

She took a few deep breaths and then began again.

"I managed to push him off me and the back of his head hit the fireplace hearth. I heard it crack, his head I mean. Then this girl came flying toward us with the knife, pushing it into his chest. She stood there, stoned faced. I didn't know if she would hurt me, too. I talked very calmly to her. The fear in her was so visible. Then she ran back to her room.

"I started to check on Adam but… you have to understand. He had just raped me."

"What happened next?" asked Reese.

Tears rolled down Sara's cheeks as she relived the nightmare.

"I went into the bedroom and the young girl was standing in the middle of the room. She was crying. The big guy wasn't in there. When I asked her who she was, she told me she was Kei Lien Chandler. I was shocked. I asked if she was Adam's wife. I mean, she was very young, but you never know these days. But she told me that he was her father. I thanked her for saving me but she ran toward another bedroom. I followed her."

"And all of this was happening while Adam lay on the floor bleeding out?" asked Reese.

"I just wanted to make sure this young lady was okay. She really did save me. He probably would have killed me and his

327

daughter after what I saw. So, I followed her to the back bedroom and I heard a voice, a man's voice, in the room with her. He was telling her to run. No one would ever hurt her again and that he was her friend. He told her to climb out the window and run. He pushed past me. I told her to run as well, I feared for both our lives. It was the same guy that gave Kei Lien the knife. I didn't try to stop her from going out the window. I know I should have, but I didn't. I went back toward the living room and saw the big guy leaning over Adam. He said he saw what happened. He saw her stab him. And then he told me I was pretty and it was no wonder Adam wanted to do me! He was so creepy. But I felt like he really wanted to help the girl.

"Then, and I know that sounds strange, I told him to keep his mouth shut. I really don't know what I was thinking or if I was thinking at all. He could have killed me in an instant. In all my years of seeing rape victims on my table, I never once thought that someday I would be in this situation. The fear is so real. The embarrassment. The shame. The total loss of control. My common sense went out the window. I can't imagine the fear that girl must have felt, being raped by her own father. I told the big guy that I would pay him a lot of money to clean up the mess and if he didn't do as I said, I would send him to the crematory, light the fire myself and shove him in it. I handed him several hundred-dollar bills. Then he then got down on his knees and pushed the knife deeper into Adam's chest. Then he told me his name. Tim Cole. I wondered why the hell he would tell me that. I was frightened of him, but he also seemed scared of me.

"I started to leave but then, for some bizarre reason, thought about evidence. If Adam was raping her all along, there could be evidence on her clothes. So, I went back to her bedroom and found her soiled, bloody clothing under her bed. I took the whole bag. I still have it at my place. I waited in my car until I saw him leave. Then, the next time I saw Adam Chandler was in the morgue on my table. I know I should have dialed 911. sooner than I did but I didn't. I guess I…"

"Stop right there," Denton said quietly, turning to the shell-shocked detectives. "I believe that's all my client has to say, detectives."

"Just one more thing," promised Lake. "I want you to think very carefully. Did you see anyone else in the house?"

"Not that I can think of. Why?"

"Are you sure? Nobody lurking outside or elsewhere in the house?" Reese asked.

"I don't think so, but it was all a blur. I suppose someone else could have been there."

"Detectives, enough." Denton stood, shaking Emerson's hand and nodding to Reese. "Sara, I will get you out on bail. But for now, you will have to be held here."

Lake laughed. "What a nice guy, Hollingsworth. You must get that from your mother."

"I suppose you are correct, detective."

"Is there anything down in the morgue that Bill can't handle for now?" Reese asked.

Sara shook her head.

"I'm sure he has it covered, but could you send someone to my apartment for those clothes? They need to go to the lab immediately. They are in my bathroom linen closet on the floor

NOW SAY YOU'RE SORRY

behind the rack of toiletries. Here's my keys. Oh, and you will find my underwear there as well. I kept them in case I ever needed proof."

As the officers were taking Sara to her cell, she passed the familiar face of Tim Cole. She glanced in his direction. He jumped back from the cell bars. The smug expression on his face disappearing into fear. Was she going to burn him alive?

Sara didn't say one word to him.

CHAPTER 97

Reese kept her promise to Andrew Kelsey by getting him a copy of the Sergeant's death certificate. The two of them went to the bank together as planned. There were no issues letting Andrew into the room that held the safe deposit boxes. Once in there, Andrew was a bit tense.

"Are you good with this?" Reese asked.

"I'm fine. It's just a little odd going through a man's belongings. Someone you never met. Feels weird."

"Do you want to wait for another day?"

"No, I'd like this to be over with."

He found another copy of the last will and testament. It matched the one he found in Jade. There was a photo of his father and his mother, along with a gold watch. A letter was also inside addressed to Andrew Kelsey. It read,

My son,

I'm sorry for not being man enough to stay and be your father. I hope what I have left you in this,

*my final wishes, will help ease the anger you must
have felt all these years. I want you to know, I
loved your mother, but I was just too young to be
tied to a family.*
Martin Kelsey

Detective Clayton helped Andrew read the will, but an attorney would certainly have to execute the final wishes of his father. He had left Andrew all his worldly possessions, including the Strasburg Hotel. The deed was there. Detective Clayton almost let out a rip-roaring laugh, but held herself to a more professional standard.

The house would be left to his friend, Teresa Kelsey. That deed was also in the box. It appears they were never really married. No marriage certificates. The only other papers in the box were Martin's birth certificate and a photo of his son as a newborn baby.

"Wow, from poor too rich in a split second," was the only thing Andrew could say at that moment.

Reese told him not to get too excited.

"We still have to find out if Teresa and your father had a marriage license. That would change things. As his spouse, she would be entitled to his estate, including the hotel. You would only be entitled to it after she passed."

Andrew was just pleased he got to go through his father's wishes and memories.

"Reese, I still feel like he killed my mother. She had a broken heart."

"I know. I would probably have those same feelings. But look

at it this way, you might not have had that wonderful relationship with your mom had he still been in the picture. Now, you
need to move on with your life."

"If all of this is true, I might be able to afford a new face."

She smiled and gave him a hug and told him whether he did or
didn't, it would be an honor to be his friend and would help him in
any way she could. Reese also told him she would do the legwork
to find out if Teresa and Martin were really never married.

CHAPTER 98

"Well," Hollingsworth asked Sara Hunter, "are you ready for your day in court? Judge Canton is waiting."

Sara Hunter stood in her best pants suit, mid high heels, very little jewelry. She crossed her fingers and nodded yes.

"Sara Hunter," the Judge stated, "I see here you have been accused of trying to hide evidence concerning the Adam Chandler murder case. I must at this time relieve you of all duties as the medical examiner for the city of Cromwell, South Dakota. All the evidence obtained during the autopsies pertaining to this trial will be dismissed and new autopsies will be performed by a court appointed Medical Examiner. Your involvement has deemed this necessary. Do you have anything to say in your defense, Miss Hunter?"

Hollingsworth stood to address the Judge.

"Your Honor, my client was trying to protect a young woman, a child really. I'm sure you are aware of the many aspects of this case. We are asking that you forgo the bail and release Sara Hunter on her own recognizance until trial. I will take full responsibility, Your Honor."

"Ms. Hunter…Sara. I have known you for a very long time. You're a very valuable asset to Cromwell. We all know this. I am going to release you on bail in the amount of one dollar. Now, Mr. Hollingsworth, I want you to be prepared when trial starts. Do you understand what I am saying to you? We don't want to lose this asset to our community on some ridiculous technicality."

The judge lifted his gavel and let it come down hitting its mark.

CHAPTER 99

Detectives Lake and Clayton paid a visit to Kei Lien's bedside one more time. This time they arrived with the photos of Sara, Tim Cole and Randall Cummings.

"Kei Lien sweetheart, how are you feeling today?" Reese was trying to be very cautious not to frighten her. "Do you think you can you look at some pictures for me?"

Kei Lien was awake, but not interested in seeing any more photos. She just wanted to sleep. Mary Elizabeth raised the back of her bed to a more upright position.

"Kei Lien, please open your eyes. The officers just want to see if you know the people in the pictures. I promise you can go back to sleep when they leave."

Kei Lien opened her eyes, "Where is Daniel?"

"I'm right here. Nothing to worry about," Daniel answered, moving closer to her bed.

Daniel was there most every day now. Kei Lien was lucid one moment and the next she was anxious, but mostly she just slept. Minh was there as well to see what the officers were going to ask her.

"Hollingsworth will be joining us right after Sara's bail hearing." Lake said.

But he had barely finished his sentence when Denton walked in the door.

"Kei Lien," Reese began, "do you remember seeing this woman in your house the night your father died?"

"Yes, she told me to go out the window and run."

"Why did she say that? Do you remember, Kei Lien?"

"My father was hurting her like he hurt me. She was yelling at him, hitting him, but he just kept doing those bad things to her and pulling her hair. I didn't want him to hurt her like he hurts me."

Kei Lien instantly began gasping for air.

"Am I in trouble?"

"No, you are not," said Mary Elizabeth, patting Kei Lien's hand. "Now take a nice deep breath for me."

Kei Lien inhaled deeply.

"Ok, now blow it out gently."

Mary Elizabeth nodded to Reese to continue.

"What happened next?" Reese asked.

"My friend Tim was there. He handed me a knife from the sink. I took it and walked over to my father. I yelled – NO! NO! NO! – and then I ran at him and shoved the knife in him. That nice lady got up and thanked me and then she told me to go out the window and run. My friend Tim told me that, too. So, I did."

Reese held up the photo of Tim Cole.

"Do you remember seeing this person, Kei Lien? The one here in this photo?"

"Yes, that's my friend Tim."

"Just one more picture. Do you remember if this person was in your house that night?"

It was Randall's photo.

"Sort of," Kei Lien said. "I only saw him for a minute, by the door."

"Kei Lien, is that the only knife you have? Like the one in the sink?"

"No, there are more. I think they are in the cabinet over the window. I think they are there."

"Thank you, Kei Lien. You can rest now."

Mary Elizabeth offered to show everyone out. She knew Daniel would want to say goodbye to her in private, so she closed the door behind her.

He moved toward Kei Lien's bed smiling at her.

"I am so proud of you for doing so well answering all those questions."

He leaned over her to tell her he would be back later, but felt the heat coming from her face.

"Mary!" he yelled.

Startled, Mary Elizabeth swung around and re-entered the room running toward the bed.

"What's wrong with her? She's so hot," Daniel said. Tears and now fear began to take over his intellect.

"It's the infections. I can only give her meds to comfort her now."

Daniel, feeling defeated, his medical training had gone right out the window. He was now just a concerned friend, feeling sad and helpless. Mary reach over and patted his shoulders to comfort him. He decided he would stay for a while longer, with her nurse nearby of ,course. He pulled a chair alongside the bed and gently held Kei Lien's hand, laying his head on the soft blanket that covered her. Mary left the room quietly, after giving Daniel a kiss on the side his forehead.

"I will be in the kitchen if you need me," she whispered.

CHAPTER 100

"Well, Detectives," Denton Hollingsworth stated. "I think we have everything we need. Kei Lien's video confession and her recognition of all else involved. Everything seems to be in order for court. With the video, I doubt the judge will insist on an appearance of Kei Lien considering her frail state."

"What about Sara?" asked Lake. "I don't think she intended to keep the bloody clothes, do you? And besides that, she is also a victim. Adam Chandler raped her."

"I understand the situation detective," Denton said. "But she did pay Tim Cole to keep his mouth shut and to clean up the mess. So, I really don't know what her fate will be. But she is a kind, respected woman. She was willing to go to jail for Kei Lien. I'm sure that will make a difference to the court."

Back at the station, Captain Brown held a debriefing in the squad room.

"I would like to commend everyone for a job well done. This was a tough case and I appreciate all the long hours required to bring those involved to justice. It's in the court's hands now, but our job is not over. There are certainly lessons we need to learn from this case. We need to do better for our community. A young woman was held captive and abused right under our noses and it went undetected for years. As residents and peace officers for the city of Cromwell, we need to build stronger relationships with our community so something like this never happens again. We also have some work to do to build stronger relationships with one another. We lost two of our own. Did it have to end that way? We must do better. We will do better. I have already started researching training opportunities that will help us handle mental health issues more effectively. I'm also in contact with some of our local organizations to discuss ways we can work together with our residents to keep our city a safe place for all. Stay tuned for updates soon. Nonetheless, I am proud of all of you. This was not easy for anyone. Dismissed."

The sentencing for each person involved took place in the Cromwell Court House one month later. Even though each trial seemed long, the jury deliberations were swift. The verdict for all parties, GUILTY.

SARA HUNTER

"Sara Hunter you are released to do 1300 hours of community service, plus revocation of your Medical Examiner License." The judge continued. "All the clothing you took from Chandler's home was sent to the lab. The DNA proved Mr. Chandler and Sergeant Martin Kelsey - as well as countless others still yet to be identified - had victimized Kei Lien Chandler."

Sara was not surprised by the sentence.

"Sara Hunter, do you wish to say anything at this time?"

"Yes, Your Honor. Thank you to the City of Cromwell. It

NOW SAY YOU'RE SORRY

has been my pleasure to serve as your Medical Examiner for so many years. I know I deserve my sentence. I am fine with it and I am quite ready for a change in my life."

RANDALL CUMMINGS

"Randall Cummings, you are being sentenced to life in Cromwell State Prison for your part in the murders of Adam Chandler and Sergeant Martin Kelsey. Do you have anything you want to say, Mr. Cummings?"

"Yes, Your Honor. I am sorry for what I have done and for allowing myself to be intimidated by my boss and Timothy Cole. Your Honor, I wish to emphasize that Teresa Kelsey, or whatever her real name is, took part in the death of her so-called husband. I know the jury may not believe that, but it is true. Also, she did sit on her sofa and watch him take his last breath. She agreed to the wrapping paper after she heard why Cole wanted to put the dog tag in Chandler's brain and wrap him up. I'm also sorry for being the reason that Officer Sorenson committed suicide. I will have to live with that the rest of my life."

The rest of Randall Cummings life was short. He hung himself in his jail cell.

TERESA MASON / TERESA CHANDLER

Before Teresa's sentencing, she made every effort to pay her way out of the whole situation. She thought she could buy the lawyers and the judge.

"Teresa Mason, the jury has found you guilty for your role in the murder of Adam Chandler and Martin Kelsey. You are hereby sentenced to 25 years to life in the South Dakota

Women's state prison. It has also been brought to the court's attention, because you are not the legal spouse of the deceased Martin Kelsey, and you have no documentation to prove otherwise, a last will and testament will be made available to you and your attorney, stating: you do not own the Strasburg Hotel and have no legal claim to ownership. Therefore, any profit made after his death, will have to be paid to the rightful owner of the Strasburg. Is there anything you would like to say at this time Ms. Mason?"

Teresa lowered her head. Then raised it again and said, "Fuck all of you!"

"Guards, please remove Miss Mason from my court room."

TIMOTHY COLE

The verdict for Timothy Cole was last. He was eventually, after two attempts, allowed a sentencing by jury.

"All rise, the Honorable Judge John Orrick, Jade District Court presiding."

"It is the court's opinion, based on the facts of this case and the findings of your psychiatric evaluation, that you are a danger to all you encounter. I, along with the jury, believe you were fully aware of all the heinous acts you committed. You do know right from wrong. You are hereby sentenced to death by lethal injection. In the meantime, you will be placed in the South Dakota State penitentiary to await your demise. Do you have anything you wish to say Mr. Cole?"

"Yes, Your Honor. I was bad. I love my mother and I should be put back into that place where they wire your head and make it hurt."

"Mr. Cole, you burned down that place. It was called the Saturn Psychiatric Center. So, you won't be going back there. And you won't be placed in any mental health facility."

Timothy Cole glared at Judge Orrick.

"I know one thing," he snarled, "the first chance I get Judge, you're next."

A toothy grin formed across Tim's mouth and then he began to laugh.

"Remove Mr. Cole from my court room at once!"

The gavel came down. "Court adjourned."

Reporters from all over the country were hovering like vultures on the courthouse steps waiting for the outcome of this bizarre case. As Reese exited, she noticed a tall redhead in the crowd and marched right up to her.

"I'm going to take a wild guess here," Reese surmised. "Would you happen to be from Washington DC?"

Reese knew full well who she was from her media ID pass.

"Yes, I am. Can you give us any answers on how Miss Chandler is doing? Why she is not in court?"

Before Reese could get out one snide remark, Emerson approached.

"Brenda, how nice to see you. Reese, this is my ex. I told you about her. Brenda this is my fiancée, Detective Reese Clayton."

Microphones were shoved at them, cameras were popping everywhere, but Reese didn't notice one of them. She just smiled and continued down the steps next to the man she loved.

CHAPTER 101

Detectives Lake and Clayton found Andrew Kelsey just four blocks from the courthouse.

"Andrew, my man, are you ready to be a business owner?" Emerson slapped him on the back.

"I believe I am. Thank you both for all the help."

"You do know you have plenty of money now to repair your face?" Emerson asked.

"Emerson! What a cold thing to say," Reese said. "This young man is our new friend and that was insulting."

"I know what he means," Andrew said. "I might just do that after I get settled into this new life. I'll need to hire all new staff to help run the hotel. Then I'll feel more comfortable leaving the business in other hands while I take care of me."

"Great attitude and great plan. We're here to help if you need us."

CHAPTER 102

Daniel stayed long hours with his friend when he wasn't needed in court. Sometimes she would awaken and want to talk a bit. Other times she would have panic attacks if anyone was near her. It was a tough time for all of them. The trials, her illness. All of it was beginning to weigh heavily on Daniel. She was in a good frame of mind the day the judges handed down the sentences. Daniel was once again hopeful. He prayed for her to be normal, whatever normal would be for her. His feelings for her were different, becoming stronger than he wanted to admit.

Minh and Mary Elizabeth had become very close and decided it was time for a new life. They would sell Minh's home and move into Mary Elizabeth's until they married. Daniel was very happy about that. It was his dad's time. His time to start a new life.

On this day, Daniel approached Kei Lien's bed very cautiously, not wanting to frighten her.

"Kei Lien, how are you today, my friend?"

Her eyes were closed. Daniel touched her forehead with his hand. Once again, she was burning up with fever. Mary

Elizabeth came around to the side of her bed. She held Kei Lien's hand so she would be comfortable and not panic. It was at that time she knew Kei Lien was nearing the end of her life in this world.

"Daniel," Mary said. "Is there anything you would like to say to Kei Lien? I believe she can still hear your voice."

Daniel's eyes began to well with tears. "No, please no."

"She is very ill, you know that." Minh said, standing very close to his son with his hand on his shoulder. "You know there is nothing more we can do for her, except let her go. Let her find peace."

Daniel leaned over Kei Lien to kiss her forehead. Her eyes opened slightly as his lips touched her skin. Daniel was holding one hand. Mary Elizabeth was holding the other. Tears began to slip down the side of Kei Lien's face. Daniel's tears blending with hers. A single ray of sun beamed through the window and struck the cut-glass flower vase on the nightstand. It was like a prism and created a rainbow throughout the room. Kei Lien, her eyes now staring at the ceiling as a strange, but calming shadow of a figure floated across the room. Kei Lien uttered her last word.

"Mom."

CHAPTER 103

Daniel found it very difficult to go to Kei Lien's services, but, as always, Dad was there to see him through. Kei Lien was cremated. When Daniel and most of the city were leaving the funeral home after her memorial service, Mary Elizabeth Hollingsworth stopped him.

"Daniel, may I speak with you for a moment? I have something for you from Kei Lien."

Daniel looked at the envelope she handed him. "What's this?"

"It's a note. She asked me for paper and a pencil on one of her good days. Your father and I thought it better to wait until her passing to give it to you."

Daniel hung his head staring at the envelope. He opened it and pulled out a small piece of paper and began to cry. Inside was a letter scrawled in the hand of a child.

Dear Santa,

Thank you for bringing me Daniel.

EPILOGUE

Daniel could no longer be sad. He knew the meaning of the letter. He was fine with it.

Kei Lien's cremains were given to Minh as her guardian. Her urn placed on the fireplace mantle until Daniel was ready.

On a bright and sunny afternoon, Daniel was packing his belongings. After weighing his options, he decided that in the long run it was his destiny to return to medical school. He wasn't sure what direction his degree would take, maybe surgeon or maybe nursing, but regardless, it was a new beginning for him.

Daniel asked his dad for Kei Lien's ashes on the day he was to return to school. He knew right where to place them.

He took one last long walk into the woods until he reached Sweetwater Lake. He took off his sneakers, socks and rolled up his jeans then waded into the water. He squeezed the urn tightly to his chest, his heart beating against the metal. Before he opened it to pour her ashes into the clear, cool water he glanced upward and said, "Kei Lien…I love you like a sister. Rest easy and know you will forever feel clean, loved and never again will you have to say you're sorry."

The End

ACKNOWLEDGMENTS

Thank you does not begin to express my gratitude to those in my life that have encouraged me to continue writing, even when I had days upon days of doubt.

To my loving husband Al, for spending a lot of time waiting for me to shut down the electronics, only to realize I needed to return to my computer to write down an idea or two. For letting me know how much you care. I am also grateful you have a talent for golf, a sport that kept you from getting bored while I was writing, at least in the warmer weather. You will forever and a day be my squeeze. I love you.

To our daughter Crystal Dovigh, our angel on earth, for the hours of time you invested reading and re-reading every draft of this manuscript. Fixing a phrase, crossing a t, dotting an i. For offering critiques and suggestions that helped bring my vision for the characters and story to life. Thank you for teaching me how to navigate this white screen, eye reddening, sometimes mind-boggling machine on which I wrote this manuscript. For knowing when I needed to vent. For encouraging me to keep going. You are smart. You are beautiful inside and out with a heart as big as Texas. You are the very best part of our lives and of course you will forever and ever be our baby girl. I love you. The story may be mine, but I could not have done this without you.

To Jeff Dovigh, (our wonderful son-in-law), Christine, Jackie and her mom, thank you for taking your time to read and offer your critique on my manuscript. For encouraging me to aim for the stars with your kind words.

To Jeff Larson of Jeff Larson Law firm in Sioux Falls, South Dakota, I thank you for taking the time to explain a little bit about the laws in your state. Also, for being what I call a touchable human being. Your insight, as well as your love of South Dakota, shines through with every word. It is because of you that I made the Captain of my fictitious Cromwell Police Department, the first Lakota female to ever hold that position.

To Attorney Melissa Fiksdal of Jeff Larson Law, thank you for your words of encouragement in writing this book. For information I may have missed when speaking to Jeff. You are both a treasure to the state of South Dakota.

To Lockwood Zahrbock Kool Law firm in Sioux Falls, South Dakota. Rhonda Lockwood & Rachel Preheim, I thank you for your help with questions on admissible facts in rape cases. South Dakota must be an amazing place to live. The people I spoke with are so friendly and willing to help. Wishing all of you the very best.

To Pauline Bartel, many thanks for your professional critique of this manuscript, your ideas on what to keep what to omit, suggestions, all made a difference to the final product.

To my dear friend and author Attorney Todd Monahan, for your time, advice and suggestions. I have the greatest respect for you. Thank you for being there for me.

To Author David Wilson, my new friend, thank you does not begin to describe the gratitude I have for you. Thank you for taking the time to read my manuscript and provide thoughtful suggestions and changes. I also appreciate all of your guidance on how to navigate the world of self-publishing. You never hesitated to answer the phone or answer an email when I had a question. It helped me tremendously.

To Dr. John P. DeLuca, Author and good friend, many thanks for reading my manuscript and providing me with a thoughtful critique for the back cover of my novel.

To Caroline Teagle Johnson, my designer, who's incredible talent has taken my vision from thought to cover creating the backdrop for which this novel takes on a life of its own.

Finally, to my siblings, Irene Mieczkowski, Joanie Hoffman, Linda Biittig, and Edward Biittig, their spouses along with the rest of my wonderful family extended and otherwise, here on earth and those who have taken that journey to an afterlife. I love you all.

BARBARA FOURNIER, author of *Now Say You're Sorry*, a detective mystery set in South Dakota, remembers her first writing classes at a community college in the Hudson Valley. She never imagined seeing her name on the cover of a book nor sitting at the desk of a bookstore signing her creation for the first time.

She is also the author of *After Our First Hello* a memoir on her personal and professional life as owner and operator of two hair salons a career that spanned 35 years.

Now retired, Barbara and her husband of nearly fifty years reside in upstate New York. They have one beautiful daughter and son in law.

You can follow Barbara on Facebook at Author Barbara Fournier. Check out her website at barbarafournierauthor.com.